An Open Question

Immaculate Conception School, Mahwah, New Jersey, USA, 1953–1957

Maria Goretti was poor,' Sister Mary St Patrick stands at the front of the room under the crucifix with the familiar white body crumpled in agony. She fixes us with a stern holding eye as she tells the story for the first time. We are second graders, seven-year-olds.

Poor is good, in stories of saints, and bad outside them. We already know that. We're ordinary Americans, rich beyond dreaming for most of the world. Our families own houses, cars, a little land for the houses to stand on and for us to play in. Our town, Mahwah, New Jersey, is zoned for an acre. You need that much land, to live here.

The poorest children in the school are the ones whose fathers work at the Diocesan seminary. You can tell by their lumpy homemade sweaters and the way they bring their lunches in paper bags or plain black lunch boxes made for men on building sites, instead of bright-coloured ones like ours.

'Maria Goretti never went to school,' Sister says sadly. A few bold boys mutter *Lucky duck* and Sister frowns warningly. She has fifty or sixty kids to teach, in first and second grades combined. She's harassed and sometimes mean. She assigns work to one grade while she teaches the other. If you finish your work while she's busy, you're allowed to pick a book from the cupboard and read. Some kids take advantage of her absence to talk and laugh and fly paper airplanes or spitballs at each other. There's an old, rickety, paint-stripped folding chair in the back of the room called the Punish Chair. To be ordered *To the Punish Chair!* is weirdly scalding and terrifying. It could be the Electric Chair, for the fear that crackles around it.

'Maria Goretti had no shoes,' Sister seems to find this romantic. We study our scuffed, boring school shoes, thinking about new shoes, especially *good shoes*, suede or patent leather saved for Sunday Mass and parties.

There's a statue of the Virgin Mary on the classroom windowsill, one bare foot about to step down on a snake. Her eyes are raised to heaven. She doesn't see the snake. Sister says she crushes the snake under her foot, but the story is about to happen, the triumphant ending still up in the air with her small white foot.

If Sister catches somebody tasting a nickel, she'll say *Never put money in your mouths, children. A coloured person might have touched it.* When the Catholic kids who go to public school come to learn their Catechism before they make their First Holy Communion, she warns us not to speak to them. They go to public school, they're different. It's 1953.

We've come in from the playground after lunch glowing and warm, even girly girls like me who walk up and down the long driveway with their arms around each other's waists, telling secrets. Sister always tells us a story. It's a ritual.

'The Goretti family was a large, happy family,' she goes on. Of course it was large. Most of us come from big families, though we don't quite realize yet that there's a connection between that fact and the Church. And of course, it was happy.

'Maria was the oldest girl in her family. She helped her mother gladly, taking care of her baby sisters and working in the kitchen even on the hottest days, never complaining,' Sister fixes us with a baleful eye.

I'm an oldest girl too, and even though I'm a spoilt American living in the lap of luxury, I have plenty of chores to do. I've had a bellyful of them. And babies, babies galore. I sit in the rocking chair with them and when they don't go off to sleep after their bottles, I press their eyelids down, lightly but firmly. They flutter softly against my fingertips like butterfly wings, before they give up.

'A father and son, Giovanni and Alessandro Serenelli, shared the Gorettis' house. Giovanni was often drunk,' Sister pronounces with satisfaction, 'and Alessandro had Bad Companions and read Indecent Literature.'

Bad Companions and Indecent Literature are tools of the devil. It's clear where Alessandro is headed.

'Maria was a very pretty little girl with long brown hair and big brown eyes. But she didn't care about being pretty,' Sister glares at us. Sister Mary St Patrick is not pretty, unlike Sister Mary Rose who teaches third and fourth grade.

She's so beautiful, for a nun, our mothers say sadly about Sister Mary Rose, as if her beauty is a disability. But it's not. It's an ability, perhaps *the* ability, and everybody knows it.

'One day after her First Holy Communion, Maria had put her sister to sleep and was sitting on the landing on top of the staircase outside the kitchen, sewing.'

She had *put her baby sister to sleep* just like I put my baby sisters and brothers to sleep. Maybe she held their eyelids down, too. American two-family houses have outside staircases to the second floor entrances. I get the picture. I don't sew, but I do get inside her, the big little girl sitting on her staircase.

Or maybe she gets inside me. For an instant, she *is* me. There's a different nun telling the story now. It's 1957. I'm ten, going on eleven. I'm a grown-up. I've had responsibilities for a long time but seriously, really, for the past year, ever since my little brother died.

I held him and rocked him and tried to force the rubber nipple between his reluctant gums. Sometimes I poured a little bit of milk out into the sink and screwed the top on his bottle again, after he'd gone to sleep. I did it so my mother wouldn't get her stricken look, when she saw how little he'd taken.

'Maria was praying on the step as she sewed.'

At ten, I dare to doubt it. She was daydreaming. She was doing nothing, except in her head. She was wasting time.

Couldn't she have any time to herself? But I know the answer: no. She was the oldest girl. She didn't have her own room – and neither do I.

For a long time, I think the word *body* means the secret, odd-smelling place between the legs, because of the way people say it. They rush the word *body*, wanting to get it out of their mouths. And the word *purity*, that keeps coming back in the Maria Goretti story, baffles and troubles me. What does it mean? If I don't know, I might not have it.

Later on, of course, I understand what Maria Goretti gave up her one and only mortal life for. In exchange, she was canonized forty-eight years later in St Peter's Square, because there were too many people for the basilica to hold. You can pray to her now. Or even sing to her.

There's a song called *Maria* in the 1957 hit musical, *West Side Story*. The song is about the hypnotic effect of your name, Maria, how it magnetizes us. It's a love song. But this isn't a love story, it's an act of exorcism. I'm afraid of that hypnosis, that magnetism. I'm sick of you, all of you Marias with your (un)holy purity. But I'm even sicker of you than the rest, Maria Goretti, because your story is the sickest of all.

You attract the wrong people for the wrong reasons. The right-wing, crypto-fascist, socially ultra-conservative clergy really get off on you. You're from the sado-masochistic school of female saints. You may not be anorexic, but you're certainly hungry. The sickos love you. They love blood, these religious ghouls. They talk about bathing in it.

They love you as a model of Catholic girlhood, not in spite of but because of your poverty and illiteracy. You have no intellectual pretensions, no ambitions, no aspirations beyond your station. Your only wish is to serve God where you find

4

him – in the kitchen. You worship Him by cleaning, cooking, sewing, all the feminine arts we're turning away from, getting bored with in the late 50s.

Timid, mute, you offer no resistance to anything except sex. You have no voice. You assert nothing but purity, blankness, obedience, virginity, suffering. How the Fathers of the Church adore you, their perfect daughter. You'd never demand anything; not the vote, equal pay, let alone equal opportunity, let alone the right to control your own fertility or (God forbid) express your own sexuality. The American clergy, especially, go wild for you. They take you up, celebrate you, thrust you down our throats until we gag on you.

We puke you up. We turn our backs on you. We believe the story they tell and show it by rejecting you. We leave you sealed in the glass coffin they made for you, like Sleeping Beauty. We aren't interested in your brief life on earth, as they put it. Familiarity with you breeds complete contempt.

- or not quite complete. Because we remember you, we oldest girls. We grow resentful of our long apprentice motherhood. We want something back, something that was stolen from us. We dream you. You haunt us, you whisper in the night. Like all ghosts, you have another story to tell and you need someone to tell it. No one has ever written *you*. They write their own obsessions with purity or poverty. You're a holy virgin martyr, or a downtrodden member of an oppressed class under a feudal landowning system, a representative of others equally starved and blank.

They all think of you as a victim. But I hate professional victims and I want something else from you. I want it to come through me like memory: part invention, part history. I need to pull you out of me like the daughter I never had. You'll talk back to me and contradict me and become someone surprising, if I succeed. You'll go your own way, not mine.

It must be lonely, being holy. Most saints are set firmly on pedestals, but not you. Your images tend to be cast low, under altars, on floors like the one where you fell. There you lie, your arms up to fend off your attacker. You're like a grown-up baby, looking up at those who kneel to pray around you, raising your arms to be picked up. Everyone wants you down there, including we liberal, lapsed, atheist/agnostic, wishy-washy, occasionally nostalgic ex-Catholic women. I'm talking to you because I'm troubled by you. I don't want to be, but I am. You're part of me. You keep knocking at my door. I want you to go away. I never liked you, as you know. But who the hell are you?

A Reply

I've been dead for more than a hundred years and I'm stirring, awakened like the Sleeping Beauty with a question, not a kiss. Who am I?

Everyone assumes they know. My family, my friends, my acquaintances, the doctors, the priests, the popes, the hagiographers, the intellectuals, all thought they knew about me. Those who wrote about me wrote backwards from the moment I was canonized in 1950. I was long gone by then. I'd already been dead for forty-eight years.

I suppose I could join the party, late though it is. But it's a sore point for me, that party. I missed it, and I never had another one. I ache for the beautiful clothes they put me in. I had a skirt and blouse for my First Communion. They were nice. But for my canonization, for my corpse, they went all out.

They dressed it like a princess. Let's call it her, even if she was only a gilded statue with my bones inside. Except the ones they'd kept, carved up for little glass reliquaries.

She really was Sleeping Beauty, Saint Maria Goretti in her glass coffin, asleep in all her glory. They loved her asleep. But I wasn't there. I was dead.

Parties were not something I missed. I was too busy missing a full stomach, a half-full stomach. A stomach full enough not to hurt from hunger.

I missed shoes and school and hair that didn't crawl with lice and itch all night. Not that it kept me from sleep. I was too tired for that. I scratched as I slept. The next morning there was blood, I had scratched so hard. This was not anything unusual or terrible. It was life.

I missed words. I had few. Even those, I hesitated to use. I was

7

shy and wild. I might be beaten. I might commit a sin – but no, it wasn't that. I was afraid to speak. It seemed a daring thing. To speak, you needed to know more than I knew. You needed to be more than I was.

Taller, to start with. I was short and stumpy. Stunted. I was not pretty. Saint Maria Goretti is very pretty on her holy cards, her banner held aloft at the canonization I missed. What did they do to her, to make her so pretty?

They have a kind of clinic at the Vatican where they perform cosmetic surgery on dead human beings. They invest in the dead. Thousands and thousands to pay for a canonization, from the start of a Process through to the triumphant finish.

I was hairy and ugly, more like a wild boar grunting and snuffling with hunger. My face was puffy in the wrong places. I lacked fine cheekbones and sensitive lips. I had coarse, heavy jowls and a tangled mass of red, squirming hair. There are no real pictures of me. We didn't take pictures. Why would we? We didn't have cameras. We didn't stop time to hold it in a shutter. We didn't freeze smiles. No one thought us worth photographing. We agreed with them.

They must have siphoned out some fat from my cheeks with Vatican lipo. They must have yanked a few molars out to make the cheekbones sit so well, with just a small indentation underneath. One thing about operating on the dead, you don't need to bother with anaesthetics. Of course in my case, they operated without anaesthetics while I was alive.

There are two pictures of me they give out on holy cards. Neither one is me, but one is closer. Cleaner than I ever was, but closer. It shows a rather suspicious-looking young girl with full, round cheeks. She has a full face and full lips. She's not exactly pouting, but she looks a bit wary. Her cloud of clean-looking hair is definitely red. She has a somewhat large, even slightly bulbous nose and bold greenish eyes. Her forehead is short. She's not ugly or dirty, but somewhat plain.

Isn't it funny that there are no plain saints? Every single one is beautiful, with Mary at the top, the Queen of the May. We all have

8

to look like her, and she has to look like Miss America, Miss World, Miss Universe – I dread to think of the surgery she's had, not just on her face. Replacing hymens can be done. It's quite common in some countries. I wonder what they use? Tissue from an animal?

Back to Saint Maria Goretti, in the second picture, the improved, face-lifted version. A facelift is a bit radical for someone not yet twelve, but never mind. They have to get rid of those coarse, heavy jowls, sculpt her into a classic oval. Then they tilt her eyes upwards to the skies under dark, trimmed brows. Nothing unruly. And – this is key – nothing red. The mass of red hair and thick red matching eyebrows have to go.

Red is for the Magdalene and her contingent of hymen-lacking penitents. Virgin saints can't be spiced with ginger hair. Saint MG's hair is dyed a deep, rich, serious brown, placed in neat waves on her shoulders. It's so thin and tame, I think they must have torn some out. Then they permed what was left, just to add some respectable waves.

The gleam of her lemon-yellow halo shows a perfect central parting. The light is cold. Her lips are thin. Her dark lipstick matches the purple martyr's robe under the gauzy white cloak I'd tear off her and flounce around in, if I could. She neither smiles nor frowns, in the way of saints.

There's something meek about her chin. Mine jutted, just slightly – I had a stubborn streak. Her hairline is pulled way back from a high, ivory forehead. Her dark, compliant hair lifts off its smooth expanse in even waves all the way down, showing off her clear complexion, her faintly, girlishly rose-tinted cheeks.

She's slim, Santa Maria Goretti. It's funny that the poor are fat. We eat almost nothing, but we balloon with bad food that bloats us. Saint Maria Goretti had a different diet from mine. I was burnt by the sun, over an anaemic pallor. I probably had malaria from the mosquitoes in the swamp where I lived.

The Vatican forgot she was a peasant saint and overdid the nose job. There's a religious romance of peasantry and poverty, but they don't want to get too close to the real thing. I don't blame them. Poverty stinks.

Saint Maria Goretti's nose looks a bit like Eugenio Pacelli's. He became Pope Pius XII, who canonized her. In fact if you look closely, her whole face looks a bit like his. She was his daughter, in a kind of masculine virgin birth. Popes like the idea of virgin daughters, like all fathers.

Saint Maria Goretti's hands have never known hard work. They're a bit like his, too, though not quite as sensitive or aristocratic. But her fingers are long, her nails nicely curved in half-moons, filed and buffed and painted with clear polish. The manicurist forgot herself a little. Not a burn, not a mark on those hands. The right one has a rosary draped around it, the left holds a sheaf of lilies. I never saw a lily, except in pictures of the saints and in church at Easter. I liked poppies that grew wild, daisies and cornflowers.

I did say the rosary every night. The prayers were a blur but we said them, exhausted and starved as we were, hoping to reach someone or something with our desperate SOS. Saint Maria Goretti has no rings under her eyes. She was never tired.

Her neck is white. They must have bathed her in a deep tub and scrubbed off layers of skin, brown and filthy. It had become a kind of hide that kept me warm in winter. She couldn't smell like me. I doubt that she smells at all.

She looks very cool. Butter wouldn't melt in her mouth. Butter! Even the thought of it melts in my mouth.

We'd have nothing to say to each other. She'd hardly speak to me and I'd be tongue-tied in her presence. But you asked me who I am, and I'll tell you.

I haven't come back just for you. You also have an agenda, whether you know it or not. I haven't come back for that. I've come back for your girls, your daughters. You say you don't have one, but you do. They're all around you, these daughters. Everyone has agendas for them, Catholics, Muslims, Jews, atheists, all the rest Whether you try to keep them out of school or push them to study harder and go further, whether you cramp and diminish them or stretch them on the rack of your ambition, you want the best for them; your best.

They're tired. They should be running, leaping into the air, rolling down hills, not shaking their hips and trying to be sexy or sitting at desks, trying to study. They should be laughing and crying and dreaming in private, in peace. They have no space. The staircases are empty.

They're an endangered species, girls – wild, anarchic girls. I'll tell you who I am. I'm a girl-child. I can't be moulded or harnessed or made into a model of anything. I'm not my moon-faced twin. I'm a spirit that moves as she wishes. I'm like a boy but with a different cast of fantasy, another stream of energy, another body and another will.

Listen to me, priests and anti-priests alike. All those who think you know me, listen hard, whether you kneel at my shrines and mumble to the white-faced virgin with the well-coiffed hair – why are you so interested in her hymen? Do you ever wonder? – or you sneer and snigger and feel superior because she died for a little plug of blood and mucous. All of you who think you know who I am, shut up and listen. I'm telling my own story, the story of Maria Goretti, the oldest girl in her family.

My story, like everyone's, begins with my mother's story, which begins with her mother's story, and so on back to Eve, or back past her to the ape-girl they've found in Ethiopia. They call her Selam, which means peace. She was three years old when she died where a freshwater stream from the uplands formed a shallow lake and preserved her fossil in sandstone sediment. It stirred my dust, her discovery.

But now I'm climbing back inside my mother. I'm listening to her thoughts and overhearing her memories. She's a little girl and I'm hiding in her head.

Your mother's had a hard life, Papa used to tell us when she lashed out, when she beat us and screamed at us. He was right.

I'm wearing your life like a dress and I can tell you, Mamma, it makes me feel more like Saint Joan of Arc than Santa Maria Goretti. It was never a dress. It's more like a suit of armour, very heavy and very, very hard.

11

1

Senigaglia (later Senigallia),
La Marche, Province of Ancona,
Kingdom of Italy, 1871

'It wasn't God's will that you stay with them, Child.'

Assunta was five years old. This was the sixth time she had been fostered and sent back to the poorhouse. The first three times, she had been too little to realize what was happening. But the older children at the poorhouse in Senigaglia always kept count.

'I thought they liked me,' she said, because she had.

'What comes to us is what God wants, not what we want.'

'Yes, Sister.'

'You know what happens, Assunta.'

'Yes, Sister,' she knew. People had to weigh up carefully whether it was worth putting food into another mouth. Local people called the orphans alleycats, there were so many of them. It was not a term of affection. She knew that, too.

'You're a good girl, Assunta.'

'Yes, Sister.'

Kittens were drowned in the same buckets people kept in their houses to squat over. Leaning down to see what was in a bucket left behind a tree in the poorhouse garden, Assunta saw a heap of curled bodies at the bottom of the cold, still water, tiny pink mouths open, newborn eyes closed tightly. She had tiptoed away as if afraid to wake them, though she knew they were dead.

'God will provide for you, as He always has.'

'Yes, Sister.'

It was a sin to drown a baby or put a pillow over its face, though it happened. Usually babies were left alive on the little shelf in the door of the Casa, where she was now. The shelf turned outwards to the world and then inwards, where the baby was removed and brought inside. Sometimes it was dead, like the kittens.

'You have Our Blessed Lady, your mother in heaven. You have the same mother as God, Assunta, you're a lucky little girl,' Sister Bernice said. 'Aren't you?'

'Yes, Sister,' Assunta said. The orphans were often told how lucky they were.

'You can go and help in the laundry now, Assunta,' Sister Bernice smiled at her.

'Yes, Sister.'

Sister Bernice sighed. 'Why don't you go to the chapel and tell Our Lady how much you love her?'

'Yes, Sister, thank you, Sister,' Assunta turned her steps obediently towards the little chapel. She liked the chapel. It was quiet. But you were not allowed there without permission.

'Bad luck Assunta. Maybe you ate too much, eh?' Georgio, an older orphan, wagged his finger at her in the corridor and made a gobbling noise.

'No I didn't,' she said forcefully. Her stomach hurt at night, keeping her awake, making her heavy and slow in the morning when she had to get up and work again. There were animals to be fed. She had only stolen a tiny portion of their food, enough to keep going. They had to keep going, too.

'Caught you at the chicken feed. I know.'

'No,' she shook her head proudly. 'They never caught me, Georgio.'

'Good for you. Did the old man catch you? Eh?'

She shook her head.

'Bravo,' he nodded respectfully. 'You're quick, Assunta.'

'I am,' she said. 'And I paid for everything I ate.'

'Ah, they made you beg,' he nodded.

14

'Of course.'

'But you're not pretty enough to get much.'

Assunta nodded. It was true. 'And I'm not little enough any more,' she added, because it was also true.

'No,' he said sadly. 'To beg you must be beautiful or small, otherwise it's no good. I worked on a farm last time. Much better than begging. But the land was bad, the harvest was poor,' he shrugged.

Assunta nodded. Georgio had been in and out of the Casa more times than she had. He would be in and out again.

'Coming to work in the laundry?'

She shook her head. 'I'm going to the chapel. Sister Bernice said I could, to tell Our Lady how much I love her. Because she's my mother and Jesus's,' she bragged.

'She's everybody's mother,' he said with a shrug. 'You and every single baby in the world. And every kid, and every grownup. Good luck, Assunta. You can say a prayer for me, too, but she'll be much too busy to listen.'

He laughed as she scrunched up her face. 'If the wind changes, you'll stay that way.'

'No I won't.'

He waved at her as he went back towards the kitchen garden, where he worked. 'Good luck, Bambina.'

'Good luck, Georgio.' Ordinarily *Bambina* would be an insult, but his tone was kind. Assunta walked towards the chapel. It was quiet there and no one could tease you.

She knelt in front of the shrine and studied the statue of the Virgin Mary in the semi-darkness. If she had been in the parish church where they went to Sunday Mass, she could have sat down in a pew, ready to slide to her knees if Sister Bernice came in. But the Casa had only this small chapel, where you knelt on the floor.

Orphans were only allowed to sit for meals. Otherwise they knelt for prayers or stood on their feet to work. Real cats curled around themselves and slept underneath carts in the street. They curled up in a ball to hide in small dark spaces.

You saw them everywhere, like ghosts. But orphans at the Casa were not allowed back to their beds before night-time, unless they were ill.

Praying to fall ill was wicked but not sinful, not yet. Assunta was five. The Age of Reason was seven. After that, she could commit sins and go to hell. But if she prayed to be sick, her prayer might be answered and she could die.

If she died before she was seven, she would go straight to heaven. She tested the idea, not for the first time. But heaven sounded cold, and Assunta hated the cold. Once past the Age of Reason, she would risk eternal damnation in hell. Hell was made of fire. It was hard to be afraid of fire. It meant warmth and light. No, she would not pray to be sick. She did not want to die before she was seven, in spite of the advantages.

The Virgin Mary didn't have gold rings in her ears, like most of the women the orphans saw at Mass and even Assunta's friend Cecelia, who said having gold in your ears protected your eyes.

But you have to have them put in when you're a baby, or else it doesn't work.

Assunta touched her own ears, where there was no gold. Sister Bernice said it was better to have a gold halo, like Our Lady and the saints. She said none of them had gold earrings, earrings encouraged vanity and why would you want to have holes in your ears? But Cecelia said Sister Bernice would go blind when she was old, like all nuns.

The Virgin was smiling. God would never let His mother go blind, so she didn't need earrings. She was smiling the way dead people smiled, at nothing. Assunta had seen the smiles of dead orphans, in this chapel. Unless the nuns were right and they were smiling at Jesus as He received them in heaven.

Was Mary smiling at Him? She was his mother, after all. She fed Jesus from her breast, in the pictures that made the boys laugh. But Mary had never offered Assunta her breast. Jesus might share His mother with you, but He didn't share her milk.

16

Sister Bernice had held Assunta up and tipped her down to plant a kiss on a cold forehead.

You are kissing a happy little saint, Sister Bernice whispered.

It was like kissing the relics of saints the priest held up on their feast days. You didn't want to see the holy splinter of bone in the glass case. At least they didn't skin the bodies of dead orphans to make relics, even though the nuns called them saints.

Orphans were told to look down when they walked through the street to Mass on Sunday. People looked at them and looked away. But the orphans scanned the faces of the people they passed. When they passed ugly, crippled, drunk, hunchbacked or mad people, they joked with each other in loud whispers:

That one's your old man! You can see the family resemblance!

That whore is your mother, they spat out when they passed a woman. All women were whores, except for the nuns. The nuns might be cruel, but they were not whores. They had never left babies on the shelf in the door of the Casa. That was the one unforgivable sin that fell on all women who were not nuns, even rich ones in expensive clothes. Older orphans like Georgio could tell what every item of clothing had cost. He liked to add them up in his head and announce the total.

When she comes back for me, the whore, I'll spit in her face, Georgio liked to say. *I'll slap her right across her filthy face and tell her to go straight to hell.*

At night the orphans dreamt that real mothers came back for them. They threw their arms around smiling phantoms and held on for dear life as they were picked up and carried far away from the orphanage, into the warm world of families and food.

Senigaglia was on the sea. Once when it was very hot, Sister Bernice took the best orphans to walk along the beach and feel the cool breeze. There were striped beach huts in rows like cheerful little houses. Afterwards Assunta dreamt of living in one, listening to the waves. A real kitten could live in a

17

box. She could live in a hut. She had been foolish enough to confide her dream to Cecelia.

What? But no one lives there, Assunta. People use them to change their clothes when they go to bathe in the sea. You don't know anything, do you? Cecelia shook her head and her earrings glinted.

Assunta wished she had kept silent.

I want to live in a villa, Cecelia's voice was triumphant as she told her dream. *With marble floors and a grand staircase I can sweep down in my beautiful long dresses like a princess.*

But you aren't a princess, Assunta pointed out. *You're an alleycat.* Disappointment made her blunt. *We're all alleycats.* Usually the orphans avoided the word.

Assunta wants to live in a beach hut, Cecelia had informed the others when they sat down to their meal of coarse bread and thick, chewy beans, that evening.

You can eat fish right out of the sea, Assunta, yes?

Georgio said that, and she had not seen that he was joking. It seemed like a good idea. Real cats and their kittens ate fish, when they could get it. She liked fish. She liked all food.

And seaweed to go with it, he added, and the orphans laughed. *Raw fish and seaweed! You can wear it, too, seaweed. You can make a skirt out of it, Assunta. You're a good seamstress, yes?*

Assunta laughed along with the rest. But her dream was spoilt. She had learned a lesson that day. If you told people something important, they took it away.

And now she was back on her knees in the chapel. She had expected too much from the people who fostered her. It was for them to expect things of her. She had to work hard and not complain if she was sent out to beg. It was almost impossible not to expect something in return, but you couldn't.

But surely the Blessed Mother was different? She expected Assunta to do her duty, and she did it. She could expect something back from Our Lady, even before she went to heaven, couldn't she?

18

She closed her eyes and prayed silently, as she had been taught: *I love you, Blessed Mother.*

She saw the statue's pale smile behind her eyes as she whispered *I love you, Blessed Mother,* out loud. Maybe it only counted if you said it out loud. Then she waited.

She's everybody's mother. Every baby in the world, every kid, every grownup. You can say a prayer for me too, but she's much too busy to listen.

Georgio knew more than Sister Bernice. Assunta stood up, still looking at the statue. Maybe another time, when Our Lady was not so busy. But her footsteps were heavy as she left the chapel.

She got permission from Sister Bernice to visit the chapel again. Each time, she told the Blessed Virgin she loved her and waited for a sign that her love was returned. Each time, Our Lady was too busy with her other children.

She was like a foster mother. If there were other children in the family, they were preferred. You were a problem for them and they let you know it. They found ways of hurting you, pinching and pulling your hair. They stole your food. They said horrible things about you.

You might get a quiet or stupid child, if you were lucky. Then you could scratch and bite them and get their food. But you could be lucky with one and not so lucky with another. There was always someone on the lookout for a victim.

You might be the replacement for a dead baby or child. But something always went wrong. In the end, you were not worth the mother's milk meant for the real one. It dried up and you were returned to the Casa.

Still, it was better to be fostered than not. There was a bit more food and a bit more attention, even if it meant more bruises. You had more chance of not being a *happy little saint.*

Now there was only Mary, the busy Blessed Mother. Assunta needed to sort out where she stood with Mary. Words came hard to her, she had to force them into her mouth and out again. She waited for her chance and one day in the laundry, she tackled Sister Bernice.

'Sister?'

'Yes, Assunta, what is it, Child?'

'You know the Blessed Mother, Sister?'

'I hope so, Child.'

'She's everyone's mother, isn't she, Sister?' She had said it.

'Of course she is,' came the calm reply. 'You know that, Assunta.'

Assunta waited. But she had to know. 'Is she a real mother or a foster mother?'

'How could the mother of God be a foster mother? What's got into you, Child? Mary is the mother of all God's children. Now, Assunta, enough questions.'

Georgio was right. Mary was everyone's mother, including the children who had perfectly good mothers of their own. Why couldn't she be their foster mother? Then she could be the real mother of the orphans. That would be fair.

Assunta's *mere earthly mother*, as Sister Bernice said, had left her on the shelf in the orphanage door on the day she was born. The shelf turned like a wheel. Tiny babies could be found before they died, or not. It was draughty. It was up to fate, or God, or Sister Bernice, who was also busy.

Christmas was coming and the story was told and re-told of the stable and the poor baby Jesus who didn't have a bed, only a manger. But his manger was soft and warm, with lots of hay. The animals breathed on Him. No one ever called Him an alleycat, or left Him on a shelf or shooed Him away when he was old enough to beg. Baby Jesus had a mother kneeling on one side of him and a father on the other, as well as shepherds and angels and wise men coming to give him gifts, including gold. How could they say he was poor?

After Christmas, when she had turned six, Assunta stood in front of Sister Bernice again. The nun frowned and touched the long rosary that hung from her belt, her fingers twisting a bead. The rosary pealed softly like a tiny bell as she walked, and warned the orphans she was coming. She cleared her throat before she spoke. 'I have good news for you, Assunta. You're being fostered again.'

Something was not right. Assunta could tell by Sister Bernice's face and her fingers, still working the polished black beads on the long silver chain.

'God is good. You're a very lucky child,' Sister Bernice said.

Assunta nodded. That could mean anything, or nothing. 'Yes, Sister.' Of course God was good, what else could He be?

'The couple live in Corinaldo.'

Not in the country, then. Corinaldo was a village. She would love to be sent to a farm, as Georgio had been. But they usually asked for a boy.

'There are many dangers in the world, Assunta. Victor is a pious man.'

A pious man. He would not try to trap her then and remove her shift. Sister Bernice tried very hard to be sure of this. But would he give her enough food to eat?

'Still, you will have to mind yourself and go carefully,' Sister Bernice went on. 'Pray to Our lady constantly to protect you. Never try to attract attention to yourself. Do you understand?'

'Yes, Sister.' That much, Assunta understood. Attracting attention brought trouble.

'Mary,' Sister Bernice smiled as she said the name, 'Victor's wife, Mary, is a seamstress. You will be a great help to them. You must always be grateful and work hard, Assunta.'

'Yes Sister.' Assunta had learned how to disappear when she wasn't wanted and come back when she was. She would be called a daughter of the house, but she would not be. It was best not to pretend, at least to yourself.

'Remember to avoid the near occasions of sin,' Sister Bernice was saying.

'Yes Sister.' That meant not being trapped by a man. She might have to aim her knee, as Georgio had taught her. She would have to set her face, as she had taught herself. The

21

same dangers existed in the Casa as outside. Didn't Sister Bernice know that?

'Keep the prize of heaven always before you,' Sister Bernice said. 'Where all pure souls will meet and be together forever.'

'Yes, Sister.'

'I remember when you came to us, Assunta,' Sister Bernice said. 'You were a tiny scrap of a thing, wrapped in a blanket with a scrap of paper attached. It said you had been baptized and your name was Sunta Angiolina Ida.' Sister Bernice laughed. 'Imagine, for such a tiny scrap of a thing!'

Sister Bernice had never said these words to her before. Once upon a time she had had a mother who could read and write. This mother had baptized her, wrapped her in a blanket, then left her on the poorhouse shelf. The Baptismal name her mother gave her *and written on a scrap of paper* was *Sunta Angiolina Ida.*

'Of course we had you baptized again, and gave you a name appropriate to your station in life, Assunta,' Sister Bernice smiled.

Assunta's smile felt like the one on the face of the statue in the church.

Sister Bernice held out a little rosary made of string. 'This is for you, Assunta. Keep it and pray with it. I will pray for you, too.'

'Thank you, Sister.' She took the rosary from Sister Bernice's hands, red and raw with cold water and hard work like her own. She had felt those hands across her bottom and even across her face, when Sister Bernice was especially busy and tired.

The little foyer of the Casa where they sat was very quiet. There might be a dead baby already there on the shelf, turning blue. But no one had left anything or anyone while they sat there. Surely even a tiny kitten with its eyes locked shut would make some sound before it died?

Asuunta worked the string with her fingers, where Sister Bernice had braided it into a tiny cross. You said the Creed on that. Then there was a knot for the first Our Father, then ten knots for ten Hail Marys, then a little space and another knot for a Glory Be to the Father, then a big space for the next Our Father which began the next decade. Five times ten Hail Marys, five Our Fathers and five Glory Be's. You had to go around three times and do fifteen decades, for all the mysteries: Joyful, Sorrowful and Glorious. She knew them all. She said them to herself as her fingers felt the knots. They were uneven, some slightly lumpier than others. The knots seemed to tighten in her stomach as she touched them.

'Are you counting them, Assunta?' Sister Bernice laughed, her eyes crinkling up under her coif. 'You're a funny little thing.'

The knots inside Assunta's stomach pulled tighter. Nothing must be shown, nothing must be seen. She had to leave with her head held high.

'You know, Assunta,' Sister Bernice said, 'you can pray the rosary for the holy souls in purgatory. There are indulgences attached to it.'

Indulgences meant days off from the time a soul had to spend in purgatory, before it was pure enough to go to heaven. Souls in purgatory burned in fires as hot as those in hell, but only for a time.

'You can pray a soul right into heaven, if you keep on praying,' Sister Bernice said cheerfully. 'Pray to Our Lady, Assunta. Say her rosary every day,' she urged.

Assunta knew what she was saying and not saying. Sister Bernice would never say *Pray for me*. That would be selfish. She was telling her to pray her own mother out of purgatory, to forgive her and pray her into heaven, where they would meet again and be together forever.

She looked up at the nun's face and then away. The knots in her stomach tightened again. 'But you can't pray for a soul that has gone to hell, Sister,' she heard herself say.

'Oh, Assunta,' she put her hand on Assunta's arm. 'God is merciful, Child,' she said. 'Always remember that.'

Assunta nodded. 'Yes, Sister.' The knot in her throat would choke her. She waited for a second and then moved her arm away carefully.

'Goodbye, Assunta. I will pray for you,' Sister Bernice said. Her voice was disappointed.

'Thank you, Sister,' Assunta said. 'Sister,' she hesitated.

'Yes, Assunta,' Sister Bernice leaned forward hopefully. 'What is it, Child?'

Her voice was almost soft. Assunta forced the words out as she had done before, when she had asked about the Virgin Mary's other children.

'Do Victor – and Mary – have other children?' It was not what she had meant to ask.

Sister Bernice smiled as she gave the good news. 'No. They have no other children, Assunta.'

Assunta took a deep breath. The smile encouraged her. She said the words. 'The note you found, Sister – the one that was pinned to me when I came here?'

'Yes, Child, what of it?' Sister Bernice's voice was impatient. The smile had disappeared.

Assunta's voice scratched her dry throat. 'Where is it?'

'What was that? Speak up, Child.'

'Where is it?'

'Where is what, Child, for heaven's sake?'

'The note. The note my mother wrote,' Assunta said. She had never said *my mother* before. Her voice sank over the words, almost to a whisper. 'The scrap of paper with my name on it, where is it?' She asked, louder.

'Good heavens, Child, who would ever keep such a thing?' Sister Bernice looked at her with disgust 'A filthy scrap of paper written by a filthy –' she stopped.

Mothers who left their babies in the door of the Casa were filthy whores. Georgio said so. But for Sister Bernice to say so – or almost – was different. Assunta felt her face burn as if the nun had slapped her.

'It's time for you to go and get your things now, Assunta.

Forget about everything except doing your duty and praying to Our Lady,' her voice was bitter as she said *forget about everything*.

'Yes, Sister,' Assunta stood up and let Sister Bernice kiss her on both cheeks. She knew her skin was as cold as the foreheads of the dead orphans under her own kisses, when Sister Bernice held her up and whispered that they were saints.

'Come back in half an hour and they will be here.'

Assunta left the foyer and climbed the stairs. She was dazed and numb. *Forget about everything*, Sister Bernice had said in that new, bitter voice. She meant *Forget about me*, because Assunta had not cried or thanked her for her kindness.

Cecelia and Georgio were waiting in the dormitory. They had sneaked away. They would go without supper, if they were caught. She smiled at them, a different smile from the dead one she had given Sister Bernice.

'I have something for you,' she said. 'I only have one, so you'll have to share it.'

She held out the little string rosary. They both reached out, but Cecelia was faster. She laughed as she grabbed it. Then she got down on the floor and moved the little circle of string back and forth across the concrete.

A black and white paw scrabbled out from under the bed. The alleycats hid real kittens wherever they could, and kept them alive on scraps of food. Kittens were also abandoned by mother cats who ran away or died.

Assunta saw again the look of disgust on Sister Bernice's face when she asked who would keep such a thing as the *scrap* of paper she had thrown away when she rescued the tiny little *scrap* that was Sunta Angiolina Ida. She watched the kitten play with the little rosary. The white string was dirtier now than it had been before. The kitten latched its paw on a knot and Cecelia pulled it free. Then she let the kitten have it till the little black and white body was caught in a gnarl of string and had to be set free again. The string was shredding in places under its sharp claws, the knots sprouting little furry tails.

A different kind of smile twisted Assunta's lips.

'Leave it, let's go,' she stood up and they followed her because she was leaving the Casa, she was being fostered and that made her the leader. She looked back from the doorway. The kitten had clawed the little string rosary under the bed. The knots made a noise on the concrete floor like tiny spatters of rain.

Sister Bernice inspected the dormitory every morning and night. She always swished a broom under the beds. Assunta turned and left the room and the kitten that had escaped drowning, at least for now.

2

Corinaldo,
Province of Ancona,
Kingdom of Italy, 1873

'Welcome to your new home, Assunta,' Mary smiled down at her and touched Assunta's small hunched shoulder shyly. Her smile showed brown teeth with lots of gaps. Her face was lined and her eyes had purple rings under them.

Assunta froze under the heavy red hand that reminded her of Sister Bernice's. It was quickly removed and Mary's face fell into even more lines. The brown teeth were hidden, and the gaps between them.

But Mary kissed Assunta goodnight as she curled away in her cold, hard bed. Assunta wanted to hiss and spit at her like the kittens the orphans tried to catch. It took a very long time before they let you near. Most people gave up long before a kitten allowed them to touch or stroke it, let alone pick it up and carry it home with them.

Assunta watched Mary's gnarled hands come close, then move away again. They were different, after all, from Sister Bernice's hands. Mary was a seamstress, not a laundress. She was not a mother, either, or a nun. She had never spun the wheel in the door of the Casa, from the outside or the inside.

Mary's brown smile became a half-smile, then a tiny pucker as Assunta's stomach pulled into a string of lumpy knots and she felt her own face tighten with it.

Alone at night, curled up into a ball, she could see the string rosary and the black and white paw swatting at it from under Cecelia's bed. Only the thought of Cecelia and Georgio could make her lips turn in a weak, wobbly smile like Mary's, and she tried not to think about them.

Mary was like most people. Her smiles shrank and vanished, her kisses missed Assunta's cheek. Assunta waited patiently for them to stop. Sister Bernice had turned from hopeful to bitter in a moment. It took longer for Mary's voice to go flat and dull, except when it was sharp with impatience or anger. Her eyes slowly lost their gleam and eventually her hands stayed in her lap, unless they were landing a slap. Finally the kisses stopped and Assunta knew by the easing of the knots in her stomach that she had won.

Victor was small and dark. He had a wispy grey beard and a loud, spluttery cough that never went away, even after he cleared his throat and spat a shiny, sticky lump onto the ground.

He took care of a few sheep for the farmers who worked plots of land outside the village. He led them up into the fields that surrounded Corinaldo where they cropped the grass all day, and back again in the evening. In between he limped through the village, coughing and spitting as he begged. Sometimes he lay in the square by the church and dozed. People moved away quickly, when they heard him coming.

The sheep were lucky. Assunta had tried grass before, and you could get something from it after the rain, when it was soft. You could chew the end of a piece of grass so that a soft white meat came out of the pale tube, down near the stem. It was only a tiny bit, but it was something. If you nibbled fast, like the sheep, you could get enough to make your stomach stop hurting for awhile.

There was never enough polenta or dried beans to boil for the three of them. The bread was so hard Assunta had to work tiny pellets in her mouth with spit before she could swallow it. Victor had a small plot of vegetables, but they had to be sold, not eaten. The soil was dry and the crop was never very good.

28

Mary was older than Victor. She took in darning and mending and sometimes she was asked to make a dress for a special occasion, like a wedding. But Assunta soon understood that this had happened much more often in the past, and she could see why. Who would want a dress that held the smells of Mary and Victor's house? How could anything beautiful come out of the filth and grime they lived in?

Yet, somehow, it could. When she was asked, Mary could make a perfect dress out of pale, delicate fabric and hand it over without a stain. The swishing skirt, the ruched bodice would be invisibly stitched, glistening with light caught from somewhere in the cave of the house. She taught Assunta as she worked and though Mary was impatient with mistakes and wanted the work done fast as well as accurately, Assunta was glad to be her apprentice.

But Mary's eyes were failing and her knuckles were swollen and sore. As time went on, she passed more and more work to Assunta. She resented the mundane darning and mending she was asked to do. Often she paid it little attention and her darns were lumpy, her stitching uneven.

Assunta quietly undid it and did it again, before it went back to a customer they could not afford to lose. She had to do this unpicking and re-stitching secretly, at night, when Mary was asleep. But sometimes she was caught at it, and her foster mother would fly into a rage and beat her.

It amazed her that the days passed and she kept on going. The little house grew dirtier, despite her efforts to clean it. Victor was too exhausted to wash when he came in at noon and at night from his combination of sheep-herding, begging and gardening. He was too old for the hard physical work. They were both too old.

It was easy to understand why Sister Bernice had frowned and fidgeted with her rosary when she told Assunta she was being fostered again. She was too young. There had been no one exactly right for Mary and Victor at the poorhouse in Senigaglia, and they had settled for her.

Assunta saved them customers who might have not only gone away but complained to friends and lost them other work. The village was small and word spread fast. People began to realize something had changed, and Mary had more work than she had had for years. She also knew what was happening, though she never said. But every now and then she would catch Assunta out in her secret night-time labour, and there would be a price to pay. Assunta accepted the beatings as her due. Failing to hide something was always punished.

Somehow the years passed and she grew taller and sturdier in spite of hunger. When she was twelve and it was time for her First Communion, she worried about what she would wear. There was no money for a First Communion dress. She would stand out from the crowd of children in their procession down the aisle in the village church.

Even the other orphans from the Casa would be better dressed. Assunta met them sometimes, when she begged in the streets. Georgio and Cecelia had been fostered in the country, both at the same farm. When she heard, it had made her wonder if Sister Bernice's string rosary had brought them such a rare piece of luck.

Victor and Mary were the poorest people in Corinaldo. They were ragged and filthy, and so was she. Normally she was too busy to think about such things. But Assunta's stomach knotted when she heard Mary asking their customers for old clothes to make over for her First Communion, even though she knew there was no other choice. She also knew the customers were in on her secret and they would be generous in recognition of the work she did for them.

Before she could make her First Communion or her First Confession, she had to go for instruction from the parish priest along with the other children from Corinaldo. Mary walked her to the priest's house and knocked on the door.

'She can come in,' the priest's housekeeper said when she opened the door, pointing at Assunta.

Mary let her hand go and Assunta walked up the step and into the house as the door was closed firmly behind her. She wondered if she would ever see Mary again, or if she might live with the priest from now on. She hoped so.

'Come into the parlour with the other children,' the housekeeper said. 'Father,' she said as she delivered her. 'Here's Assunta from Mary and Victor.'

'How are you, Assunta?' The priest asked her.

I'm hungry.

I'm very well, Father,' she said, and dipped a curtsey as Sister Bernice had taught her, long ago.

'Good, good,' he patted her head.

She had an urge to grab his hand sink her teeth into it, like a kitten. Maybe then he would see her.

In his terms, she *was* very well. Victor never laid a finger on her. Even the beatings and slaps, he left to Mary. There were fewer of those, these days. Assunta was stronger, they were weaker.

She watched the other orphans as the priest asked each one in turn the same question: *How are you?* They all said *Very well thank you Father.* They must have weighed things up, too. If they spoke out, they would be blamed and not believed. They would be sent back to the Casa in disgrace. No one would ever foster them again, and Sister Bernice would know what they had said. Words were not for them. They only brought trouble, even words on a *scrap of paper* with the name of a *tiny scrap of a thing.* Both scraps were gone now. She was Assunta, sturdy and fit for hard work. *Sunta Angiolina Ida* was as dead as the orphans whose foreheads she had kissed.

The priest seemed blind to the fact that some of the children were clean and well-fed while others, like her, were tired, hungry and only clean on top, despite the effort Mary had made to scrub her down.

Assunta's skin was raw, chapped, chilblained, broken and bruised from work, burnt from cooking and ironing. The scars and bruises were there for anyone to see, along with the dark circles under her eyes.

She could see hunger in a face. The priest must know what it looked like. It was all around him. The bones came up out of the skin like the roots of trees breaking the surface of the ground. The cheeks puffed out under the bones and the body puffed out, too, from bad sour grain.

The housekeeper came back with a tray of biscuits and tea. Assunta and the other alleycats leaned forward as one and secured the plate of biscuits between them, before the children from the village who had real parents could make a move. They were slower. They had no need of the priest's biscuits.

'No, no, Assunta, you have to share,' the priest singled her out and made her open her fists. There were three biscuits clenched in each one. 'You may have two,' he told her. 'Go on, put the other four back.'

He didn't make anyone else share. The other orphans were bigger and might have refused. Assunta put the four biscuits back on the plate. Her face felt very red and the other children made faces at her, orphans and the rest.

'God loves all his children equally, whatever their station in life,' the priest said as they munched their biscuits.

Assunta fought against choking. She took a swallow of tea and didn't eat any more.

'Remember, children, of those to whom much has been given, much will be required,' the priest went on.

Did he mean the children with beds, or at least mangers, instead of blankets on cold floors? The children who let others take biscuits out from under their noses, because they had more at home?

'You are all among the fortunate, as you know.'

Assunta took another swallow of tea, as his glance burned her. He thought she was *among the fortunate*. But her fortune had been the shelf in the door of the Casa, then years spent doing her best to please in poor, crowded, dirty houses where

32

there was never enough food, and then the poorest, filthiest house of all.

Could the priest read her thoughts? If he did, he would accuse her of being ungrateful. It was a great sin to be ungrateful. Victor *left her alone.* He was pure, and she had remained pure. To the priest, like Sister Bernice, that was all that mattered.

What could impurity be like? She had seen it and heard it. It was hellfire and damnation. But like fire, it made heat. Bodies sweated, lips were flecked with foam. She'd seen animals. They shivered and whimpered. Still, they did it. Like hell, it might be better than cold heaven. But it was a sin to think so.

Her First Communion clothes would be a skirt and blouse, not a dress. They were white with small black spots on the skirt. They were clean and neat, the best clothes she had ever had. She lifted them to her nose to smell the precious starch that was only used for customers' clothing.

Before she received Jesus in Communion, she had to make her First Confession. Mary and Victor walked with her to the church. They walked slowly, as they always did. Assunta had passed the heavy iron over their freshly washed clothes, but they were still rags and of course there was no smell of starch. She caught the pitying looks from those they passed.

Their leathery, sweaty hands held hers tightly and told her silence was expected of her, as always. There must be no telling of family secrets to the priest, no talk of hunger or overwork or beatings.

She could tell the priest she was often dizzy with hunger and thought she might faint. She could say she ate grass sometimes. She could say she was beaten for making sure they kept their customers.

But when she climbed into the confessional, she felt very small. The big wooden box was tall and dark around her. She remembered how the priest had made her put the biscuits back on the plate, and she felt even smaller.

'Bless me Father for I have sinned,' at twelve she was well past the Age of Reason. She had been sinning for five whole years.

'Yes my child,' the priest agreed with her.

Assunta confessed morning and evening prayers unsaid. She confessed her envy of the girls from the village who would have white dresses that floated them up the aisle. She saw the dresses as she spoke, soft and billowy.

'That is vanity, my child,' the priest said sharply. 'It is many sins in one. The sin of covetousness can lead to greater sins of theft,' he said.

Assunta was silent. Her pride would never let her steal, except for food, and then only when she absolutely had to.

'Vanity leads directly to impurity,' he said, 'and that is the worst sin of all. It makes Our Lady cry, do you understand?'

His deep voice rose. Victor and Mary would hear him, outside in the church.

'Yes Father,' she whispered.

'One day you will have a husband, I hope,' the priest said, 'and you will bear children to the honour and glory of God. Until then, you need to be vigilant of your chastity.'

'Yes, Father.' The words seemed to swirl around her in the darkness.

'Your purity should blossom like a lily in the midst of weeds. Remember what Our Lord said of the lilies of the field.'

She was silent, lost in the tall confessional. She didn't remember what Our Lord said and even if she had, she couldn't speak.

'He said that lilies neither toil not spin, but not even King Solomon in all his glory was dressed like one of them. That is what you must be, a beautiful lily for Our Lord and Our Lady. That matters far, far more than any earthly white dress. It is the pearl of great price. It is what separates us from the animals.'

What separates us from the animals is that they have more food.

34

They suck from their mothers like Baby Jesus. Her mind spat back the sinful words without her willing them. But they were still a sin, and she had ruined her confession. She said her Act of Contrition in a shaking voice. Was she sorry? She was sorry for Victor and Mary's house, for cold and dirt and hunger and that, too, was a sin.

How could she not want a soft, white, new dress for her First Communion? What did she know about pearls and lilies? Her stomach knotted and she knelt rigidly behind the little screen the priest spoke through.

'For your penance say the fifteen decades of Our Lady's rosary and meditate on all the holy mysteries.'

'Yes Father.'

He gave her Absolution and she left the confessional to tiptoe up the aisle to Our Lady's shrine. She looked up at the statue smiling the same smile as the statue in the Casa. It was hard to imagine the statue crying, even for impurity.

She got up from her knees after one decade of the rosary. That was long enough. That way she would not seem to be such a great sinner, and Victor and Mary would forget what they had heard, if they had heard anything. They were both quite deaf.

But as they walked her home, chaining her to them again with their heavy hands, all she felt from them was relief and gratitude. They could tell she had not described their lives, in the confessional. They had been afraid of losing her, and they couldn't survive without her. As they became weaker, she did more and more of their work. Lately, she had led the sheep up the hillsides for Victor more days than not, before and after long hours of sewing and ironing and cooking in the cramped, dark house.

As she walked up the aisle on her First Communion day in her made-over clothes, she felt like someone else, someone whose name might be *Santa Angiolina Ida.*

'God never sends anyone a cross too great for them to bear,' the priest said from the altar.

Yes He does.

Why did she think things that were sins? She had already committed a sin by not saying the whole of her penance in the church in front of Victor and Mary, because she was ashamed. And there were other, lonelier sins she could not confess. She did not even have the words for them. But she had the shame.

She would never be pure of heart. There were no lilies in her life, no pearls. They were for Sunta Angiolina Ida. She might have been pure of heart, but she was gone.

Help us, Assunta prayed as the priest droned on, directing her prayer to the statues, to Jesus in the tabernacle on the main altar, to the proud parents in the congregation, to the priest. *We're not alleycats. Cats have more to eat than we do.* Assunta opened her mouth and closed it with the words still inside. She felt the old knots tighten in her stomach, one knot for every word she didn't say, going round and round and round, the same words every time.

Maria's Memo

Mamma has more long, gruelling years to go, before I come onto the scene. I know it's cowardly of me, but I can't go on watching her suffer and seeing what it does to her.

Different kinds of lives go on in the same world at the same time. Mamma was twelve when she made her First Communion. The years are passing quickly, as they do, even though the days and weeks are slow. It's 1884. She's sixteen, and nothing has changed.

But what was the other half of the world doing, while Mamma was starving? I'd like to see another child, someone totally different from her, someone, for example, like little Eugenio Pacelli, who will become Pope Pius XII and canonize Saint Maria Goretti, seventy years later. It's fun to play with time, now that time has stopped playing with me. I'm going to take a peek at Eugenio's eight-year-old life.

3

Via Monte Giordano 3
(now Via degli Orsini)
Rome, Italy, 1884

'In nomine Patris et Filii et Spiritus Sancti,' Eugenio Pacelli swept a graceful sign of the cross from his forehead to his heart and then to each shoulder. At eight years of age he was aware of the whiteness of his hands and what his mother called his *long, sensitive fingers* as he began the Mass, wearing a piece of spotless damask that had once been a tablecloth. She had made it over into a chasuble, cutting and seaming a hole for his head, tailoring and trimming it to frame his thin form. She ironed it for him often.

'Amen.' She whispered the response devoutly from where she knelt behind him.

His grandfather muttered his *Amen* from the chair where he dozed and fitfully attended his grandson's performance of the Mass. But if Eugenio should make a mistake, the old man would be wide awake in a second.

'Introibo ad altare Dei,' he and his mother both thrilled to the familiar words. *I will go to the altar of God.*

Women could not serve Mass, of course. The responses were for an altar boy to make. Eugenio was an altar boy. But when hc celebrated the holy sacrifice of the Mass in their parlour, his mother made the responses from a respectful distance. His grandfather had to be left in peace with his prayers and memories.

Eugenio knew every word, every gesture of the Mass. He

played this game every day, if he could. If he missed out a day, he felt lesser for it and he sensed that his mother did, too.

Eugenio is a born priest. He had heard his mother say it, then seen her colour as his father gently reproached her.

We must not presume, Virginia. If God wants the boy to be a priest, we will be honoured beyond our deserving. But it is not for us to say.

She had bowed her head as she was bowing it now, for the Confiteor.

Nonetheless, his grandfather had said, and shrugged expressively. Only that one word, not enough to defy his son's authority in his own household. But enough to thrill Eugenio and affirm his mother's judgment, without harm or offence. A judgement that his father shared, yet felt he had to temper with a reminder that in the end, God would decide.

Diplomacy came easily to his grandfather. Before Eugenio was born he had served Pope Pius IX, the famous and beloved Pio Nono, longest-serving pope in history. Marcantonio had retired from his long and distinguished service to the papacy as a Marquis twice over, with stories that had become as much part of Eugenio as the life of Christ and the lives of his favourite saints.

'I confess to Almighty God, to blessed Mary ever virgin, to blessed Michael the Archangel, to blessed John the Baptist, to the holy apostles Peter and Paul, to all the saints and to you, Father, that I have sinned exceedingly in thought word and deed. Through my fault, through my fault, through my most grievous fault,' Eugenio squeezed his eyes shut and tapped his chest with his tight right fist in an ecstasy of guilt and penitence, knowing his mother was doing the same. A sneaking glance told him that his grandfather's gnarled old fist had found its way as if by reflex to his own chest, though his eyes were closed and no words came from his slack lips.

What were his mother's sins, apart from her ambitions for him? Four years before him, there had been his sister Guisppina, then two years after her, his brother Francesco. But her two older two children, wonderful as they were, had not satisfied her soul. God wanted more of her. He wanted Eugenio, her born priest.

It was harder to understand why she then found it necessary to bring his sister Elizabetta into the world, when he was four. But it was not a sin. She was a married woman and had certain obligations. He knew vaguely what they were, more by a process of elimination than anything concrete. They were the things the Virgin Mary had not done.

'Kyrie eleison,' he intoned the only Greek in the Latin Mass. *Lord have mercy.*

'Christe eleison,' his mother responded. *Christ have mercy.*

The Virgin Mary was his real mother. She was pure and spotless and had had only one child, Christ. Twice a day his mother led her children to her shrine in a corner of the parlour to pray to her, and the entire family said her rosary there every night.

When the time came, he washed his hands from the clean oil cruets his mother had given him, shivering a little. The apartment was cold. After the Mass he would warm his hands at the little charcoal brazier that they used for heat, unless his grandfather required it. But for now he offered the cold up for the souls in purgatory, many of whom must owe their flight to heaven to the cold at Via Monte Giordano 3.

He was coming to the Canon of the Mass, the heart of the sacrifice. He would pronounce the words of transubstantiation, practicing for the day when his pale fingers would be empowered by Holy Orders to change the bread and wine into the body and blood of Christ. Once he was a priest, he would say Mass every day of his life, until he died.

'Hic est corpus meum,' he genuflected as he raised his arms and looked up at his hands, positioned to lock a white sliver like a small moon into place between them and hold it up for all to see. He could feel his mother behind him, willing him on. There was no white disc yet, of course. But its fragile image was there. They could both see it.

41

This was his test. He celebrated his masses *a cappella*, without the three bells that rang out in churches to warn the faithful that the moment of consecration was near. Every priest had to find the degree of concentrated silence in himself that drew his congregation with him in the supreme moment. Alone on the altar with his back to them, he was the conduit through which they would reach the Holy of Holies. But Eugenio had to do it without the dramatic assistance of the bells.

He looked out of the corner of his eye and saw that the silence had roused his grandfather. He had succeeded. He had embodied the specific intensity that dug an old man from his doze. He would awaken others, from sin as well as sleep. It was his destiny, and the two people in his congregation knew it.

He took the beautiful old silver cup that had been in the family for generations and held it in his hand as he pronounced the words 'His est sanguinis meum, this is my blood of the new and eternal covenant, the mystery of faith. It shall be shed for you and for many in the forgiveness of sins. Do this in commemoration of me.' He genuflected as he held the cup up high.

He knew his mother was looked forward to the time when he would place the body of Christ on her tongue. He had little hope of being in time to give the Eucharist to his eighty-year-old grandfather, thereby making these apprentice masses even more important to the old man. As he read out the list of saints to be remembered, he felt their greater ambition for him. Even his father would acquiesce in that, for Eugenio and all his children as well as his wife, his father and himself. What else was worth striving for, if not the ultimate crown? To be with Christ and the Virgin Mary and the blessed saints in heaven, that was the aim of every baptized soul.

His grandfather had lapsed into sleep over the long recital of saints' names. The climax of the Mass was over. Eugenio recited the rest without thought of rushing or mumbling, though many priests did. His masses would be meticulous.

'Ite Missa est,' he said regretfully. *Go, the Mass is ended.*

His mother bowed her head for his blessing, not so low that she couldn't watch his hands inscribe the cross in the air. They looked at his grandfather, tilted sideways in sleep after his brief rally. Eugenio blessed him as well, smiling. Then he helped her up from her knees. She leant forward, her serious, distinguished face soft with love, and kissed his cheek.

'It was beautiful, Eugenio,' she said softly. 'Now I must go and see to our supper.'

'God expects us all to do our duty,' he said. It was in place of a homily, and made the Mass feel more complete.

'Play your violin, Eugenio,' the old man startled him by requesting. 'Go on. Otherwise I will feel melancholic,' he threatened, gesturing towards the chair that was always turned to the wall in the austere parlour. 'Go on, warm your hands and play the Schubert *Ave Maria* for me and your mother.'

Eugenio went to the charcoal brazier and held his hands over it. He looked at the chair his grandfather had indicated. It was a symbol of the papal territories that had been ripped away from the pope with the unification of Italy. Victor Emmanuel had struck the final blow by seizing Rome. Now the pontiff had only his little Vatican City, as it was known; but even that was not officially his.

Marcantonio refused to recognize the new Kingdom of Italy. His grandfather had worn one glove all his life, no matter how cold the Roman winter. His father did the same. It was the custom among those, like the Pacellis, who were Black Nobles, the elite who waited faithfully and worked zealously for the restoration of the papal lands.

His grandfather had hoped to have a hand in that restoration, but instead had lived to see more and more indignity meted out to the Holy See. At least he had seen the pope brought back to Rome in triumph, after he had been forced to flee.

He had told Eugenio the story many times. One of the pope's ministers had been stabbed to death in broad daylight, and the next day the pope's summer palace above the city of Rome was sacked by the same filthy rabble from which his assailant had come.

Our Pio Nono had to be disguised in a plain black cassock, old Marcantonio shook his head mournfully, *he bore it with such patience, like a saint. An old cassock and a big, wide pair of spectacles, to hide his face. Imagine, he stayed away for a year before he came back. And after that,* his voice sank as Eugenio waited for the last line, always the same, *our Pio Nono never left the Vatican again until the day he died.*

Eugenio was haunted by the spectre of the prisoner pope, waiting for a release that only came with death. In his imagination, Pio Nono still roamed the Vatican clad in his plain black cassock and big spectacles, though he knew his father went to the Vatican every day to work as Dean of all the canon lawyers for Leo XIII, who was Holy Father now.

Pio Nono had proclaimed the doctrine of papal infallibility, after his return to Rome. He had already proclaimed the doctrine of the Immaculate Conception, declaring that the Virgin Mary, alone of humanity, had been conceived and born free of the taint of Original Sin. His grandfather had been by the pope's side for those historic proclamations from the papal throne.

Yet for all that his grandfather had achieved, including the founding of the influential Vatican newspaper, *L'Osservatore Romano*, Marcantonio had had to bear the loss of the papal holdings. It was the tragedy of his life, of all their lives.

Eugenio reached for his violin on the shelf next to the most important books. His father's beloved *First Principles*, a meditation on death by Saint Alphonse Liguori, had pride of place. His father read from it every day, and every year he took a devout band of pilgrims with him to a Roman graveyard, where they stood for an hour and meditated on death.

He took up the violin and found that his fingers moved nimbly enough. He began the Schubert *Ave Maria*, his mother's favourite, and she came to the kitchen doorway to nod and smile at him, wiping away a tear at the same time.

He played with his eyes on his grandfather and when the old man's eyes opened, his own closed. Eugenio offered up his playing for the intention that the chair be taken down from against the wall and used again, and his father wear two gloves, when the papal lands were handed back.

It would not happen while his grandfather lived. But he had made his noble contribution and now his mind must be fixed on heavenly things, not earthly matters. He had seen his son become a distinguished and important Vatican lawyer, if not quite as distinguished and important as he had been. Eugenio's older brother Francesco would also study law, as he would himself. The day had not yet come when he could announce his vocation to the priesthood, except through his practice masses, always celebrated when his father was not at home, though he knew about them, of course. No one would have dreamt of deceiving him. There could be no deceitfulness in their pious household.

His hopes soared with the notes his long fingers drew from the strings. What those hopes were he could hardly think, let alone say. But what was left unsaid, even unformulated in the mind and heart and soul, was seen by Almighty God.

There was an earthly crown, as well as a heavenly one. It was rare to bring them together. When he was six, Eugenio had asked his grandfather why the pope needed so many lawyers. Old Marcantonio had smiled grimly.

'The devil is very busy around the Holy Father, Eugenio.' He had made the sign of the cross hastily, to ward off the devil as he said the name. 'Where there is such holiness, the Evil One redoubles his efforts. There are many who would undermine and slander the pope and seek to further reduce the power of the Holy See. There is a need for the keenest legal minds – among which,' he had added humbly, 'I hardly count my own humble powers – to attend the pope and see to his many earthly concerns.'

'You protected the pope, Grandpapa,' Eugenio had said, smiling. 'My Grandpapa protected our Papa, and now my papa protects our Papa!'

'Yes, it's true,' his father had smiled and agreed when the remark was relayed to him that evening. 'But you must never joke about the Holy Father, Eugenio. It could be disrespectful.'

Eugenio remembered the exchange vividly. He had been slightly crestfallen. He would never be disrespectful about the pope. Later, though, he had heard his father repeat the joke to his mother. They had both commented on how quick-witted Eugenio was, at such a young age. Then there were other murmurs, too low for him to hear.

His father brought a little bit of Vatican City, shrunken as it was to one hundred and eight and a half acres of uncertainly held territory, home with him every day, just as his grandfather kept the invisible landscape of the former papal territories inscribed like faded but beautiful old maps on their walls.

'Only the pope wears not just a crown but a triple crown,' his grandfather had told Eugenio when he was still a small boy. The beehive-like crown was placed on the new pope's head at his coronation with the words:

Accipe thiaram tribus coronis ornatam,et scias te esse Patrem Principum et Regnum, Rectorem Orbis, in terra Vicarium Salvatoris Bostri Jesu Christi, cul est honor et gloria in sacula saculorum. Receive the tiara adorned with three crowns and know that thou art Father of Princes and Kings, Ruler of the World, Vicar of our Saviour Jesus Christ on earth, to him be honour and glory forever. Amen.

His grandfather was surprised and delighted when Eugenio, aged seven, recited those Latin words to him from memory. His father had explained the more spiritual interpretation of the triple crown as symbol of Christ's three roles: priest, prophet and king.

Thou art Peter and upon this rock I will build my church and the gates of hell will not prevail against it. I will give you the keys to the kingdom of heaven; whatever you bind on earth will be bound in heaven, and whatever you loose on earth will be loosed in heaven.

Those words had been with him for as long as his memory stretched. Their symbol on the papal coat of arms were the two crossed keys in a saltire or cross of St Andrew. The gold key stood for heavenly power, the silver one for earthly power.

His father loved to tell the story of St Andrew's Cross. When the apostle Andrew was crucified, he requested that his cross be in an 'X' shape, because he was not worthy to have the same shaped cross as the one on which Christ had died. *That*, his father always ended the story dramatically, *is what is meant by humility.*

His mother came out of the kitchen and sang while he played, her lovely soprano soaring on the Latin words: 'Sancta Maria, Mater Dei, ora pro nobis, peccatoribus. Nunc et in hora, mortis nostrae, et in hora mortis, nostrae.' *Holy Mary, Mother of God, pray for us now and at the hour of our death.*

Eugenio opened his eyes as he heard his grandfather's low voice. They would die. They would leave him. It must be. But they would leave him in the Blessed Virgin's care, and he would entrust their immortal souls to her. His lips parted to form the *Ah* sound as he joined them in Schubert's long *Amen*.

Maria's Memo

How could that person possibly have seen me for what I was? How could he have any idea of what or who I could have been?

But Mamma is growing up fast and things are taking their course with her. Or is it Providence, plotting her way through life?

In any case, change is on the way, and my life is about to begin as both halves of me come together for the first time. How momentous these meetings are. Nothing a pope does begins to compete with them, really, does it?

4

Assunta felt the priest waiting as she knelt in the confessional and recited her list of sins, always the same ones apart from the sin of envying white soft dresses. That sin was past, and she would never confess one like it again.

Nor would she give the parish priest the satisfaction of saying the words he waited to hear. Corinaldo was a small village and people knew how things stood with Victor and Mary. Someone would have told the priest.

She waited for her Absolution on a cold, bleak day in winter. The years had rushed by since her First Communion seven years ago, though each day was long. She was nineteen now, and what of it? Nothing had changed.

'Listen to me, Assunta,' the priest said when he had spoken the Latin words of Absolution and she had begun to rise from the kneeler in the confessional. 'I have something to say to you.'

She waited, shocked by hearing her name from the murky depths of the confessional. Was he going to speak to her again of ingratitude and impurity? She braced herself against his accusations.

'I know of a young man, a good, strong Catholic young man, who is looking for a good, strong, Catholic wife who will work hard and bear him children to the glory of God. Do you think you might be that young woman, Assunta?'

She was mute with shock.

'He is a poor man. You will be a poor man's wife, but God is good and you are used to that,' the priest went on. 'Shall I arrange a meeting, here at the rectory?'

'Yes, Father, thank you, Father,' she answered. Her own

voice sounded dull and thick in her ears. It carried no excitement or anticipation. But she was sealed against those things.

'Very well then,' he sighed. 'I will arrange it, Assunta.'

Even the statue of the Virgin Mary looked different, as she walked down the aisle in a daze. Victor and Mary no longer accompanied her to Confession and she knelt for a long time, going round the rosary and trying to take in what the priest had said. How would she tell them, helpless and bedridden as they were?

But it was clear that they already knew. Her marriage was a reward for her silence. Their lives were narrowing and would soon close. The end would be hard, but hastened by hunger. They were sending her away before she had to see it. It might have killed her, too. Such things happened.

Assunta was grateful to them, for the first time. It was a warm feeling. She wondered whether she would have warm feelings for Luigi Goretti, or he for her.

Would he be disappointed in her, as Mary and Sister Bernice had been? She hoped she would find it in herself to be different with him. He was a man and no man had left her on the poorhouse shelf, or thrown away the scrap of paper with her real name on it. There was the priest, of course, who saw nothing. Except that he had, that was why she was meeting Luigi Goretti. But Luigi was another sort of man again, not a priest. A man who desired a woman.

Would he desire her? Assunta had never asked this question before. She knew she lacked beauty. She was not exactly big, but she was ungainly, bulky despite her hunger. It had always been an advantage, until now.

'Luigi is a good man,' Victor rasped.

'He needs you more than we do,' Mary added, and he nodded.

Mary's words cast a chill over the glow of gratitude Assunta felt towards her foster parents. How could anyone need her more than they did? Was Luigi crippled? Was he ill? She was filled with trepidation when she went to the priest's house to meet him. It was clear she had no choice but to accept him. The choice belonged to Luigi, or perhaps not even to him. It belonged to the priest and her foster parents.

'Sit down, Assunta,' the priest said to her. 'Luigi will be here shortly. I wanted to have a word with you first.'

Perhaps he would tell her the details of Luigi's disability. She took the chair he indicated. It was soft and welcoming and she sank into it, hoping there might be biscuits.

'St Paul tells us it is better to marry than to burn,' he began.

'Yes, Father,' she kept her eyes down. She liked the word *burn*. The priest might see her liking in her eyes.

'Therefore I feel it's time for Luigi Goretti to find a wife,' he continued.

'Yes, Father.'

'He lost his mother very young, Assunta, and he lived with his father and stepmother until recently. Not an ideal arrangement,' he pronounced.

'No, Father,' she agreed, though it didn't sound so bad to her. Perhaps the stepmother didn't like him, or preferred her own children, the ones who had come warm from her body? She had known that situation, in some of her early foster homes. It comforted her that his real mother had died when he was a child. It brought the idea of him closer.

'But now his father has died, God rest his soul.'

'Amen,' Assunta replied.

'And it's time for Luigi to go out into the world and make his own way,' he continued briskly. 'It's because of this that he has come to Corinaldo, to work on the land. He is badly in need of help, Assunta.'

'Yes, Father.' She understood. Luigi Goretti needed her to work, as everyone had always needed her. But would she belong to him any more than she had belonged to them?

'Your purity is to your credit and the credit of your family, Assunta,' he said.

Your family. The word startled her. Was he inviting her to challenge him, to answer *I have no family*? He knew she wouldn't speak, now of all times. When Luigi comes, I shall retire to the desk in the corner and look over some papers,' he said. 'I shall remain in the room to protect your virtue and make certain nothing is said or done to upset you, nothing of which Our Blessed Lady would not fully approve.'

Our Lady would be there too, of course. Her image was certainly present. While he spoke, Assunta counted three statues and five holy pictures, three of Our Lord and two of Our Lady. There was a Sacred Heart, a Crucifixion scene and a Good Shepherd. Mary was shown with a serpent's head under her bare, uplifted foot. Assunta looked away from that one. The other statue showed Mary with the Baby Jesus, so really there were four of Our Lord.

'When you are married, Assunta,' the priest startled her again. 'There are certain things – certain unclean things that a man and a woman should not do together, even when they're married. I will explain to you what they are, when the time comes.'

He smiled at her and she smiled back, blushing. What could he mean?

'It will be up to you to keep your marriage pure in the eyes of God,' he told her. 'Men cannot be held responsible for their urges, which were given to them in order to assure that the human race continues. It is part of the duty of a wife to gently assist her husband to fulfil this sacred task in the natural way God created for men and women to fulfil His divine purpose. Anything that does not tend towards this end is unlawful and an abomination unto the Lord.'

It was an old joke. *Ah, your new father has it off with his sheep*, Georgio had taunted her when they heard that Victor was a shepherd. The little holes of animals were pink and round and exposed. Men might drive themselves into their wives that way, too, without the fear of conceiving another mouth to feed.

'I understand, Father,' she said firmly, and the priest looked startled and almost disappointed. Then there was an uncertain knock on the open door and a firm *Enter, Luigi* from the priest, who motioned Assunta to remain in her chair. Luigi Goretti stood in the doorway and she knew she would have no problems of that sort with him.

She also understood what Mary had meant when she said *He needs you more than we do.* Assunta had been chosen for the bulky strength and sturdiness of her body, not in spite of it.

Luigi Goretti was small and pale. He was more handsome as a man than she was pretty as a woman, but more delicate as well. That was his handicap. She had been chosen to compensate for his weakness with her strength. She was not an alleycat any more, she was an ox, and she would work like one for the rest of her life. She saw it all in a flash, as Sunta Angiolina Ida's scrap of paper was torn into a thousand pieces and cast to the wind.

Luigi was dark-eyed and intent. His deep-set brown eyes blazed in his thin face and kept him from being ferret-like. No one would ask her whether she liked him well enough to marry him, not even Luigi himself. But she decided that she did.

If he was disappointed, he hid it well. She smiled at him. He deserved a smile, and she knew that real smiles improved her appearance. They were not easy for her to find.

Luigi smiled back. He had combed his hair carefully. The priest gestured him into a straight-backed chair, facing her. He sat with more dignity and confidence than Assunta felt. She struggled to remain on the edge of her chair, thinking ahead to when she would have to rise. She might be an ox, but she did not want to look like one.

'I hope you and your family are well, Assunta,' Luigi said formally, clearing his throat.

I have no family. Give me one! 'Thank you, yes. And I hope you and your family are well too,' she replied.

'We are.'

'I have good health, thanks be to God,' she assured him

'I, too, thanks be to God,' he echoed.

'I am eager to change my circumstances,' Luigi continued after a glance – for reassurance, or permission? – at the priest. 'My mother died when I was very young and I lived with my father and stepmother – she is a good woman and she treated me well, of course,' his voice told Assunta the opposite was true. 'But my father is dead now, and I have land of my own to tend, with a house to keep. I need a wife to keep it for me and help me in all my endeavours, to the honour and gory of God,' he ended in a rush, raising his voice slightly for the priest's benefit.

She understood what he hadn't said. His position in the house kept by his stepmother had been bearable. In the absence of his father, it was not. He had rushed into working a small strip of land, the best he could get. It had taken all his energy and it was more than he could manage. She knew his story as well as he did.

'My mother left me in the door of the Casa in Senigaglia on the day I was born – with a note that said I had been baptized,' she would not tell him the rest, not yet. But she would begin with the truth. 'A Sister at the Casa told me about the note, which she had destroyed. I was fostered many times and then when I was six I went to my present family, and I have worked there ever since.' She paused. He would know what she meant by *I have worked*.

'I would also like to change my circumstances,' she went on bravely, meeting his eyes, 'and have a family and home of my own. I would keep it very well,' she promised. 'I can cook and sew and work in the fields and take care of animals – I am used to hard work,' she said simply. 'I have never known anything else.' Let the priest make of that what he would.

Luigi looked back at her and smiled. 'Perhaps,' he said respectfully, 'we might also be kind to each other, Assunta.'

'Yes,' she nodded hopefully. Would she be able to learn what kindness was and how to give and receive it? It might be her hardest lesson yet.

'Very good, my children,' the priest stood up from his desk and came towards them as if, now that kindness had been mentioned, the conversation might stray into dangerous territory. 'You seem to have settled matters in an exemplary way for pure sons and daughters of our Holy Mother Church, and we shall read the banns beginning next week. You may meet here on Sundays, after Mass, for a few minutes each week.' He beamed at them as he extended this hospitality. 'It's as long as you can be spared from your work,' he reminded them.

'Thank you Father,' Luigi said. 'I would like to give Assunta something, if I may. As a token of our betrothal.'

The priest nodded. 'Yes, Luigi, all right.'

Luigi reached into his pocket and took out a small white box. 'This is all I have from my mother, Assunta. She made my father promise he would give them to me for my wife, when I became engaged.'

He said the word *wife* formally and seriously. Assunta took the box with trembling hands. She opened the lid and inside there were a pair of pearl earrings mounted on tiny, thin gold half-hoops.

'Thank you Luigi,' she said, winking back tears.

'Gold is supposed to protect your eyes, not make you cry,' the priest said.

Cecelia was right. Assunta wanted to ask if you had to be a baby for the protection to work, but she didn't. The priest shook both their hands and then Luigi grasped Assunta's hand enthusiastically. She enjoyed the pressure but did not return it, in case the priest noticed. She had her earrings clenched in her other fist.

Luigi left first and then the priest ushered Assunta out. Mary and Victor were waiting. They looked curious, but said nothing.

57

'We have arranged matters,' the priest told them. He looked at them as if he might be thinking of what Assunta had said to Luigi about her life, and sighed. 'Assunta has something to show you.'

Assunta opened the little white box and showed them the earrings Luigi had given her. She got a better look at them herself than she had dared to, before. They were much prettier than Cecelia's.

'It's good that you're a seamstress, Mary. You can pierce her ears with one of your needles.'

The priest was letting them both know that he had seen the earrings and he expected to see them again. Assunta felt offended on their behalf. Mary and Victor were harsh, because life was harsh. But they would die before they took her earrings.

'Yes, Father, of course,' Mary said.

'We shall marry them as quickly as possible,' he told her.

'That's for the best, Father,' she agreed.

Victor murmured his assent. Walking home between them, Assunta felt Mary squeeze her hand as she said softly, 'I hope you will think of us kindly, Assunta, in your new life.'

There was so much she could say. There was also a temptation, surprising but powerful, to throw herself into the arms that had tried to embrace her when she first arrived from the Casa. But it was too late. It had always been too late, from the moment Sister Bernice threw away the scrap of paper and the scrap of Sunta Angioline Ida along with it. Perhaps even before then, when the same hands that held the pen had placed her on the shelf in the poorhouse door and spun it like a wheel of fortune. But now the wheel of fortune had unexpectedly spun again.

'I will try to think only of my new life and the future, Mother, not the past,' Assunta said in a neutral voice.

'Of course. And I hope it will be a happy future, Assunta,' Mary replied.

When they got home, Mary took her sewing box out and

58

Assunta prepared herself to have holes put in her ears. She would have gone through much worse things, to have the earrings.

Mary was quick and it was done without fuss. She left threads in Assunta's ears until they healed. Then she could put her earrings in, in time for her wedding.

Assunta took the earrings out to look at them again, when she was alone. She could hardly believe they were hers. The milky light of the pearls made her think of the priest talking about *pearls and lilies*, though she couldn't remember what he'd said. But she held pearls in her hands, and soon they would shine from her ears. The little gold half-hoops twinkled.

She was escaping from Mary and Victor because of their shame. They should never have taken her from the Casa. Everyone in the village said so. As for the priest, he shared the blame with Sister Bernice. Assunta's marriage had come out of silence and shame, like everything else in her life. But she still hoped it might be different.

Maria's Memo

Papa was lucky in Mamma, I see that now. He might have had a slight edge when it came to looks. He might have been more respectable. He was not a bastard.

He was a quiet, gentle man, my poor Babbo. He needed someone like Mamma. He was not a man to coax life from the thin, hard soil. The only crops he ever succeeded in growing came from her flesh.

Because of Mamma, her children would be strong. Perhaps it was said, with easy brutality: 'Their children must be strong, above all. Nothing else matters.'

Almost certainly, it was said. Mamma was a conduit for children and the crops to feed them. Tilled soil, tilled flesh. The dual curse of Eve. Later they'd say she was a conduit for me, a peasant woman willed by God from all eternity to be the mother of a saint. And Mamma would try as hard as she could to believe it. Perhaps she succeeded.

But first she would learn more hard lessons. She thought she had learned them all, when she had only just begun.

5

Assunta would be married in a red blouse and a black skirt, with a black scarf on her head. Her wedding costume was carefully chosen. Mary took her to the market in Corinaldo, where people from the village wished her well and blessed her. She wore her earrings for the first time, and they were much admired.

'Everyone loves a bride, Assunta,' Mary said, almost reproachfully. 'Afterwards they will forget you,' she added.

Assunta smiled at her warning. Did Mary think she was a fool? Hard work and hunger were lasting. Nothing else. But she was much younger than she looked. She was not beyond the reach of longing. She had not learned to will herself past hope. She could be tempted over the threshold of feeling once more, perhaps for the last time. How could she refuse to go?

Her new clothes were unheard-of luxuries, though her entire trousseau had cost very little. But it was a lot to them. When they got home and she was smoothing out the white nightgown, Mary turned to her.

'Assunta, you know you have to submit to your husband in certain ways,' she said hesitantly.

'Of course, Mother,' she said impatiently. How could Mary think she had reached the age of nineteen without knowing all about it? Mary's face changed, and she realized she had missed another chance to be a daughter. Mary wanted to tell her things she might already know, in order to bring them closer. And she had ruined it. Would she always ruin the moment when closeness was offered? Would she ruin it with Luigi?

The week before the wedding, Mary went with her to see the little house she would share with Luigi on the land he was working for its wealthy owners.

'They could have done better than this,' Mary said as they went in. 'It's as small as our house.'

It was. But it was clean, and more light came in through the windows.

'We will make it better,' Mary said determinedly. She spread the tablecloth she had presented to Assunta the night before, from her own trousseau.

'It's so fresh,' Assunta said. When she was alone in the house, she would sniff the starch.

'It has never been used,' Mary said.

'Never?' Assunta was startled.

'There was no occasion for it,' Mary said simply, pulling the corners to even the cloth on the rickety little table in the kitchen.

Assunta felt a stab of pity for her.

'These belonged to my mother,' Mary explained as she placed two white plates on the cloth. 'They have also never been used.'

The white dishes had passed unused from generation to generation. Assunta was not the only one who harboured another life within her, a life as beautiful and fragile as the white plates that were never used and therefore never chipped or stained. Mary might not have had another name, but the clean, faded linen of the tablecloth and the fine white plates spoke of something other than the life she had lived with Victor in their dingy little house.

'I wish I had more to give you, Assunta,' Mary said when she had laid out the cutlery and placed an empty pitcher on the table. 'At least you have your earrings,' she smiled.

'Yes,' Assunta touched one carefully. She wasn't used to them yet. She checked often to make sure they were still there.

'But I do have one more thing,' Mary took a large bundle from the depths of her old string bag.

64

Assunta felt something like dread. She was threatened with feelings that could weaken her, just when she needed to be strong. On the other hand, she wanted to feel something for Luigi. He had not placed her on the shelf in the door of the Casa. But neither had Mary.

'I'm very grateful to you for these things, Mother,' she said woodenly.

'I know you are, Assunta. Come,' Mary led her towards the bedroom.

Assunta hesitated on the threshold. It was a room she would enter with Luigi Goretti. The thought frightened her. She would rather not think about it until the day, or the night, had arrived.

'Come in, Assunta,' Mary sounded cheerful, unlike her usual self.

Assunta entered the room behind her. Mary was spreading a patchwork quilt over the bed. It was made from swatches and remnants of stuff from customers' clothes, old hem-lengths from shortened skirts, useless bits of material from dresses she had made to order. Assunta saw several patches of soft, silky fabric she had rubbed between her fingers with her eyes closed, then opened them to feast on the flowery prints, the deep pinks and reds and purples. She had watched the finished dresses leave the house with the same ache she had once felt for a perfect white Communion dress.

Mary had made the quilt for her without her noticing, just as she had re-worked Mary's mistakes in secret. It was a sly, silent way of thanking her for that.

She touched a piece of pale pink silk, remembering the underskirt it had made for layers of tulle. She fought tears. Mary had starved her and beaten her. How dare she turn around now and do this for her?

'It's only scraps,' Mary said, pulling the quilt straight over the bed.

Scraps. The word made Assunta's tears spill. Mary moved

65

quickly and she was held in an embrace she seemed to be returning, or at least not resisting.

'Scraps for a scrap,' she said thickly, when she could.

'You're not a scrap. You're a good girl, Assunta.'

Good meant *useful*. But she leaned down to touch the quilt again, on a square of black velvet. She wanted to wrap herself in it like a cocoon. Perhaps what flew out would be beautiful.

'You must have this, too, Assunta,' Mary handed her a clean white cloth, neatly folded.

The cloth was like the rags they used for their monthly bleeding, but without old bloodstains or ragged edges.

'Put it beneath you on the bed. Leave it there till morning. That way Luigi will see that you were pure for him,' Mary said. 'Afterwards you can burn it. You will not stain the linens.'

There was always a grain of doubt about the purity of any bride. Assunta heard the priest's voice in the confessional, murmuring about *lilies and pearls*. Purity was not like that. It was bloody and messy and the white cloth was needed to absorb the necessary stain of it.

'It's all right, Mother,' she said, smiling. Women knew what purity meant, even if priests did not.

Mary nodded and smiled weakly back. 'I knew you were a good girl,' she said. 'I'm proud of you Assunta. You have been a good daughter,' she pushed the words out with an effort. 'A better daughter than I have been a mother.'

Assunta gathered the frail body into her arms without a word. There was nothing she could say. Mary was weak and she was strong. She had been the mother and Mary the daughter, except for today.

'Victor is a good man, Assunta,' Mary said, taking her arm as they left the house. 'He protected me, and then he protected us. He could have left us,' she said, nodding as Assunta glanced at her in surprise. 'But he stayed. A man can always leave and have only himself to feed. I am certain that Luigi is also a good man.'

Assunta was startled. As they walked, she puzzled over what Mary was trying to tell her. A man could always leave. It had been true of Victor years ago, if not now when he was old and weak.

She saw the justice of Mary's words, as they walked back together over the stones and cobbles of Corinaldo. Even Mary, ugly and old as she was, would have been preyed upon by other men, if not for Victor. At the very least, she would have been whispered about. Whatever might be said of them in the village, Mary's reputation was never in question.

If Victor had left and Mary or Assunta had slipped, there would have been no pity. Necessity would have made no difference. Better death than disgrace.

But the worst might have been said of them, whether or not it was true. They needed Victor to defend their honour. Useless as he was, without him they would both have been lost.

Just scraps, she heard Mary say as they walked back through the dusk. Her frail body felt relieved at Assunta's side, even relaxed. It was a bit like walking back with Mary and Victor from her first confession, but different. That night, unable to sleep, she puzzled it out.

If Assunta had not been able to demonstrate her purity on the white cloth her almost-mother gave her for the purpose – no longer flown from the window like a flag on the morning after the all-important wedding night, but still every bit as essential – blame would have fallen on her, of course, but then, close behind her, on Mary. A mother was responsible for her daughter's purity. The father did his part simply by being there and, though not in this case, giving her his name. Victor would not be blamed if the white cloth remained white. Mary would have fallen short and she would pay for it, along with Assunta. Purity was not white but red, blood red.

Mary was ill for several days before the wedding, and Assunta sensed that she would be abandoned by the two

67

people the priest had called her *family*, before she could leave them.

She would find out later that Victor had tried to make his way to the church. He was lamer and slower than before, and he had given up and gone home. No one from the village had offered to help him. They were tired of Victor and Mary, their need, their filth. No one wanted to see it or them, not even Assunta, who was more relieved than saddened by their absence.

Two strangers, selected by the priest, stood up for them as witnesses. Assunta found herself imagining Cecelia and Georgio in their place. Were they still together on their farm? They might be anywhere, including heaven. Or hell. *God is merciful, Assunta*, she heard Sister Bernice say. She said a quick prayer for all of them, even her almost-parents, trying to be merciful back. It might help with what lay ahead.

Luigi walked her to their house, arm in arm. It was not like being walked to confession by Victor and Mary. People they passed smiled and wished them well.

'You've made a miracle here, Assunta.' Luigi smiled warmly at her and shook his head in amazement when they stepped inside the house.

She drew him into the bedroom to see the quilt. Let him think she was shameless. She couldn't wait.

'How beautiful!' He cried.

'Yes,' she nodded. 'Now come, let us eat before we work, Luigi.'

He smiled and obeyed her. She was home. The house reminded her of the shanties on the beach she had longed for as a child. She poured out the soup as Luigi walked around, inspecting everything.

'Sit down while you can, for heaven's sake,' she told him. She marvelled that the words came easily to her. She sounded like a wife. Again Luigi smiled and obeyed.

They had bread and soup. There was wine, a present from the priest she didn't open yet. They sat at the table and ate.

She had taken up the precious white cloth, to save it for their evening meal. They would use it, but she wouldn't waste it.

'The soup is delicious, Assunta,' Luigi said.

She smiled at him. The soup was tasty, but thin. She had put a few vegetables in it. The broth was made from a mutton bone.

'Victor gave me the bone. One of his old sheep did us a favour and died, Luigi,' she joked with him across the table, amazed at herself.

'It was kind of him,' Luigi said. 'I must give him my thanks.'

'The sheep?' She asked. 'I think it's too late, Luigi.'

'Victor,' he started to say, then laughed.

'I've already thanked him for us both,' she said, adding thoughtfully, 'who knows? Perhaps he bashed its skull in with a rock.'

'Assunta!'

She shrugged. 'You're right. Probably not. In any case, it was ready to die. The bone had to stew for three days to get any goodness from it.'

'It's very good,' he said.

Assunta was the one who saw the world as it was, and Luigi let it shock him as she had learned not to. Or so she thought.

'It was a kindness on their part, not to eat it,' she said grudgingly. 'The smell was everywhere, in that terrible house.'

'I hope you left them some, Assunta.'

'Of course,' she lied easily. She had felt almost guilty, covering the pot to take it away with her. She had tiptoed to where Mary lay, thinking to ask her about returning the pot. But Mary was deeply asleep and Assunta looked at her white face for a second, then tiptoed out again.

'We can save the priest's wine for the evening, Luigi,' she told him. 'There's work to be done this afternoon, eh?'

'Yes,' he nodded. 'If it's not too much to ask, on your wedding day?'

'No,' she silenced him. What else would they do but work? The other thing, the making of children, could not be done in daylight by decent people. They would wait and work together in the field and begin to know each other that way first. She was not ashamed to be known by her work. It was the best thing about her.

Luigi changed his clothes first in the silent bedroom, while Assunta cleared away their meal. They would not observe each other's nakedness now, in the glare of the afternoon. She was grateful that darkness would fall and they would see by candlelight, when the time came.

There was soup left for evening. She covered it carefully, and put away the bread. They had a bit of fine pasta from the market, too, a small luxury. She would boil it and make it with olive oil and garlic pounded into a sauce. When Luigi came out of the bedroom, she went in and dressed quickly in her old clothes. Then they went together, to work the land.

Assunta saw right away that it was not good land. The soil was thinner than their soup. Only the coarsest grain, a kind of thick, dark, bulbous wheat would be harvested from such land, and it would take hard work to raise even that. She understood Luigi's urgent need of a wife to help him, but what could they pull from this stubborn land?

Still, they had to make it yield. She went to work with a will. He seemed encouraged by her gusto, and they laughed and joked as they worked side by side like comrades. It was a good beginning.

In the evening they ate hungrily and drank the wine the priest had given them. It tasted sour, but it made Assunta feel softer. The soup was better than it had been, and the pasta was delicious.

'We should go to bed. It's been a long day,' Luigi said when the food and wine were gone.

There was a hint of command in his voice. He was her husband, and it was her turn to obey him. This time he let her go first into the cold bedroom. It was summer, but the room was damp and chill. She shivered as she undressed and put on the new nightgown Mary had bought her in the market. It was white linen, clean but unadorned.

She spread the cloth carefully on the bed before she lay down. She hoped it would be over quickly. She had combed out her hair. At least for this it did not matter so much what you looked like. She was tired. It had been a long day. But she had to stay awake for her husband.

Luigi came in, moving quickly and nervously as he undressed. The easy jokes of the afternoon were gone. They were alone with a mystery.

He climbed into the bed next to her and she turned to him. His warmth was welcome. They clutched each other and then they kissed. They went on clutching and kissing until suddenly he was on top of her and then inside. It was quick, urgent, and seemed to hurt him as much as it hurt her. There was a look of pain on his face, or was it pleasure?

There was very little blood. Two large blackish-red clots in a plug of mucous made her a good woman, instead of a good girl. Some women bled like pigs. Did that make them better women? She saw Luigi look at it in the morning, before she took the cloth away to burn it. Her virginity had been there for him to take and he had taken it.

Their days fell into a pattern. They ate, worked, ate again in the fierce heat of the day and went back to work long before it had cooled. They ate their final meal of whatever was left in the evening, and Luigi lay on top of her briefly. There was no more pain. And then they slept.

Soon her monthly bleeding stopped. Her body softened, demanded more food and sleep than she could give it. She wept at night with tiredness, silent tears that slid from her eyelids. Luigi did not draw his body across hers. He let her sleep as much as she could. She was grateful to him. He tried to give her some of his food, but she refused. He was already much too thin and pale.

She had always been hungry, but never like this. Hunger gnawed at her and she dreamt she was eating her baby. It

71

was soft and tender and she devoured it greedily. She woke in shock and guilt that melted to relief.

The birth was long and hard. She cried and whimpered, but kept herself from screaming. The midwife congratulated her on her courage, but her face was worried when she looked at the tiny baby.

'He's so small,' she sighed. 'You will have to feed him often, Assunta.'

Assunta heard her through a haze. Even so, she understood that in order to have enough milk for her baby, she needed to eat more and work less. She told Luigi what the midwife had said when he crept in to see his son, and he nodded. They had always spoken to each other of important things with few words, from the first afternoon in the priest's house.

They gave the baby Saint Antonio for his patron saint. He was the patron of lost things, and one of Assunta's favourites. He had saved her many beatings, at the Casa and afterwards.

She had found something she hadn't known was lost. A bewildering mixture of strangeness and familiarity swept through her when she held her streaming, bloodstained son. He took hold of her from within with a cry, a squeak. His face was the first thing Assunta had ever adored. It was the face behind the host the priest held up at Mass, the only face that mattered.

Her own hunger had never knotted and twisted inside her like Antonio's. He cried feebly from hunger and she stuffed her knuckle in her mouth to stop herself from screaming and scaring him. Her milk was too thin. He stopped suckling to yelp with bitter disappointment and frustration and his little broken cries cut through her more than her labour pains had done. She tucked her nipple back into his mouth, but he grew discouraged and began refusing it.

She understood him. Her understanding split her open, like his birth. He was losing hope and he was too small to survive despair. She smiled at him and sang to him. She kept up a feverish, desperate cheerfulness and said the Joyful

Mysteries over and over again as she held him in her arms. He must feel only joy around him. If he took gloom from her milk, it would poison him.

He lived for eight months. She would not let him go. He slipped from her slowly and she held on tighter and tighter as he slid towards darkness. She made him fight when he was too tired. She fought for him. She wrestled with him. She prayed and sobbed to the Blessed Virgin Mary, because there was no one else.

Luigi made certain another child was conceived before Antonio died. They needed children to help them with the land. Luigi was also was weaker than he had been. The land was draining him. Only Assunta was steelier and stronger, with a strength that came from shocked grief.

She had loved Antonio more than God. He had been everything to her and she to him. She was the wife he would never have and he was the husband Luigi could never be. Her love for him was wild and fierce. It came from somewhere in herself that she had never been before. It excluded everyone and everything else, despite Luigi's nightly visits to her body. He could have it. Her heart was taken.

But Antonio was gone and her heart had gone with him into the ground. Now she was empty, despite the new life in her womb. People around her were sorry, but pleased about the new baby. Babies often died. It was not unexpected. The important thing was to keep on.

The tiredness was worse than the first time, but the hunger was less. Her child had died of hunger, how could she eat? She forced herself to eat enough not to starve the new one before it was born. She was tempted to overwork and let the child bleed out of her, rather than watch it suffer as its brother had done. But Luigi made her stop working. He wanted this new baby.

It was a boy, bigger than the first and more robust. God was good, people said. Assunta was silent. Angelo thrived on the little she had to give him. He sucked so hard on her nipples that he seemed to draw milk from her depths. Antonio had not had the strength to draw on her hidden reserves, to create them with his need. This one did and then, just for good measure, Luigi gave her another child, in case the second one also died. With two, she would feel safer. She laughed at Luigi, but he was right. She had a new fondness for him. He had known what she needed before she did. That had never happened to her before.

This time she gave birth to a girl. Luigi smiled down at her. 'You will have company, Assunta,' he said. 'A daughter will comfort you.'

He knew that she was still not over the loss of Antonio. She smiled weakly back at him. He understood so little, after all. As if she would ever recover.

He seemed to see it in her eyes. 'At least she will help you in the kitchen.'

'Poor thing, she's just born and already you put her in the kitchen,' she protested, laughing a little. She felt the first stirrings towards her daughter. 'I will pierce her ears,' she said. 'We need a little pair of earrings for her.'

He nodded. 'Of course.'

Then Assunta wondered if it was the right thing, after all. What good had her earrings done her? Luigi was right. The baby girl would be in the kitchen soon enough, if she survived. Where else did women lead their lives, except in the fields? How could two females be company for one another when they were always exhausted, starving, bearing or burying children? Her lips set in a line. Better that this daughter should die.

But somehow Luigi Goretti found a little pair of earrings for Maria Teresa, and she lived.

Maria's Memo

I'm in the world now, Mamma, and you don't want me. You know what's in store for me. I'm a girl. It isn't pretty and there is no mystery.

You think there are no mysteries left, that you have plumbed the depths. You are mistaken. Things can always take a different course. But somehow that's the one thing you never learn, despite what your life tries to tell you.

You were abandoned as a newborn infant. Perhaps you thought of it when you had Antonio. The thought made you hold him tighter, but he still slipped from your arms.

They told you to look at Jesus on the cross, but watching your baby writhe with hunger made you smile wryly at the Crucifixion. Only a man could think his own suffering supreme.

Perhaps your own mother couldn't feed you? Did you think of that? Perhaps she saw what lay ahead, when she placed you on the shelf in the poorhouse door. Besides, you had Babbo to protect you and she had no one. She might have kept you if you had been a boy. But no woman could protect a girl-child by herself.

Papa loved me. I was his song-bird. You smiled your wry smile when you heard him say it. You were an alleycat and I was a song-bird. What more was there to say?

Nothing had ever been as you expected. You thought each kind of suffering was the worst and also the last. When Antonio died, you thought you'd reached the bottom of the pit of suffering.

You should have known by the time I came along that life has one name: change. Any fairy tale could have told you that fortune changes in the wink of an eye. But you never heard a fairy tale. You tried to look for reasons, for punishments and rewards.

How many ways are there for God to torture human beings? My answer is two: love and the lack of love. People can make up their minds not to love, like you did. But love isn't in their power. God is love, and love is strong and cruel.

I was a girl as your own mother had been, and you. I was embedded in your flesh even after I was born. I never entirely left you as your sons did. After me came Mariano, then Sandrino, then two more daughters, Ersilia and Teresa.

But I was the oldest girl. I was your apprentice. You depended on me. I was destined for the kitchen, as my Babbo said when I was born. When people speak of the world's oldest profession, they make a mistake. The world's oldest profession is motherhood. It's a hard profession, one that has to be learnt. Whores get more time off. No one can fuck twenty-four hours a day and eventually, anyway, they retire. It's true they can be beaten, hurt and even killed. Yes, and mothers?

A baby is a tyrant like no other, even babies like myself and my brothers and sisters who soon learn not to wear themselves out crying. No one will come when everyone is out in the field, getting the harvest in. Perhaps that's the world's oldest profession, for men and women alike: coaxing food from the reluctant earth. It combines the labours of the whore and the Madonna. The soil must be seduced to make the grain stand up. The shoots need tender care. Madonna and whore, both are needed to make food, to make life.

In any case, it's time for me to live.

6

'My Babbo!' I broke into a run.

Papa turned and smiled. His hand went to his forehead and wiped away the sweat. I ran faster, to jump into his arms.

'Slow down little one, you'll fall –'

Too late. Down I went into the hard caked earth with a thump that skinned my knee, breaking the scabs from the last time.

'You have to slow down, Marietta,' Papa came towards me, puffing as he hurried.

'I'm not crying Papa,' I said proudly.

'No,' he sighed, half-laughing. 'You're always brave, Marietta. But it would be better not to fall, eh?'

'But if I never fell, I wouldn't be brave,' I argued with him.

He scooped me up and piggy-backed me to the house. I felt bigger than Papa. But I loved it when he gave me a piggyback and I knew he did, too.

'I'm a bird in a tree,' I sang as we left the field behind in the late sun. It was still hot. It was always hot, except in winter when it was cold. 'I'll sing for you, Papa.'

'My songbird,' Papa said, as I knew he would. 'Shh, Marietta,' he said then, and slung me down to the ground.

He was sweating again, and stooped. He bent over like an old man when he walked, his face all folded up. I tried to smooth it with my stumpy little fingers, but it always folded up again.

'Listen to the birds,' he said.

I was silent. It was our game, our time. Every evening I ran to meet him and we walked home like this, stopping to listen to the swallows that swooped and dived in the evening, flying together first one way, then turning, all together, and flying the other way.

'Why do they do that, Papa? How do they know?'

'It's a mystery,' he said.

I loved it when he said that word. The birds were a mystery, something familiar and strange in our lives.

'They have a signal,' he explained. 'We can't hear it but they can.'

'A secret signal?'

'A secret signal.'

Like we do, I wanted to say. But he had picked me up again and we were striding towards the house. Our time was over, until tomorrow.

'Marietta, your father is too tired to carry you,' Mamma scolded from the doorway. 'Put her down, Luigi.'

'It's all right, Assunta,' Papa laughed, but his voice scraped his throat.

I loved being carried. But Papa's face was even more folded than before.'

'Marietta, stop making that nasty face. If the wind changes you'll stay that way,' Mamma said.

What way? I couldn't see my face. But I went ahead of Papa into the house, where there were no birds. Our house was dark and it smelled. The rooms were small. I was like a little animal penned up and once I was inside, Mamma's shadow fell across me like another pen in which I was held tight.

Mamma wasn't easy with me like she was with Angelo and little Mariano. They didn't test her like I did. I didn't understand it, but I knew it. More secret signals between people, like birds.

'Now, Marietta,' Mamma put me up at the table. 'Soon you'll be able to help me,' she sighed.

'You'll be a big girl, helping your mother,' Papa said, coming from the kitchen where he had splashed his hands and face with water.

I nodded because I never disagreed with him. But I knew what Mamma wanted. She wanted me so quiet I was almost not there. She wanted me to play dead, so that if I died it wouldn't make too much difference. I couldn't say what she wanted but I knew it. Another secret signal. Once I was big enough to help her, I'd be swallowed by her shadow.

Mamma stayed in the house all the time now. My brother Mariano was still little and there was another baby coming. It was her job to stretch the food we had, to feed us all. The miracle of the loaves and fishes was nothing, compared to what she did every day.

'Your papa needs his rest, Marietta,' Mamma scolded. 'He works hard and he's tired.'

I looked down at my plate. It was cracked like Papa's face. I knew he was tired, better than she did. I brought him joy, not pain. It wasn't only work that tired him, but worry. Papa worked as hard as he could, but it still wasn't enough. He had to work as hard as he couldn't. The harvest could fail. If it failed, he failed. If he failed, Mamma failed. Her milk became too thin and then the baby would fail, too. Papa couldn't let that happen again.

I was a child but I knew these things, not in words but in my bones. I knew how much my parents feared losing another child. Fear made Papa pull me close, and Mamma push me away.

But one day Mamma led me outside and showed me a family of cats she had spotted under the tree behind our house. She had a strange, soft look on her face as she squatted and stared at them.

'They have a nest, like birds,' I laughed.

She smiled. She let me give them water and a little grucl and said I could try to tame one of the kittens and have it for my own.

I watched the nest of kittens for hours, patiently waiting, making the mother cat trust me. Mamma had taught me that cats needed patience. They were suspicious by nature.

I shared my food with the cat family, even though I was hungry. There was never enough, but I was used to that. I saw that giving them food made me almost part of their family.

'I'm a little wild cat. Meow!' I called to Mamma when I came inside.

She looked up with a start. 'Don't say that, Marietta,' she scolded me. 'The cat is a cat and you are a little girl, a child of God.'

'But the kittens are God's children too, aren't they, Mamma? Doesn't God want them?'

'Come, let me brush your hair,' she said instead of answering. 'You look like a little wild thing.'

I wanted to be a little wild thing. I played while she worked. I was pleased by the world that burdened her. I couldn't help it and neither could she.

Sometimes I made Mamma laugh and then I laughed again and clapped my hands like Papa when I sang. To make Mamma laugh, to make Papa's face smooth, these were my aims.

I succeeded in taming a little orange kitten, the same colour as my hair. I was six. I loved my Sole, my sun. He was my toy and my friend.

Sole and I danced for Mamma. I held his front legs and sang, while he protested. Mamma protested, too, but she liked it. When we couldn't make her laugh, I took Sole outside the house to play under the tree. When Mamma was silent and sad, it was best to go away. Her mood turned and she lashed out like Sole's mother cat.

She hit Angelo more than me. He was noisier and naughtier. But I also came within the yardstick of her anger, unless I took myself away.

Meanwhile, God had not run out of ideas where Mamma was concerned. She thought she had nothing left for him to take. She measured out her love for us, thinking measured love brought less pain. But she had another love she didn't

80

measure, because she didn't know it was there. She was busy preparing for the new baby. The midwife came in the middle of the night and I woke with a sense of bustle and noise and breathed in strong, familiar smells like the ones I made when I crouched over the bucket, and when I skinned my knees. There were cries like Sole's when he was outside at night. I went back to sleep and woke to a different cry. My third brother, Sandrino, was with us now. He grew quickly, and though Mamma was busier than ever, she smiled more.

One night after I had gone to bed, I heard my parents talking. They were still in the kitchen, or I would not have heard their words so clearly, or the things they didn't say.

'Assunta,' Papa said, 'we have to leave here.'

I listened hard. Leave Corinaldo! It was home. It was the world.

Mamma grunted like I did when I fell down and skinned my knee, then spoke my thoughts. 'Leave Corinaldo? Our home?' Our land?'

'The land doesn't feed us, Assunta, and it never will.'

'But Luigi –'

'I can't work any harder, and it isn't enough.'

She was silent. What Papa said was true. But he had only come to Corinaldo after his father died.

'You have no roots here. You would tear me from the soil where my child is buried, Luigi?'

'Assunta. We have other children now, and we must feed them. Be reasonable.'

'My soul,' she sobbed. 'Soil,' she corrected herself and I heard in her voice that they were the same.

'We can't lose another child, Assunta.'

'God wouldn't let that happen,' she said and I heard the rustle as she made the sign of the cross.

'If we stay here, who knows?' He sighed. 'Even God couldn't save Antonio.'

'Luigi!'

81

'God expects us to help ourselves,' he went on. 'The only way is to leave here.'

'But if we leave,' she paused. 'We're lost.' The lostness was in her voice.

'Has Corinaldo been so good to you, Assunta?'

'Has it been so bad? It doesn't matter, good or bad, Luigi. Corinaldo, Senigaglia, they're what I know.'

'I'm sorry, Asssunta.'

'Sorry? For what, Luigi? Nothing has ever been your fault, never, never.' She was weeping again. 'It's my fault, I bring bad luck –'

'Don't say that! God will punish us if we lose faith.'

'And how will that be different?'

'Assunta!'

I was shocked and frightened. My parents never spoke like that. But I heard Mamma thinking. She knew Papa had a stronger faith than she did. He was a simpler, better soul than she was. But his goodness made it hard for him to understand her.

'Luigi, when you left your village to come to Corinaldo, didn't you feel you were leaving your mother behind?'

'My mother? But my mother was in heaven!'

'Heaven? Not even purgatory?'

'My mother suffered so much at the end, I knew it was her purgatory,' he answered.

He had looked upon his mother's agony with faith, not horror. Mamma was defeated by his faith.

'Very well, Luigi, we will do whatever you think best.'

Neither Mamma nor I slept that night. We saw the winding, hilly streets of Corinaldo and the smooth weave of the mountains around it. We watched the birds circle the village in the morning and evening and listened to their cries.

Mamma was leaving her dreams, wispy as clouds; her memories, dark and jagged as cliffs. But she felt something almost like Papa's faith, for Corinaldo. A place held a spirit. It didn't watch over you like your Guardian Angel, but it held you. Unlike an angel, you could see it, touch it, smell it, taste it and hear it all around you. The mountains were a kind of protection, not angelic but rounded and real, made from the earth and linked to the sky. They defined the horizon for us. They defined us. They had always been there and they would remain. But we were leaving.

There was nothing to be done, but Mamma's faith quailed before another trial. Her heart would be smashed again. I saw it in her face the next day, and then I turned my attention away from her.

Leaving Corinaldo was my first adventure. It taught me what adventure was. Once you learn, you never forget. I wasn't fearless, but I was excited. Papa said we'd see the sea, we'd see Rome. These were names to me.

'Sole will be with us, Mamma,' I reminded her, lifting him up so that she could see his little orange face. I thought it might comfort her. But her eyes filled and she waved both of us away.

Sole would bring us luck. I was glad he was orange and not black. He could never bring bad luck. Thirteen was bad luck because there were thirteen at the Last Supper, where Our Lord was betrayed. Three was holy, because it was the number of the Blessed Trinity. But deaths came in threes, so it had another side. These things were part of our lives. The bright star of Bethlehem gleamed behind the shooting stars we saw at night, beautiful and troubling. A shooting star signalled another soul gone home to God. Our world was filled with signals we tried to read and understand.

Mamma clung to her rituals and beliefs, in the time before we left Corinaldo. Her almost-mother had taught her these things. We knew Mary, our not-quite-grandmother. She was very old and frail, like Victor, our almost-grandfather, but somehow they clung to life. They wanted us to be theirs, as they had wanted Mamma. But she was not theirs, and neither were we.

But Mamma's almost-mother came to the house often, in

83

the time before we left. She and Mamma grew closer as they were parting. Mary and Victor had always been there in Corinaldo, near but far. Now they would only be far.

Mamma decided that Angelo and I would become grown-ups in the faith, before we left Corinaldo. We would receive the sacrament of Confirmation. This ordinarily happened at the age of twelve or thirteen, after First Communion, and I was only seven, but we were about to make a dangerous journey.

'Confirmation leaves a mark on your soul that can never be erased, like Baptism,' Mamma told us.

I knew what she felt. To her it was the mark of Corinaldo we would receive, like a little map or flag the bishop planted firmly in the soil of our souls. They, too, had come from Corinaldo, mingling *soil* and *soul* as she had done when Papa told her that we had to leave.

Besides, we needed more protection from the devil now. We knew every nook and cranny of our village, there was nowhere he could hide. Once outside Corinaldo, he could be anywhere.

I didn't much like the idea of Confirmation. Mamma hinted that more would be expected of me afterwards, though she never said exactly what. Perhaps the mark on my soul would attract the devil's attention. She talked about the devil a lot.

I was shy when it came to the Confirmation ceremony, and had to be held in the arms of a woman of the parish like a baby. I had not only *not* become a grown-up in the Church Militant, I had become an infant again, like Sandrino. Mamma was angry with me, though she couldn't show it. I was quite happy with the way it had gone. I had answered my question, an easy one, the first one in the catechism: *Who is God?*

God is the Supreme Being who made all things and keeps them in existence.

Afterwards the priest invited us to have some cakes. They were sweet and delicious and I began to change my mind about Confirmation. The priest came up to me and pretended

84

to be very serious in a way that made it clear he wasn't, as he asked me another question.

'Do you know the Holy Father's address, Marietta?'

'Rome, Father,' I stuttered.

'And where in Rome does the Holy Father live?'

'Do you mean the street, Father?'

He smiled. 'No, Marietta, the Pope does not live in a street but a whole city of his own, called Vatican City because inside it is the Vatican, the palace where the Pope lives. If you ever want to visit him, remember that.'

'The Holy Father lives in the Vatican, Vatican City,' I repeated, and everyone laughed.

My mother's almost-mother helped us pack, not that there was much to take. It all fit onto a small handcart. We had one shirt each, and one set of sheets for our beds. They were washed once a year. Our clothes were washed more often than that, but not very often.

Everything was washed before the journey. Mamma scrubbed at our clothes with hard soap. It was suddenly important for things to be cleaner than they had ever been. Even we were scrubbed. It hurt. We didn't take kindly to this unusual treatment, especially Angelo and Mariano. Our skin was tough, but some of the toughness came from dirt – and we wanted to keep the layers we had. Being clean left us more exposed.

I had ridden with Papa before, on the cart drawn by the ox. I loved the sensation of being moved along while I was still. First we had to crouch one by one over the bucket. There would be no time or place once we were on the move, Mamma warned us. Papa took the bucket and emptied it outside in the gutter, and then he rinsed it out to bring along with us.

We were gypsies, me with Sole clutched tight. We had to take the diligence to Scnigaglia and from there take the train to Rome, where we would meet Senator Scelsi's steward, who would take us to our new house on Senator Scelsi's land. *Senator Scelsi* – I said the name to myself like a charm. *Senator*

Scelsi would save us. The land outside Rome was not poor and hard like the land in Corinaldo. It was thick, like the clouds in the sky or snow on the ground, but black and warm. I imagined many things I hadn't seen, like all children.

As we left our house for the last time, Papa was tired and Mamma was sad. I clutched Sole and mounted the diligence, looking at Corinaldo all around me and saying goodbye. Then I looked ahead towards Senigaglia, a place I had heard of all my life. Mamma shivered when she said it. The poorhouse where she had been left was there, and also the sea.

It was bumpy and rough and we had to hold on tight. Mamma scolded Angelo, who was too excited to be still. His excitement made Mariano noisy, too. I wanted everyone to be quiet. I wanted to see everything and not be distracted. I wanted to feel every bump, even when I thought I might slide off my seat onto the dusty road and lose Sole forever.

I would run after Sole, if he escaped. My family would stop the diligence and wait while Papa ran, too. He would catch Sole and pick me up along with him. I comforted myself with this plan as we bounced along the road.

Sole squirmed and fought and scratched me. He wanted to run away, back to Corinaldo. I had to hold him so tight I was afraid he'd suffocate. When we got to Senigaglia, Papa would find a box for him. But in the meantime I held him and let him fight and checked that he was breathing in my hot grip.

As he quieted, I found a way of drowning out Angelo and Mariano's noise and also forgetting Papa's folded forehead and Mamma's down-turned lips. Papa was still worried. Moving cost money, even though we were moving because we didn't have any.

I began to sing, softly, hymns, nursery rhymes, harvest songs. There were enough to get me to Senigaglia without shouting at my brothers for spoiling our journey. We might not have another.

I liked singing more than speaking. I didn't have such a

good memory for words without music, but I could remember them perfectly when they came attached to tunes.

We didn't complain, or wish that things were different. God gave us what we had. But we sang our longing and He didn't mind. He liked singing. God was always listening and He could hear everyone at once. God had no eyelids. His unblinking eyes followed you everywhere, though they were called the Eye of God, as if He had only one.

It was puzzling, but I thought more about God's ears. They must be huge but beautiful, like enormous flowers. No wonder He liked music, after the dull drone of prayers. I sang about Papa and Mamma's faces, tired and strained. They were there in the words of the hymns as I *pleaded from this vale of tears.* The hymns gave longing a name and called it *heaven.* Heaven had streets that flowed with milk and honey. There must be sweet soft bread to go with them, and rich yellow cheese. *My cup is overflowing,* the psalm said.

I had picked up skipping rhymes from older children in the streets and squares of Corinaldo. Many of them named someone called Maria, Marietta, one of the versions of my name. People liked to place their daughters under the protection of God's mother.

Singing was another way of moving. If I sang while the wheels moved under us, I moved inside while we moved into the world. I loved wheels. Mamma was found in a door that turned like a wheel. It was different for her. Her face was white and shut.

Every now and then Angelo would decide to notice my singing and mock me, but I was busy learning the world as we rode along. Other people lived their other lives in other houses. I was old in some ways, raw in others. The prospect of school was sinking further away every year. I had to learn what I could, as I could.

The air changed. The land flattened or humped up again. What you breathed became part of you. Every place you moved through, moved through you.

87

We had set out after breakfast, still hungry. We had not had enough to eat since I could remember, and lately it had been worse. Angelo nagged Mamma for food and she gave him and Mariano little hunks of hard, sour bread. They made faces but it kept them quiet for a time to work away at it, trying to moisten it in their mouths so they could chew it. I didn't ask for any and I wasn't given it. I wanted my mouth free to sing.

Papa told Mamma she would feel better once we left Senigaglia and were on our way to Rome. 'No bad memories then, eh, Assunta?'

She turned her head away from him as she lifted her shift over Sandrino. Papa tried so hard. He wanted to help her, but bad memories were harder to forget than good ones. I knew that at seven, and he had no sense of it as a grown man.

Sole was still now, in my lap, but I stayed alert. He'd run away if I relaxed my grip. I made my brothers pay a tribute of crumbs for their bad behaviour while Mamma and Sandrino slept. Otherwise I'd tell her everything when she woke up. Sole licked the crumbs from my fingers. Mamma woke only when we had to move ourselves and our belongings onto the train.

But between these two things came the sea. It sang. I was silent.

'You like the sea, eh, Marietta?' Papa smiled at me.

'Yes, Papa,' I couldn't say anything. The sea told me the same thing as the sky, the thing Mamma tried so hard not to learn. Everything changed as you looked. The clouds changed shape just as you saw a bear or a mountain in them. Waves stretched and fell over. Only God didn't change, and He was invisible.

Mamma didn't want to see the sea. She started awake when we got to the station at Senigaglia. I had to clamp Sole in my fist. He hated the bustle and chill of the station. I did too, but I loved climbing aboard the train. I was only anxious about Sole. Once we were settled I was happy, I had a

88

comfortable, warm seat, a box for Sole, and the world slid by to entertain me. If my stomach rumbled loudly, I ignored it as I always did. Sole was safe, and so was I. If I had a sense that things might not stay safe with us, I brushed it aside.

Mamma and Sandrino slept again, on the train, and Papa kept Angelo and Mariano quiet.

'Your Mamma is very tired,' he said.

She was always tired, but she slept because of something else. Papa never spoke of his own tiredness. He took good care of Mamma. He knew her weakness better than his own.

People looked at us. I began to sing, scrunched by the window hoping I could stay there and see out. Miraculously, I did. Papa saw to it that I was free to watch the sea and listen for the restless music I could almost hear, as I pressed my ear to the glass.

'We'll go to the sea, Marietta,' Papa promised. 'We'll go to the sea and you'll hear it and bathe in it.'

I smiled back at him. It might be so. But I turned hungrily to the glass to catch as much of it as I could while the train flashed past the first of the towns on the way to Rome.

The villages were larger than Corinaldo and they hung from mountains or were cradled in valleys beneath the hills. One of them seemed to be carved out of rock. I was beginning to realize that we were really leaving home and it would leave us, too.

Later I lost my precious window to a grumbling Angelo. I gave it up and sat next to Mamma's solid bulk as she slept on with Sandrino in her arms, not wanting to see what led away from what she knew. There were two more stops and then we were at the gates of Rome.

'But we're inside a church,' I said as the train pulled us into a huge cold building. I was bewildered. I wanted to cry. We were inside, not out. We were supposed to be in Rome, why had the train pulled into a church? Then I remembered my dignity as a newly confirmed Christian. The Pope's address was the Vatican, Rome. The Holy Ghost came to my aid.

89

'Is it the Vatican the train comes into?' I asked as we stood blinking on the platform. Papa was hauling our belongings down while Mamma herded us to one side, apart from Angelo who was helping Papa. I saw him glance at me, alarmed that I had caught on to something before him.

Papa stopped work to wipe his brow and smile at me. 'What a lovely idea, Marietta. But this is Termini, the station. It's a very big station from which people go to many different places.'

Angelo laughed at me.

'It's big and grand like the Vatican,' Papa said. 'You're not wrong, Marietta.'

But I was wrong. I didn't like the Vatican after that. Angelo went on snickering and I looked around resentfully at the station. It was huge, with stone walls and big, thick columns. Other trains stood at other platforms and I saw that Papa was right, many people were going to many different places.

'Are some of them going to Corinaldo?'

'Yes,' Mamma said immediately and mournfully. 'Some of them are certainly going to Corinaldo.'

'Are they going because they have no food?' I couldn't help myself. If people were making journeys from Rome and perhaps even from Colle Granturco, where we were going, for the same reason we had left Corinaldo, if they were going to Corinaldo looking for food, then the station was a great tangle of hunger that would never be solved.

'People travel for many reasons,' Papa said, and then he turned to bring the rest of our belongings from the train.

'They might be visiting someone,' Mamma said. 'They might be going to a wedding or a christening.'

The people around us didn't all looked pinched and hungry like we did. Some of them looked frighteningly well and strong as they cut through the crowd.

'Hold each other's hands,' Papa warned. 'We'll have to walk to our meeting place with Senator Scelsi's steward. I'll push the cart. Angelo, you help me, and Maria, you hold Mariano's hand.'

This brought a chorus of tired and hungry protests from Angelo, until Mamma began to threaten. I wanted to help Papa, not clutch Mariano with one hand and Sole's box with the other. But I could see why Papa had warned us. The crowds didn't part for us the way they did for some people. We had to push and butt our way through.

Rome air. I opened my mouth to taste it better. It was stony. Everything was made of stone. There were walls everywhere, more than the walls around Corinaldo. Rome made me feel very small. I was like Sole now, hating the bustle and strangeness, and I clutched his box tightly as he writhed and howled inside it.

People looked at us as if we'd done something wrong, and this time there was no window I could lean into. Even the beggars had no smiles for us. Of course we gave them nothing. We had nothing. I kept my eyes down, but I felt the stares.

We were ragged and dirty. We smelled. I had never thought about these things until Rome made me see them. People turned away from us in disgust. I couldn't sing as we trudged through the streets with our little cart.

How could people not remember that Jesus was born in a stable? Stables didn't smell so wonderful. Would they hold their noses if He passed, in His mother's arms? I wanted to raise my head and shout at them. But I was trembling under all those eyes. Besides, no one would listen. Beggars shouted, pleading for alms, and no one paid attention. Then Angelo and Mariano had to hold their little pink things over the gutter in a side street and people looked even more disgusted, especially when Mariano did more than pee. I wanted to go, but I was afraid if I let anything out, I'd end up doing what Mariano did.

It was harder to walk in Rome. There were so many other people walking in the same place at the same time. We didn't belong, we had no place.

'So many poor beggars,' Mamma murmured, crossing herself.

I envied them. They sang out their pleas. They were a part

91

of the life of the streets as we were not. People didn't try to walk through them, as they did with us. Again and again someone barged through the gate of our tightly-held hands. Then we came to a standstill and whoever had been cut off ran to lace up again, to be part of our chain of hands. Sometimes it was me, with Sole gargling from his box. I ran for all I was worth. I wouldn't mind so much being lost by the sea and the orange sand. But not in Rome.

'Bernardo Lantini, steward to Senator Scelsi,' a harsh voice said as a tall, man came up and shook hands with Papa.

'Luigi Goretti,' Papa said. 'Luigi,' he added, so that the man had to nod.

'Bernardo.'

Bernardo looked at us the same way other people did. 'Four bambinos,' he said. 'Senator Scelsi did not expect so many little mouths, Goretti.'

Papa smiled tiredly. 'God has blessed us.'

Bernardo shrugged. Then he nodded curtly at Angelo to help Papa hoist the handcart onto the carriage, like a diligence but smaller. It was a tight fit and the ride to the Colle Gianturco, near Paliano, was rough.

The carriage rattled and banged us through the streets. At least we were seated up high, away from the stones of the Roman streets. We didn't earn so many scornful looks as we rode along. But Rome went fast and I felt things slipping away. I clutched Sole's box and checked his breathing. He was very quiet and I wondered if Rome had killed him.

I couldn't sing. What if this was the wrong place for us? Colle Gianturco had to be the place we needed. I had imagined the man smiling, with his hands full of bread. Instead he frowned and we were hungry, so hungry I was dizzy and even my brothers were quiet.

We left the city. It was dark and quiet and the roads were not only dirt, not cobbled. The hooves of the horse made a muffled noise instead of a sharp one. I began to sing lullabyes to Sandrino, who slept in my arms. Papa smiled at me and

I smiled back. He thought I was singing because I was happy, and that made him happy. Sometimes Papa was more of a child than I was. He didn't hear the sadness in a lullaby that told a child to sleep because the world was hard and sleep was the only way out, except for death.

The roads became narrower. We had entered a small village. When the horse stopped, I was almost asleep. We all slept, except the horse and Bernardo and Papa. I jumped down, still holding Sole's box. I had to find a bucket or at least a tree.

'Come on, Marietta,' Angelo tugged at my hand.

He had already spotted the little hutch behind the house. He pretended he was leading me in the darkness, but he let me go first.

I could have gone in Rome. All I did was pee.

'Hurry up, the food will be gone,' Angelo called.

I finished and waited while his pipi made its loud whisper in the dark. Then he had to do more, and took longer than I did. When he was finished, he ran into the house ahead of me.

The house smelled of warm food. Mamma was whisking away tears of relief as she made everyone sit at the table in the kitchen. There were the usual thick beans mixed into a stew, but lots of them, already cooked and still warm for us. There was polenta which would fill us up and hard black bread made from the same thick meal, which we would have to chew in tiny mouthfuls. There were even some ripe tomatoes like little red suns, and slivers of onion like fingernail moons.

'Signor Scelsi had this left for you. He knew you would be hungry,' Bernardo was saying in his dark voice. Mamma invited him to eat with us and we were all sorry when he said yes. He ate quite a lot, but we ate faster. We fell on the food. We would have eaten the grass outside the house.

When Bernardo was gone, we scampered around our new house. There was a room for me and baby Sandrino and another one for Angelo and Mariano. The house was bigger than our old one, and colder.

'We'll soon warm it,' Papa said. Bernardo had told him to start work in the morning in the field. There was a bean crop to harvest quickly, before it passed the peak of ripeness. Signor Scelsi would ride over in one week to check his progress.

Papa had hardly eaten. How could he, when Scelsi's steward took the bread from his children's mouths? Papa had lifted and carried our belongings, looked after us and Mamma all day, but he had to pretend he wasn't hungry. Bernardo had watched us with hard eyes, when he was not eating.

My room had two small beds in it. It felt damp and chilly, but I liked it. I put Sole in the box Papa had found in Senigaglia. But he jumped out of the box and came into my bed. We slept, Sole purring me a lullaby.

The next morning was bright and clear and Papa was in the field at dawn, while the rest of us slept.

'He wouldn't let me make him breakfast before he went out,' Mamma was in the kitchen, cutting slices of tomato onto bread. She had hidden the food that was left over on the night before, afraid Bernardo might take it away.

'Take this down to your papa,' she told me. 'He must have some food before the Angelus.'

Papa would come in at noon for his main meal of the day with us. But it was only six a.m. Mamma knew I would carry the food to the field without tasting it. I would never steal food from my Babbo.

He was standing still in the field as if saying the Angelus already, the beautiful noontime prayer that echoed Mary's answer to the angel Gabriel when he came to ask her if she would be God's mother. He stood as though he had no strength left to move, and I hurried to him with the food.

His face frightened me. He seemed very far away, listening to something I couldn't hear.

94

'I brought your breakfast, Papa,' I called. I wanted to make him look like my Babbo again.

'Ah, my Marietta, thank you,' he said.

He ate, tearing the bread and chewing it quickly, swallowing even the precious tomato without tasting it. He usually held back, as he had done last night. I had never seen him eat like that before.

'Marietta, how do you like your new home?' he asked when he could speak.

'I like it, Papa,' I said to please him. As long as we could eat, I would like it.

'Good, good,' he said. 'And your brothers?'

'They like it too. Angelo will come to help you, later.'

'It might be better,' he stopped, then shrugged. 'I don't know which is better, to have his help and have to tell him what to do, which slows the work, or to carry on alone.'

In the end he sent Angelo back to the house, after a time.

'He says speed is the most important thing,' Angelo reported to Mamma, 'and he works faster alone.'

She nodded. She was trying to make a soup that would stretch the food Senator Scelsi had left us. We had eaten too much, the first night.

She was busy cooking and putting our few things away, trying to make the house feel like home. She had made us take our earrings off for the journey, in case bad people tried to tear them off. But when she looked for them, only hers were there. Mine were gone.

'I'm sorry, Mamma,' I said. I thought she would be angry with me.

'It's not your fault, Marietta,' she said. 'Maybe a poor beggar took them.'

'But what will we tell Papa?'

'Don't worry, I'll tell him.'

'All the women in Rome have gold rings in their ears,' I said.

'A gold halo is better,' she answered. 'It can't be lost or stolen. And it keeps the devil away.'

'Does the devil wear gold earrings?' I pictured him, his bright gold earrings flashing.

'Don't think about the devil, or he will come to you,' she said.

'If I think about gold earrings, will they come to me?'

She shook her head. 'Enough talk, Marietta.'

It would be useful, to have a halo. Our house was often dark and we had very few candles or oil lamps. But it was more interesting to think about earrings. I was sorry mine were gone. Mamma didn't seem very upset, which surprised me. She liked to see me in them. I went on imagining the devil prancing around with gold earrings flashing on his horns. It brought him closer to me. Perhaps Mamma was right about that, too. When you thought about the devil, he was there, especially if you had left your home.

Noon came and we said the Angelus together as the bell rang from the church. It made me feel as if we were back in Corinaldo. But Papa didn't come in from the field. Mamma sent Angelo to get him.

'Tell Papa to come now, the soup is warm,' she said.

He came in slowly, like an old man. He looked older, after the long morning's work. Mamma put the food in front of him. It was her turn to hold back. I wanted to give her some of mine, but it was gone before I had the chance. She wouldn't have eaten it. It would only have gone to my brothers.

Our first few days in Colle Gianturco passed very slowly, but not for Papa. Senator Scelsi would bring us more food when he came. Food was scarce, which made the hours long for the rest of us. There was only one small sack of beans and one of polenta. No more tomatoes, no pasta, little oil and some garlic for flavour. Papa worked from dawn till after dark, but there were still beans to harvest.

Finally Senator Scelsi rode into the field and we all went

out to see him. He had saddlebags filled with provisions for us.

'I am keeping account of what I give you,' he said to Papa. Papa nodded.

Mamma took the food from him and I helped her carry it up to the house, leaving Papa with Senator Scelsi. I had seen his face as he looked at the field and at Papa, shaking his head. But the harvest was in. He could not fault Papa. He had said nothing.

When Papa came in that night, he was grey. Mamma made him sit and eat before he said a word. The harvest was good, but there was no rest for him. It was time to begin preparing the ground for the next one.

Papa changed along with the land, as if he, too, was being ploughed. What would be planted in him, other than tiredness? Patience, maybe. He had great patience and it seemed to grow all the time. Mamma had very little patience, and hers was growing less. I wanted to ask if she had told Papa about my earrings, but I was afraid to.

The next harvest was also good, and Papa looked even more tired. Again Senator Scelsi came and shook his head. Then he began speaking to Papa in a low voice. I couldn't hear what he was saying.

'Senator Scelsi came today,' I told Mamma when I went back to the house. 'He said something to Papa but I don't know what.'

Her lips tightened. We waited together for Papa to come home. Papa was slower with this harvest. What would happen with the next, and the next? Was that Senator Scelsi's question?

'Senator Scelsi is bringing us more workers, to get the harvest in,' Papa tried to sound happy. 'A widower and his son. We'll be better off this way, Assunta. We need more workers, and they need someone to cook their meals and mend their clothes, to make a home for them. What could be more sensible?'

His voice pleaded with her. She gave him a long look,

opened her mouth and closed it. When I was in bed, I listened hard and heard her say:

'This father and son will also share in the profits, eh? We'll have less and we'll need more food from Scelsi. Will he give us enough? You look like a scarecrow, Luigi.'

'Of course he'll give us enough, Assunta. This will be a good thing – Scelsi doesn't want us to fail. He wants us to stay on his land,' Papa said.

Mamma thought our journey was a mistake, but she had thought so from the beginning. I waited, but Papa was silent. Then Mamma spoke again.

'If all else fails, there's always your good friend. You know who I mean, Luigi. Domenico Cimarelli.'

'Yes,' Papa agreed. 'Domenico would do his best to help us. Count Mazzoleni is very good to him.'

'But not the others,' Mamma said. 'Domenico is your friend, Luigi. You must keep him for us, when the others have gone. They won't stay forever, this father and son?'

'I don't know how long they'll stay, Assunta. That's for Senator Scelsi to decide.'

Mamma said something I didn't hear, and Papa didn't answer. But Papa had brought us here and he knew what was best. I fell asleep to Sole's purr and woke up cheerful and curious as well as hungry. I was a child and harder to squash than Mamma and Papa. Besides, I knew less.

The two men lived in a cottage across the road from ours. They smiled and were friendly. There was no harm in their eyes, no judgement. They were glad to help, the father, Giovanni, said, cuffing his son, Alessandro, to make him agree. They ate with us, and there was more food because of them. Scelsi gave a more generous ration to three workers, and now the Serenellis would help us pay for what we ate. Sometimes Bernardo came on foot to watch the work. He hid behind a tree, but I saw him and told Papa when he came.

Mamma worked hard, cooking and mending for them and

us. She grew sharper and less patient and I had to help her more, especially as she was expecting a new baby. But I liked our life at Colle Granturco, and I liked the Serenellis. Any change made life more interesting.

But Giovanni didn't work like Papa, and Alessandro had been at sea before he was called back to help his father. He had to learn how to work the land. Giovanni liked to lie under a tree and drink wine. He had had a terrible accident on their farm, and his right hand was withered. He blamed everything on his hand, and he blamed his hand on the world.

Mamma treated Giovanni with courtesy, and he accorded her the respect due Papa's wife. But she looked at him with suspicion and a kind of fear. He muttered to himself when he was drunk and she frowned and looked away, thinking he was mad. I was frightened of him too, but I was more interested. Talking to yourself is something children do without thinking. Giovanni seemed more like a child than a man to me, and that was interesting.

Mamma had another baby, a girl this time. No one talked about earrings for her. It would have meant a new pair for me, too, but I was still happy to have a sister. I pretended I was grown up and served the men under Mamma's instructions for the first day after Ersilia was born. I thought of my Confirmation, that had made me an adult in the eyes of the Church, and I tried to behave like one.

But when Mamma came back into the kitchen with the baby at her breast, I was only too glad to be a child again. I was better off playing with Sole outside and escaping from back-breaking chores.

'We're nothing but slaves,' Giovanni ranted when we sat around the table in the evening. 'That bastard Scelsi makes us pay too much for his rotten food.'

'Please, Giovanni, not in front of the children,' Mamma said.

'They need to know how the world works. Some own the land and some work it, eh, Alessandro?'

Alessandro grunted agreement.

'Yes and what about that little snake Bernardo?' Giovanni asked.

'He works for Senator Scelsi, just like us,' Papa said.

'He makes his living telling lies about us. Scelsi will make us work until we drop down dead, the bastard!'

'Not that word, please, Giovanni,' Mamma said.

He opened his mouth and closed it, shaking his head.

'Senator Scelsi also has a family to feed. He does his best for us,' Papa said in his worn voice.

'You can't believe that, Goretti. As for his family, let them starve! I wish they would starve!'

'Giovanni,' Papa looked sad. 'Please don't say that about anyone.'

'Luigi's right,' Mamma said. 'If you curse the children of Signor Scelsi, it will come back on your children.'

'My children,' Giovanni leaned across the table to cuff Alessandro. 'They know I'm right about Scelsi. Eh, Alessandro? Eh?'

Alessandro was fifteen and very shy. He turned red and nodded. He wasn't used to being around women, Mamma said. He had been a sailor, and there were only men on ships.

'Eh? Speak up, be a man!' Giovanni went on, leaning across the table to his son. 'You know I'm right! And so do you, Goretti, even if you won't say it.' He started blustering and muttering about Scelsi and how, one day, things would be different.

'Ask him,' he dipped his head towards his son. 'He knows. He says nothing, but he knows. He reads it all and keeps it all up here,' he tapped his head. 'Eh, Alessandro?'

Alessandro nodded, blushing. 'One day things will change,' he muttered.

'There, you see? He knows!' Giovanni shouted. 'Tell us about the revolution, when we'll spill Scelsi's blood! Speak up, Boy!'

'Giovanni,' Papa said. 'Please.'

100

Alessandro pushed his chair back, nodded to Mamma and fled to their cottage across the road.

'He has a devil in him, that one,' Mamma said later, about Giovanni.

She said it when I was meant to be sleeping. But it gave me a new idea of the devil. He could be inside you. How could you get him out? I had to ask Mamma.

'The devil will always run away if you make the Sign of the Cross,' she said, making it as she spoke. 'And you must try not to think of him,' she added.

The first part was easy, the second was hard. His gold earrings flashed as the devil danced around me to their music. Even if he didn't sing, he hopped and danced. He only went away when I forgot about him. As soon as I remembered, he came back.

One afternoon Senator Scelsi came up on his horse to inspect the fields and found Giovanni fast asleep in the hot sun. I was bringing the men some fruit from Mamma, and I watched as the horse came to a standstill and Senator Scelsi watched Giovanni sleep. Papa and Alessandro stopped working in the field.

Senator Scelsi got down. He let his reins drop and his horse stayed where it was as he stood over Giovanni, who went on snoring.

'Papa, wake up!' Alessandro shouted, just as Senator Scelsi took off his hat and hit Giovanni in the chest with it.

'Wake up, man! I see that what Bernardo says is true. You're a disgrace, a drunken sot who stinks of wine in the middle of the afternoon. What's wrong with you?'

'What?' Giovanni woke with a start and almost toppled over onto his side. He put his hand on the ground to steady himself.

I almost laughed, he looked so funny. But Alessandro and Papa had reached the tree, and they were white-faced and frightened.

'My father has not been well, Your Excellency,' Alessandro began.

He sounded very grown up, and I thought Senator Scelsi would listen to him. But his face was red as he turned to Alessandro.

'There's nothing wrong with him but laziness and too much wine. You're lying to me, Serenelli. And you, Goretti, have you also come to lie about this good-for-nothing you allow to sleep while you work?'

Papa stood white and shocked, but he answered with dignity. 'No, Your Excellency, I was not going to lie.'

'No? Humph!' Senator Scelsi moved towards his horse. 'You're all liars and lazy drunks.'

'Excuse me but I am neither, Your Excellency,' Papa said. 'I work hard for you, and so does Alessandro.'

'He does,' Giovanni said in his thick voice. 'My son works as hard as anyone.'

I was proud of my Babbo. But Senator Scelsi climbed up onto his horse and looked down at Giovanni, pointing his finger at him, then at Alessandro and then at Papa as he spoke. 'I want you all off my land. I'll send Bernardo after you later, to collect what you owe me. Don't worry, he'll find you.'

'But Your Excellency,' Papa said. 'My wife and my children, how will they eat?'

'You should have thought of that before you crossed me,' Senator Scelsi said.

'But I didn't mean to cross you, Your Excellency,' Papa said. 'I apologize if my words offended you. If you look at the field, you'll see we've been doing a good job.'

'Don't grovel to him, Goretti, can't you see the tyrant wants to get rid of us?' Giovanni stood up.

'I should call the police and have you thrown off my land. Then you'd never find work anywhere,' Senator Scelsi said. 'But I won't, for the sake of the little Gorettis. But I want you gone today. Today!' he dug his heels into his horse's side and he was gone.

'Madonna, help us,' Papa sank down on his knees and crossed himself.

'A lot of good that will do, Goretti,' Giovanni spat the words at him. Papa went on praying and Giovanni threw his hat at the tree. 'He's a tyrant and a pig, Scelsi.'

'I'll go and see my friend Domenico,' Papa said, making the Sign of the Cross again and rising from his knees. 'He'll help us if he can. First I have to go and tell Assunta.'

Giovanni didn't offer to come and help him break the news. He stayed in the field with Alessandro, blustering about Senator Scelsi.

I followed him into the house. I was afraid of what Mamma would say, and I could tell Papa was, too.

Mamma was cooking. She looked up surprised, when he came in. 'What is it, Luigi? Are you ill?'

'No, Assunta. But I have to go and find Domenico, right away, and you have to pack our things.'

'Pack our things! Again! But why, Luigi? It's Giovanni, isn't it? Isn't it? What has he done?'

'It's not important, Assunta. What's important is to make sure we have work so the little ones can eat.'

'What has he done, Luigi?'

'He was under a tree when Senator Scelsi came,' Papa said.

'Under a tree. Drunk, you mean. He was drunk and you were blamed along with him. I've seen this coming all along. Not another step do they take with us, Luigi. Not another step.'

'We can't let them starve, Assunta.'

'They'd see us starve, Luigi.'

'Alessandro is a good worker. We wouldn't have lasted so long without him. Be fair, Assunta.'

'Fair! How is it fair that we're thrown out of our home, because of that drunken pig? How is that fair? And now you want to bring them with us wherever we're going, we don't even know,' she collapsed into a chair, sobbing and shaking her head. 'We don't even know.'

'Marietta, stay with your mother,' Papa said. 'I have to go see Domenico. God will provide, Assunta, especially if we're charitable.'

Mamma kept her head down and said nothing as Papa set out on foot to find Domenico, who worked for Count Mazzoleni. Giovanni and Alessandro came up to the house and we sat together and not together, as we ate. Mamma and Govanni glowered at each other and Alessandro kept his head down and went to their house as soon as he had finished eating.

'I have to pack,' Mamma said, getting up from the table. 'As we've been thrown off our land, through no fault of Luigi's.'

'That bastard Scelsi was looking for an excuse to get rid of us,' Giovanni said. 'That bastard Bernardo told him lies.'

He kept using the word that made Mamma wince. But this time she drew herself up as she answered him.

'All the more reason not to give the Senator an excuse.'

'He would have found one sooner or later, Assunta. They always do,' Giovanni replied.

He went off to the cottage across the road. Mamma put us to bed, but everyone was waiting for Papa and no one wanted to sleep.

'Your Papa won't be back till morning,' Mamma said. 'It's not such a short journey, eh?' She looked as if she was about to start handing out cuffs, and we closed our eyes.

It was very early in the morning when I heard Papa's voice. Giovanni and Alessandro came in after him as if they were waiting, too.

'You look exhausted, Luigi,' Mamma said. 'Have you had any food?'

'Teresa gave me a wonderful supper. And breakfast.' Papa's voice was tired.

'You've had a long walk, Luigi.' Giovanni said. 'Catch your breath. Do you want some wine?'

Mamma made a sound like 'uggh'!

'Not in the morning, Giovanni,' Papa said, and sighed. 'Domenico has found us a house and some land from the Count. All of us. But we will have to live together in the same house, this time.'

104

'You're a good man, Luigi Goretti,' Giovanni said in a choked voice. 'Alessandro, thank Luigi.'

'Thank you, Luigi,' Alessandro said.

After a few minutes, Luigi and Alessandro left and I heard Mamma crying and Papa comforting her. But I couldn't hear what they were saying and I fell asleep.

Again we were on the move, this time to go deeper into the Pontine Marshes, to a place called Ferriere. The distance was not so great but it was another journey, and not one we had expected. Mamma was tight-lipped.

'We're real gypsies now,' was all she said, but it was enough.

Gypsies wore gold hoops in their ears, like the devil and the women in Rome. We were gypsies without earrings. Mine were lost and Mamma had taken hers off again, for the journey. I imagined gold hoops jingling like tambourines, as gypsy carts rolled down the road. A halo would never jingle.

Once more Papa loaded our things onto the cart. Giovanni didn't help, though he was the reason we had to move. The Serenellis had their own cart for their possessions.

'Now we'll be in a house with them,' Mamma hissed as we set out. 'We won't be able to call our souls our own!'

'Assunta, there's nothing more I can do,' Papa said wearily.

He looked weak and pale and she was silent. The journey included a train ride from Segni to Cecchina. The land was flat and the villages were little strings of cottages and scalloped fields. I was dreaming again, singing softly and clutching Sole. He couldn't believe I was so cruel as to uproot him again, and I held him tight. He'd be off if I didn't, taking his chances without me.

Papa was cut by the disgrace of being thrown off Senator Scelsi's land, though Mamma kept reminding him it wasn't his fault.

'It's Giovanni. And now he goes with us again, with his worthless son. They're not family.'

'They must eat too, Assunta,' Papa said. 'They're our friends.'

105

'Friends! I knew we'd be sorry we'd ever seen them. People like that –'

He silenced her, with a glance at me. I knew what she meant. Giovanni's wife had died in a madhouse, and another son, Gaspare, was still there. It was a terrible thing. It made Mamma suspicious and Papa kind.

We left the train and climbed onto a cart to continue our journey. It was hot in the sun with nothing to eat or drink. But we were travelling again. I was sorry not to see the sea. The towns we passed looked doleful, not like the sculpted villages on the way to Rome. But when we arrived in Ferriere – a flat, ugly place with a smell from the marshes – Domenico and Teresa Cimarelli were there to meet us. They were smiling and seemed truly glad to see us and I liked them right away. We had never been welcomed like that before.

'Mazzoleni gave us some furniture and food for you,' Domenico said. 'It's a gift,' he said, low, to Papa. 'He said he doesn't want you to start out in debt.'

'Fine food it must be,' Mamma said sharply.

But it was. There were many tomatoes and onions, this time. There were olives and bread with oil to soften it, along with the usual beans and lots of pasta. It felt like a feast. Teresa and Domenico had warm, open faces I wished they were our parents, though I felt guilty when I looked at Papa's pale face. But they seemed so happy. Maybe Mamma and Papa would be happy here too, and look like they did?

Count Mazzoleni had given us an old dairy to live in. It smelled of sour milk and ancient cheese, but it was big enough for all of us and we didn't feel pressed by the Serenellis. They were grateful to Mamma for her cooking, and to Papa for letting them come with us.

The kitchen was on the ground floor. We could share it with the animals in winter, and carry the heavy buckets of water to it. It was where we gathered to eat together.

There were steps outside the house to the upstairs, where we slept. I shared a room with Baby Ersilia, no longer such a baby. Still, because she was so small it was almost like having my own room. I had never had a room to myself. There would be a lot more space if you could fly. The room was very tall. But it was not so very small, and I walked round and round it. I imagined how people must feel when they had mansions and palaces to walk round, how the Pope must feel in the Vatican in Vatican City. Imagine having a city to yourself! On the other hand, he might be lonely.

The work went well and even Giovanni lent his good hand as much as he could, more than he had ever done for Senator Scelsi. He persuaded Papa to take a little wine in the evening and my Babbo got some colour back in his face.

Sole and I liked the new place. There were many birds. I kept watch on Sole. He could feast on rats and mice, but not birds. That was the commandment I handed down to him, only one instead of ten. But even so, he couldn't keep it. Not only that, but he was proud of his murders. He brought me his victims to admire. I wept over the mangled birds and buried them under the tree beside the house. Why must Sole and the birds, my greatest friends, be enemies?

'That's the way God made them,' Papa told me. 'Cats eat birds, and birds eat worms. Everything eats something, Marietta.'

At least they had plenty to eat, Sole and the birds. I envied them their full stomachs. We hunted our food from the land, where it was much harder to catch.

Mamma was pleased by the house, despite the smell. Papa was pleased that she was pleased. He worked harder than ever and there was a burning determination in his eyes. Alessandro pitched in. Giovanni slacked off as usual after his burst of energy, but he pushed his son to work hard.

I was eight years old and I had a year to myself, more or less, a year in which there was no new baby – a baby year always meant more work for me – a year in which I was free, when I had helped Mamma. I could take Sole and make up a game with him, or sit and dream by myself. I was shy, but

107

not afraid. I was brave enough to frighten myself, as children do. Our baby brother Antonio became a ghost I could frighten my brothers with, even Angelo. He was in heaven. But heaven was hard to imagine. It seemed a very silent place, very clean. It seemed unlikely we would be allowed in, though the Gospel said it was easier for the poor to enter.

Maria's Memo

I suspect my earrings were sold to help pay for the first move. Mamma must have fought for hers. I don't imagine Papa was very happy about it, but he was making her move. He couldn't take her earrings as well. Besides, hers had come from his mother.

I loved our first journey. Even the second was movement and life. Every child loves this echo of being carried in the womb. An echo, a memory and something completely new, sewn together into what we call travel.

I would turn nine soon. At nine I had two years, nine months and twelve days to live. My beloved Papa had even less, and his death would change everything.

But life before he died was so ordinary, so calm. Teresa Cimarelli, Mamma's new friend, became mine too. She liked it when I told her things about my life, not that there was much to tell. I made her laugh with my stories of the devil in gold earrings.

I was shy. Only shy people know what that means, how it skins you alive. But I wasn't shy with Teresa. She treated me like a precious, important person, and because of her I wasn't so shy with Domenico, her husband, though we were not so close. They were kind to us, like godparents. They gave us extra food, and clothing gathered from the neighbours. It spared Mamma the shame of having to ask for things. Teresa and Domenico helped us as if it was the natural thing to do, laughing away any thanks.

I wonder what it was like for Mamma, being around Teresa's happiness? She was a happy woman in a way my mamma would never be. She loved Domenico. He loved her. They even liked each other. Mamma and Papa had not chosen one another. They depended on each other and Papa cared deeply for Mamma. Whether she cared about him in the same way is less certain. But it was me he really loved, just as Mamma had loved Antonio. After he died, what she loved was his shadow in us and perhaps in Papa, too.

But sometimes the simple light of liking broke through and made us glad to be together. Teresa and Domenico brought that light into our house. They had no children and they gladly shared us. It helped Mamma and Papa and it helped them. If life had gone on like that – who knows?

7

Every two weeks, Teresa took me to the market in Nettuno. I loved sitting up in the cart beside her warmth and bulk. The ride to the market was the best part, with everything ahead as we left Mamma and my brothers and sisters behind. Time rolled out like a road that went on and on.

At the market, Teresa sold the eggs and pigeons we had brought. The money would help us buy cooking oil and other things we needed. I hated it when people came up to us, which was not the best way to sell things. I wanted people to pass me without looking, to leave me alone. I liked to watch them from a distance as they went about their business. Teresa was the only exception. She could come as close as she liked.

I woke up in the morning hungry, but not too exhausted to dream or sing. The days were long, filled with colour and light and Sole and taking food to the men in the field, or calling them in to the kitchen.

Once I felt comfortable with Teresa and even Domenico, my shyness began to ease around the people I saw every day, the other workers in the field. They meant me no harm. They worked hard, and were too tired and hungry to think much about me. It was a good thing not to be thought of. It made me feel free.

My Babbo didn't look so worried. Mamma softened a bit. We shared our lives with the Serenellis, who were hungry for family life. Their hunger made it seem more precious. Teresa and Domenico on one side, Giovanni and Alessandro on the other, made our family the centre of their lives.

Giovanni was like a rough, drunken uncle. His withered

hand shook more and more. He couldn't help it and we tried not to look, though it drew our eyes. I wondered if the devil Mamma said was in him lived in his withered hand. I prayed the devil wouldn't come and live in anything of mine.

Alessandro was a quiet older brother, who could read. That's what the Serenellis brought to our table – along with their appetites and Giovanni's mutterings – wine, which Giovanni tried to share with Babbo and even sometimes with Mamma – and reading. We had never known anyone who could bring printed words alive.

Alessandro would take up the paper and, with a flourish, read off headlines and even whole stories to us, unless Mamma stopped him. Many of the stories he read held more than a grain of protest against the laws and limits laid down by the church and the state. I heard these things with interest and surprise – there was another way to look at things! – but Mamma wouldn't hear it. It could lead to quarrels, raised voices and thick silences when Alessandro stormed out and slammed the door of his room. It was not so pleasant, then, to be a big family together. Still, the Cimarellis came often, and our house became a place where people liked to be.

I ran to meet my Babbo when he came in from the fields in the evenings. He seemed smaller than in the afternoon, when I found him saying the Angelus as the church bell tolled. We said it together and I loved hearing his strong, deep voice.

But in the evening he was shrunken and grey, as if the heat of the afternoon and hard work had drained him. But his face lit up when he saw me, and he always managed to smile as we walked back arm in arm to our table.

I knew Papa, my Babbo, was our North Star, our calm centre. He was first up in the morning, last to bed at night. Mamma was just there, like the sky or the land. But Papa was the sun, stars and moon that came and went, at least for me. My brothers were rowdy and noisy and Babbo had to speak to them sternly and even hit them, though less often than Mamma did. He would never dream of hitting me. I was his little flower of the field, wild and ragged, growing how and where it could.

He caught my eye to smile or wink and something passed between us. I felt his fear that he would fail to feed us and another child would die. He was haunted less by Antonio than Mamma's sadness over his loss. Time had passed, but a corner of her still mourned for her first child. Papa could not bring light to that corner, and he feared another tragedy. Would she stay in the dark forever and refuse to come out? Giovanni's wife, Alessandro's mother, had gone mad. Would Mamma also become someone else, a stranger, if another of her babies slipped away from her?

Mamma needed Papa to protect and provide for her. She couldn't stand alone. No woman could, but she was shadowed by my brother's death and the hardships of her early life. Papa had brought happiness into her life, and he could take it away again.

Papa didn't see that by working so hard, he was ruining his health. Even if he had seen it, what could he do? He had failed on the land before, in Corinaldo. Count Mazzoleni was kind because of Domenico, and our way was smoothed in Ferriere. But Papa could not fail here, or it would go very hard with us.

Things began to change as the year turned and I turned nine. A new baby was on the way. There were many chores to do as Mamma grew heavy and tired, and soon there would be more. I would have to watch the baby while Mamma worked, or do the chores under her watchful eye. I had begun to do a woman's work when Ersilia was born, but now that I was older, I was serving an apprenticeship that would soon be useful, even crucial. Not that we knew. But a kind of knowing was slowly taking hold of us.

One night at supper, Papa slid from his chair onto the floor. Alessandro, Giovanni and Mamma tended him while I ran for Teresa and Domenico, praying with all my might. A

113

terrible fear gripped me like something that had been there underneath for a long time. But I wouldn't admit it. My mind closed like a door and refused to open.

'He's burning up with fever, Teresa,' Mamma wept when we got back to the house. Teresa, then Domenico, felt Papa's forehead. Teresa went to make a cold compress for his burning face.

'I'm going for the doctor,' Domenico said.

'No, no,' Papa said from the bed. 'I'm a bit tired, that's all, and warm from the heat of the day. Come, come, no fuss. Tomorrow I'll be back on my feet, working as usual.'

'Luigi no,' Mamma said, echoed by the other two.

But Papa was determined. 'I fooled you,' he smiled at us. 'I wanted your attention, Assunta. You've been neglecting me lately.'

Giovanni laughed harshly. Papa's act of well-being was almost convincing, and everyone wanted to believe it. The next day he set out as usual, and the next. But our house was threaded with fear. The carefree time was over. It almost returned, as time went on and Papa worked as hard as usual. But his face was white when it wasn't red with fever. He drank more of Giovanni's wine and blamed the flush of fever on that, and for his shakiness when he stood up from the table.

Twice more he collapsed and was put to bed in the evening, and twice more he staggered out to work in the morning wearing his familiar smile. When I went to meet him in the evening, I felt I was supporting him as we walked back to the house. His weight was little more than Ersilia's. He had always been wiry, without fat but muscled and strong. Now he stumbled in from work, weak as a kitten.

Mamma never smiled. Her voice was sharp with worry as she moved slowly around the kitchen. Papa was too tired to joke with her, or play with us in the evening. The younger children didn't hide from him any more. They came up and kissed him, then went away as though he frightened them.

114

'If this one is a girl, Luigi, we'll name her after Teresa, who has been our good friend and will be hers, too,' I heard Mamma say to Papa in the night.

'And the great Saint Teresa,' he answered.

Teresa Cimarelli came when Mamma's pains began, and helped the new baby girl into the world. Her kind face became softer, washed with tears when Mamma told her the baby's name.

'She has my patron saint to protect her as she has protected me,' she said.

I wished I'd been given Teresa as a first name instead of a second. I was sorry to offend the Blessed Mother, who could hear my thoughts. But there were so many Marias! Besides, Teresa was a friend, and now my new sister would have a special claim on her.

'You can pray to Saint Teresa too, Marietta,' Teresa said, as if she also heard what I was thinking.

I became busier than ever, helping Mamma. She had to rest and make milk for baby Teresa. Papa had to work harder, too. It was early spring, the air warming after winter. The warmth was welcome, except for the mosquitoes it brought. Papa's cough became deep and racking and I dreaded hearing it. It woke me in the night and made me restless, tossing and turning in my bed as I tried to pray for him, for Mamma, and for help with the feelings that welled up when I looked at my lucky new sister, with Teresa's name.

Mamma was frantic, Papa like a ghost. When my new baby sister was barely three months old, in May when the air turned from warm to hot, Papa collapsed and had to be carried in from the field. I was following Mamma's orders and trying to cook when I heard something and opened the door to see Alessandro and another worker whose name I didn't know, carrying Papa on a stretcher made from sacks twisted together. I thought he was dead.

A doctor was finally brought. He pursed his lips and shook his head. Papa had malaria, pneumonia, meningitis and typhus.

He pronounced the deadly names in a low voice. There was no need to tell us it was hopeless.

Mamma groped for a chair where there was none, backing against the wall. Nothing was familiar any more. These deadly names had crept up on us. How could Papa have become so deathly ill, so quickly? But it had not been quick. He had worked in the marshes of Ferriere for a year and three months, before he was struck down. Each month, each day had taken a toll on him.

For ten days we tiptoed around the house. We prayed. We said our nightly rosary around his bed, trying to work a miracle. I walked into Nettuno to buy medicine, praying as I went. God could not take Papa, not when we needed him so much. He was the light in our house, the humour, the kindness. He made us all lighter and kinder, including Mamma and the Serenellis.

Ten days. Nine nights. The house murmured with prayers and fear and footsteps to and from the bedroom where Papa lay. Mamma cooked him food he couldn't eat. She brought him remedies that did no good. She sat by the bed feeding baby Teresa, staring ahead of her, tearless and shocked.

Papa smiled at us when we went in to see him, or tried to. Luigi Goretti, who did the work of two men and still smiled in the evenings and laughed with his children, could hardly lift his eyelids. He tried to join in the rosary, but his eyes fluttered shut. He was not our Papa any more.

The Cimarellis sat with us. On the tenth day after the doctor had been, Papa spoke. I listened from outside the door.

'Assunta,' I heard him say, and then I could only make out 'Corinaldo'.

'Of course, yes, Luigi, I will return to Corinaldo with the children. I will do what you wish,' Mamma replied in a broken voice.

Soon afterwards, Papa started breathing loudly. We knew

116

he could not go on pushing his breath out like that, and in the afternoon it stopped.

Mamma, on her knees by the bed, put her head down and kissed his hand. When she got up the rest of us kissed his poor hand, still warm but finally released from the swamp-heat of fever. His face relaxed in death into a better likeness of our Papa.

Death had washed the terrible tiredness from his face. If he came back now, he would laugh and make us laugh. I could imagine the laughter more easily than thinking it was gone forever. It seemed such a small step, from life to death. Couldn't he take the small step back?

But as the warmth left his body and his features became fixed, it was clear that the small step was final. Death was like a ladder, put down and then pulled back. There was no return and no climbing after him.

A hush came over our house. The Serenellis told us they were sorry for our loss and theirs. They both wept over Papa. Mamma and Teresa Cimarelli washed Papa and dressed him in his best clothes and the Serenellis took his body downstairs and onto the cart the oxen would pull to the cemetery.

As I went down the stairs to walk beside the cart with Papa's body in its wooden box, I saw from the landing that my cat Sole lay in the dirt. I ran down to him, but he was dead. His mouth was open as if to let out a cry. I picked him up and put him carefully to one side. I would come home and bury him later. I couldn't cry for him now, there wasn't time.

The men who worked in the outer fields as well as our own closer ones came to Papa's burial, and the women too. There were many people present, and many tears. Count Mazzoleni rode up on his horse, dismounted and took off his hat to stand at the graveside. It was only afterwards that I realized the Countess had not come. I was dazed and dizzy since Papa had taken his small step into the next world. *He is having his purgatory here on earth*, Mamma had said as Papa lay burning up with fever. Now he was in heaven. But heaven was very far away.

'There's so much malaria that Count Mazzoleni keeps a supply of coffins for those who die from it,' Domenico told the story in a low voice as we walked from the graveyard. 'It was Luigi's job to unload the coffins when they came from the carpenter, and store them in the barn. "One of these will be mine", he said one day, not long ago,' Domenico's voice was choked. 'He thought it was a joke, he didn't know he would be right.'

I rode home with Mamma on the cart that had carried Papa. I clutched her hands and we wept together. What were we going towards? What was left for us in this world? Giovanni helped Mamma down from the cart.

'You're worn out from nursing poor Luigi, Assunta,' he said to her, his voice low and thick with sadness. 'Rest now.'

Mamma had kept vigil day and night, praying and caring for Papa and feeding Teresa. She had not believed until the very end that he was going. Now she went into their room where Teresa Cimarelli had changed the bed for her, putting on clean linen of her own. Mamma slept through until the following morning. I had to look after my brothers and sisters and keep baby Teresa from waking Mamma with her hunger, rocking her and singing to her. I had no time to bury Sole.

I missed his fur against my leg. I wanted to weep into his orange coat and feel him curled next to me in bed. But he was gone with Papa. I only hoped he would curl up with Papa and comfort him when he missed us.

There was a great emptiness in the house that night. Papa was dead and Mamma asleep as though she, too, was dead. I held my baby sister and rocked her and thought how close life and death had become for us. It was almost impossible to tell them apart. Teresa Cimarelli came with a big pot of soup for us and bread, sweeter and softer than usual. What she brought was always life.

'We'll let your mother sleep,' she said. 'She needs to be strong now.'

I ate like a hungry beast. We all did. The Serenellis were dignified and respectful and we were grateful for their presence. They had known and loved Papa, who had been loyal to them when Giovanni least deserved it. I thought of how I would miss them when we returned to Corinaldo, which would happen soon. I had heard Mamma promise Papa to take us back there. I imagined the sadness of the return journey, without my Babbo. The Serenellis would help us and then they, too, would vanish. There would be more sadness and then a new life.

The next day Mamma was up before dawn. She woke me and brought me into the kitchen to show me what to do. I knew how to make simple meals – I was nine years old, after all. But I had to learn how to make bread, how to tell when the soup was ready and the beans were soft enough and not too soft.

I liked feeding the hens. I had learned how to get on with them and avoid their sharp beaks, and I enjoyed their mutterings and sharp sudden cries. Mamma showed me how to tidy up quickly after one meal and begin preparations for the next. There was also the washing to think about, and ironing and sewing in the evenings.

As I listened, I remembered when Ersilia was born. I had worked hard for a day, until Mamma came back. But Teresa was three months old. Why was I learning how to do all of Mamma's chores now?

'You will have to be me now, Marietta,' Mamma said to me, trying to smile. 'How right my poor Luigi was when he said you would end up in the kitchen,' her eyes filled as she spoke. 'Even he didn't know how soon it would be. Still,' her voice grew sharper, 'I was doing these things when I was six, Marietta, younger than you.'

She was white with tiredness and sorrow, her face lined with exhaustion and worry. But where would she be, while I was in the kitchen? Had she promised Papa that she would return to Corinaldo without us? Was that what I had overheard?

'I have to take your Papa's place in the fields,' she said. 'I'll begin weaning Teresa right away. Otherwise we won't be able to stay here, and there is nowhere else for us.'

Now I understood. Mamma would leave the house every morning as Papa had done. She would replace him in the field and I would replace her in the house. Teresa began to cry and Mamma hurried away to give her a wet rag, instead of her breast.

The crying went on as I ran outside to find a shovel in the barn and bury Sole. I put him under the tree beside the house so I could open the kitchen door and see his little grave. I was careful not to put him near the deep hole where we took our buckets to empty.

I dug as deep as I could. Mamma was calling me and I had to go in. I knelt and tried to pray for Sole and Papa, but suddenly I was kneeling on the ground sobbing. If Count Mazzoleni had come up himself on his horse and ordered me, I could not have stood up.

Mamma came out and helped me inside, still sobbing. 'Come, Marietta, we have no time for this,' she said.

I looked up, but the sky seemed blank and empty. The birds Papa and Sole had both loved in their different ways were only tiny pinpricks on the horizon. Then we were in the kitchen, and I had to pay attention to what Mamma told me as she dried my tears, not unkindly.

'You'll be too busy to cry, Marietta,' she said, and she was right.

Maria's Memo

I can still see Mamma's face when she looked towards the fields where Papa worked. She climbed the steps to look down from the landing, her face like the faces of women watching for ships to come in bearing their husbands, ships that sailed dangerous seas where monstrous sea creatures lurked.

Our monstrous creatures were tiny things that flew in the air and whined in our ears and stung us as we slapped at them. The swamp at Ferriere was filled with mosquitoes that carried malaria, and at that time there was no cure. People – some people, not us – were just beginning to believe that the disease was borne by mosquitoes. Before then it was thought to be carried by the air we breathed, which was foul enough.

Probably we all had malaria. It stayed in our blood and made us tired. We had many colds, many stomach complaints. We didn't know what good health was, so we hardly missed it. Hunger was a condition of life, and its aches mingled with the rest. Our bones were sore with tiredness. The malaria lurked, but remained at bay.

I felt Mamma's fear along with my own. She must have had nightmares about the future, or perhaps she was too tired. As she fed baby Teresa, what did she think about? She was a stout, practical soul. Defenceless in the harsh, alien marshland of Ferriere, a widow with six children, how could she survive?

When Papa died, one of the two worst things that could happen to a woman happened to her. Pregnancy outside marriage was one. She had avoided that. But widowhood was the other, and that was not in her hands.

My Babbo had foreseen how it would be, once he was gone. That was why he made Mamma promise to go back to Corinaldo. He knew the net would tighten around us. He did his best to protect us from beyond the grave.

Women gave birth in the fields and went back to work. That was the dual curse of Eve. Birth and death were incidents. Work went on. Papa's memory held sway for a little while, and the respect due a widow who had given birth only three months before and was now working in the field. But these things would not protect her, or me, forever.

My Babbo had humoured Giovanni and shamed him into doing some work. But once Papa was gone, Giovanni had no shame. He was too weak to be anything but a bully, once Papa's shoes were empty.

8

At first I was flattered by the great trust Mamma had placed in me. I would do my best. I would learn how to cook. I liked the idea of learning something. I'd played and been a child long enough. I'd always been serious. People laughed at my seriousness. Now it was a good thing I was serious, for our family and the Serenellis. They called me a little old lady when I walked beside Teresa in Nettuno. Now a little old lady was what we needed.

The grain we had was hard. There was little rising, much pounding. Our cooking was a matter of brute force. Luckily, I was strong. Every herb had to be pounded into dust, to make the soup taste of something. The garlic had to be mashed into strong white oil to give the rough pasta some flavour, when we had it. The polenta had to be cooked so that it was soft and not dry, like the beans.

It was not so exciting to make the same things, day after day. It was hard to keep your mind on the fire and the pot and not let things burn and be ruined, and wasted, or cook till they were dry and tasteless, especially when you were hot and sweaty. You wanted to think of other things. At first I burned the soup as well as myself.

'You can't cook for us, you're a child,' Giovanni said. 'This soup,' he shrugged. 'It's like piss. Like piss,' he muttered.

'He drinks piss, that's how he knows,' Angelo whispered, a little too loudly.

Giovanni didn't hear, but Alessandro did. He hid a smile, I was glad to see.

'Don't speak to Marietta like that!' Mamma said to Giovanni. I wept and she embraced me. I had tried hard. But you

123

had to keep watch every second, and not dream. I had no time to dream, but still I dreamt.

'One has to try first, before one can learn,' I heard a familiar voice say. 'We should have some patience.'

It was Alessandro. I lifted my face from Mamma's shoulder.

'She'll soon get there,' he said. 'We should have faith in her, after all.'

'Ah, you take her side,' Giovanni grumbled. 'He takes her part,' he explained to himself.

But that was the end of it, for the moment. Alessandro had defended me. His father would bluster but not rail against him the way he did with us. He came to my rescue often, when Giovanni grimaced and complained. He shook his head at me to pay no attention. He behaved like a good step-brother.

I needed patience, just like Giovanni. I was an impatient child, though no one noticed because I was quiet in my own little world, where things moved at a lightning pace. But now I was clamped in the world of the kitchen, where things took their own time.

I was always waiting for something to be ready. There was plenty to do while I waited, and then I forgot what I was waiting for. I got lost in other chores, chores I liked better because I could dream over them and slip back into my own world again.

I had to give my mind to my work. It didn't belong to me any more. But my mind was young, it skittered and skipped and I had to call it like a dog, chase it like a water buffalo from the swamp or a stubborn ox slow to accept the harness.

Later the oxen became patient and heavy as they toiled away. I didn't want to be like the beasts that moved so slowly, always doing the same work. My mind didn't want to stay in its new traces. It wanted to play at being a grownup and think about being the lady of the house, like the Countess we caught sight of sometimes, rather than my poor Mamma. How could I want to be like her?

I didn't understand how Mamma washed and sewed and ironed and cooked and cleaned all at the same time. How did you remember about soup and babies and forget to think about yourself? I couldn't think of anything, not even God. Prayer was a luxury. The nightly rosary was a kind of dream. We knelt and said the decades and no one knew what was in my mind. The words flowed, angels floated past and baby Jesus lay on glowing yellow straw the colour of cheese.

Sunday Mass made a change in the week like the rosary made in the day, though Sunday was less of a day of rest for me now. There was still cooking to be done, Teresa and Ersilia to look after, the boys to keep in line. But I could leave the washing and sewing, for one day.

I loved walking into the church and smelling incense and beeswax. There were beautiful cloths on the altar and the priest wore lace and satin that rustled and gleamed. It was a place that had nothing to do with work and sweat and tiredness and hunger. I clung to the rosary and the church. There was danger as well as work outside their magic circles.

Giovanni said it wasn't right for Mamma to work in the field instead of Papa. He never said why, when there were many women working in the field. But it had not been her place while Papa lived.

The truth was that she shamed him. She did the work of two men, like Papa. Giovanni didn't do the work of one. Papa had worked hard and Giovanni had respected him, though he had thought him a fool. But for a woman to be capable and hard-working scorched him. He took it out on Mamma in every way he could. He took it out on everyone, except his son.

Mamma worked even harder, so that she could come in from the field to help me at noon and again in the evening. I could almost manage alone in the kitchen and look after Baby Teresa, but the final preparations for our meals would have me in tears if she didn't come in to calm me down and help me arrange things.

'She left the work to us again,' Giovanni said one evening, shaking his head, 'the woman left the field. Left the work to us.'

'He slept under a tree all afternoon,' Angelo said. 'I saw him. I saw him,' he repeated, mocking Giovanni, 'sleeping under a tree all afternoon.'

'Be quiet, Angelo,' Mamma told him. 'He didn't mean it, Giovanni,' she said quickly, turning to him. 'Everyone knows how hard you work. And Alessandro,' she smiled at him.

Alessandro looked away from her, his face dark. Mamma had told him to take down the pictures he had put up on the walls of his room. I didn't know what they were, and Mamma wouldn't tell me. She only said they were sinful and did not belong in a Christian house.

'Harder than a woman,' Giovanni jeered, recovering himself. 'No woman can do the work of Luigi Goretti.' He pronounced Papa's name with emphasis and then gave his verdict. 'The harvest will fail. The harvest will fail without him,' not quite daring to repeat Papa's name.

Mamma's face grew whiter. I looked at Alessandro and he didn't look away from me. He put his arm on his father's, and Giovanni threw it off angrily. But he was silent, for a moment. Then he lifted a forkful of the polenta I had cooked so carefully and dropped it again, while we watched hungrily. 'The Serenellis deserve better than this. It's not fit for animals. We're used to better,' he told Alessandro, 'on our farm, remember? Good bread, good wine? Before this?' He raised his shaking hand, which was worse than ever. 'This curse that fell on us, on your poor mother and your brother and me,' he shook his head and went on muttering as he ate and kept us from eating, taking huge gulps of wine with every bite.

We ate, making as little noise as we could. Even my brothers were quiet. After awhile we thought he had finished for the night, and they began to talk and laugh again.

'Poor Luigi,' Giovanni roared, banging his good hand on the table. 'Worn out from making babies, eh? Eh, Assunta?

You wore a good man out.' Then he laughed as Mamma broke down in tears and left the table. 'She wore him out,' he observed to himself, nodding as he looked slyly around the table at my brothers. 'Women, eh?' He nudged Alessandro. 'We know all about women, don't we?'

Angelo's' face tightened and his fist clenched. Sandrino watched him and did everything he did. They would have to challenge Giovanni, if he went on insulting Papa and Mamma. He knew it and so did they.

'Angelo,' Mamma came back just in time. 'Angelo, eat your supper and then we'll say the rosary.' Her voice pleaded with him.

He looked down at his empty plate and said nothing. Giovanni watched Mamma give him food from her own plate.

'You have to eat or you won't be able to work, not even like a woman works,' he bawled at her. 'Aren't you ashamed to take the food off your mother's plate?' He asked Angelo. 'They have no shame,' he muttered, 'these Goretti brats, they have no shame. Their father turns in his grave, because they have no shame.'

The mention of my Babbo got Angelo half out of his chair, but Mamma was ready. She lifted him like a baby and pulled him outside while Giovanni cackled to himself.

'Ah, the mamma's boy,' he said, loud enough for Angelo to hear. 'The mamma's boy goes with the mamma.' Then he reached across and helped himself to the food on Angelo's plate, which had been Mamma's. 'Mamma's boys don't need to eat. They don't work,' he snarled. 'They don't need to eat. They should be drowned like kittens.'

'Your brats should be drowned like kittens,' he repeated when Mamma came back without Angelo. It made her turn white and turn her back on us, and her food. I went to her, standing at the basin where we washed the dishes with water I brought from the well. She was shaking all over.

'Mamma,' I whispered. Was she mad, like Giovanni's wife and Alessandro's mother? Perhaps Giovanni had made his

127

wife mad and he would do the same to Mamma. Perhaps madness came through his hand.

She shook her head at me and smiled a weak smile as she came back to the silent table. Someone had put some food on her plate, and she ate it. She needed it, in order to work.

My Babbo had often laughed Giovanni out of his curses and complaints. But it was Giovanni's nature to look for someone to blame for his withered hand. Mamma could work, he couldn't. My brothers would grow into young men, not madmen like his son Gaspare or cripples like himself, not even crippled in the way Alessandro was, that had no name.

Alessandro was too quiet, too sullen, too fond of his own company. He was not given to drink, or jokes, or even complaints. He moved like a shadow through the house. Giovanni had to lord it over us and especially over Mamma. He had to find ways to hurt her.

As we sat down and ate our food in a new and strained silence, only baby Teresa complaining loudly over the lack of Mamma's nipple in her mouth, I felt how large Papa's empty place was.

Angelo helped Mamma in the field, but he was not so fast. Mariano and Sandrino were always getting into fights, and if Mamma heard them she settled things quickly with her hands and they came crying to me.

'You wouldn't act like that if Papa was here,' I told them.

I had to make them obey me. They were hungry, they were little boys and they had no Papa. I had enough to do, without worrying that they would hurt each other and give Giovanni another excuse to criticize us.

'Do you want to beg in the streets?' I asked them. 'That's what will happen if we get thrown off Count Mazzoleni's land.'

I frightened them into good behaviour. I called on Papa in heaven to make them mend their ways. They looked around, afraid he would appear.

Papa was in heaven but also in the cemetery, where I went

whenever I could. The cemetery was like the church, but more private. In the daytime it was like a big, grand room roofed by the sky and furnished with stones. It was my room, as much as anyone's.

Papa welcomed me silently. If there were other living people there, they nodded but they had their own reason to be there. The trees gave shade and made alcoves where I could sit. I never sat for long. There was no time. But I loved the time I stole and I came away better for it.

The cemetery was a neighbourhood where people lived underground and were never seen, though their names were carved on their doors and they were always at home. They didn't stare at me or make me shy. No one chased me away. The rules were different in the graveyard, like the church where you could pray instead of work.

I felt less sad there. Papa had a quiet place to lie and he was not so tired, now that he could sleep. I lay down sometimes and imagined what it might be like to stay there. It was better than the cold, white heaven I had heard of, filled with drifting clouds and angels. Sometimes, when there were no other visitors, I sang to my Babbo.

I was still a child. I played hide and seek among the stones by myself. I hid when other children came. I needed peace and quiet, but the graveyard was a popular place. We all went there for the same reason, to get away from our borrowed lives on borrowed land. The silence gave us something back, like the silence in church. Maybe even more. No one told us what to think about in the graveyard, except of course the stones. But when I thought of Papa I thought of everything he loved, especially the birds. I looked up and saw them again and wondered about their secret signals. Sometimes I lay on what was called hallowed ground and watched them, not thinking of anything. I felt the devil wasn't there. I wasn't certain God was, either, though He was everywhere. But the graveyard felt very empty, with an emptiness I came to with relief.

129

The men escaped from the house to the field. Mamma was glad enough to leave the kitchen. For me there was cooking and tidying and caring for the baby, sewing, washing, going to the well for water. There was no end to the work in the house. There was always something I should be doing and doing well, so that Giovanni couldn't complain about my darning or cooking. I was clumsy and gave him plenty of cause for complaint. I never answered him back. I had to keep going under his red, watchful eye.

Walking to the well could have been another escape for me, but I always had to hurry. We needed a lot of water and there was never enough. It made Giovanni roar and I spilled some on my way back home when I thought of him.

The well was another place that belonged to everyone and no one, like the church and the graveyard, but you had to join in the jokes and chatter with the other girls and women. I liked being with women after our house, which seemed full of men, but I couldn't join in, I was too shy. Besides, they joked about Mamma and Giovanni and I wanted to cry. I heard my name whispered and they tittered around me while I tried not to listen.

The heavy buckets of water had to be carried home, and I had to think before I dipped a cupful. The men needed water to drink and wash. Giovanni would gulp and splash and waste my precious water that was never mine, although I fetched and carried it. Sometimes I heard his voice in my sleep. At first Alessandro tried to help me. But as time went on, he took pleasure in making work for me like his father.

My whole body groaned when I woke in the morning. I had to force my sore, tired arms and legs to move. They were also children I had to shout at. I had to make them afraid so that they obeyed me.

I could sleep on my feet. I could sleep at the fireplace. It was like a little room, small but warm. I sang under my breath, not to amuse myself but to stay awake. The baby liked it. But there were days when I was too tired and sad to sing, days when I could not escape to the cemetery and I only wished to be carried there.

I sang to escape the devil, who was certainly in the kitchen. Sometimes the fireplace made me so hot I had to run outside to look up at the sky and leave the devil behind. The red fire looked like an open mouth as it flared up. I could fall down into it and be swallowed up. But I had to steel myself. I had to light the fire and keep it going while I put things into the heavy black iron pot that hung above it.

Giovanni became worse and worse. I wasn't stupid. I heard the gossip at the well. He thought Mamma was his by right, with Papa gone. The busy tongues at the well said that she would let Giovanni into her bed, sooner or later. She was a widow, what else could she do? But I knew how much Mamma hated him. She had always looked down on him. She would never take him into the bed she had shared with Papa, the bed where Papa died.

'There are too many Gorettis,' Giovanni growled as he rationed our food more and more. 'They have to make do with less,' guzzling his wine and eating. 'Less for them,' banging his fist on the table.

Alessandro shared his portion with the children. It made me soften towards him. It made Giovanni mumble at him, but it also shamed him and made him less cruel, for a time.

One day when I had fled to the cemetery, an idea came to me. I was ten now. I loved the church with its crucifix, its shrines and statues. I knew the stories of Jesus and the Blessed Mother and the saints by heart. I sang the hymns I loved. The church was my indoor cemetery, my refuge. When I made my First Communion I'd be part it in a new way, gliding up the aisle with the others on Sunday to stick out my tongue and receive Jesus. I could ask Him to help us, Mamma and all of us. He would find us a way out.

I would not be ground under without a fight. I didn't want to disappear, to sink without trace. I wanted to wear a white dress, a veil like a puff of cloud settled on my head. I wasn't

131

finished dreaming. I had never been to school and now I'd never go. But I might get some education. Only in the catechism, it was true. But that was something. Right in the midst of our darkness, I saw a path open up for me. It was a chance, the only one I had.

I spoke to Teresa first. Mamma was too busy and too tired. With Teresa's help, I made a plan. Something fierce had risen up in me. I was bullied by everyone, even the children. Alessandro defended me sometimes, but I couldn't rely on him. He was afraid of his papa. Everyone attacked me, because there was no one else. I had to fight back.

I was a member of the Church Militant, after all. I was supposed to fight! I would learn. I was hungry to find out how things worked. I was swamped by the house, the work, the swamp that had killed my Babbo.

The catechism might tell me why people died, especially fathers. God was a father. Could He explain it? If the catechism failed, I could ask Him when he came to me.

'Mamma,' I said to her one evening as we sat sewing in the dim light, 'When can I make my First Communion?'

'But Marietta, we have no way of getting a dress, a veil, shoes, my poor darling. I have to see you living like a beast in the field,' she complained. 'Besides, you'd need to learn the catechism and I cannot let you go to school. I need you here.'

'Yes, Mamma, I know,' I said. *She* had to see *me* living like a beast in the field! She was asking me to pity her! 'But the Countess Mazzoleni,' I pronounced her name with authority, 'has a housekeeper called Elsa Schiasi, who instructs children in the catechism. Teresa has spoken to her for me,' I had Teresa on my side, with Domenico behind her. I couldn't fail, though I was surprised by Mamma's resistance. 'Elsa Schiasi has agreed to take me into her class,' I told her. 'It's all arranged.'

We had seen Count Mazzoleni at Papa's funeral, but the Countess had not come. Like the count, she rode up sometimes on her horse to the edge of the field. The Count came to talk to the workers and the Countess came to deliver parcels of food at Christmas, or when one of the workers was sick. She had brought things when Papa was dying.

I hadn't seen her then. I could only see Papa. But I had seen her before and I knew she looked like the women in Rome, with soft hair piled on her head to show off the thick gold hoops in her ears, and beautiful clothes you wanted to touch. Maybe that was why she stayed so far away. But now I had said her name. I had dared.

Mamma took a deep breath. 'But you're needed here, Marietta.'

'I can do the housework fast, and go to Conca two or three times a week. And Teresa will help me with the washing. I'll work harder than ever. I know how to work hard, just like you do.' She knew it was true.

'Oh, Marietta.' She sighed.

The sympathy in her voice meant trouble.

'I wish you could have a wonderful First Communion, at least. But Giovanni will grumble if the soup is not on the table, and then where will we be, eh?'

She was telling me her story, without words. Giovanni would take advantage of any weakness, any sign that we were not coping. He wanted Mamma. It was what people expected. But he was a drunk and a brute whose withered devil-hand shook. He was sly and mean. He would never treat Mamma or her children well, whatever he said. She would be lost and all of us with her. He could not be a stepfather. He had proven that by his will to starve us out until she agreed.

I had to help her fend him off. She was safe in the field. There were other people there. As long as I in the kitchen I guarded her, blocking Giovanni's way. I lay in her bed at night. If I was gone, he'd have a chance to corner her. She couldn't spare me, because I spared her.

'If you wait,' she cautioned me. 'Wait for a time and then we'll see what comes,' her voice became vague and weak.

'Nothing will come for us now.'

'Giovanni will make it impossible,' she said. 'How will you manage the house? The children must also be fed,' she added.

'Teresa will help me. You've taught me well. Giovanni hardly complains any more, because nothing is burnt and everything is done. I can do the same work in the same way, only faster.'

She nodded. 'I'm sure you can,' she said. 'Faster than I could.'

It was true. I almost felt sorry for her. I had woven my plan around her like a web, and she was already caught in a web. But I couldn't afford sympathy.

'My class begins next week,' I told her. My voice shook. How could I abandon her? I needed the ruthlessness of the young, and it came to me. I would have my time. Others besides Teresa and Domenico would be on my side, and Mamma knew it.

I was looked upon kindly. She was a widow, and widows reminded people of what they wanted to forget. Widows wore black and made people think of the shortness of life. They looked at Mamma and thought of how Papa had worked for his family as they were working for theirs, and how he had died of the malaria they feared.

My Babbo would want me to make my First Communion. He had made Mamma promise to move back to Corinaldo on his deathbed. I had hoarded my secret knowledge of her broken promise. Sometimes I thought she knew I knew. But now I was going to use it as a weapon against her, to get what I wanted.

'God will take care of us, Mamma,' I said. 'He will see that my First Communion does not make things worse for us. Papa will be so happy for me, in heaven. He'll see that our lives can be good, *even here in Ferriere.*' I waited a second. 'Maybe someday we can go back to Corinaldo,' I said. 'That would make Papa happy, wouldn't it?'

Mamma sat heavy and still, as if I had wounded her. She was used to the silent disapproval around her. Never had

Mamma needed a family more. Her almost-mother was far away and she could be no help. Her almost-father was dead. Mamma was thirty-one, and she was old. Giovanni made her less of a threat to other women, but he gave people more to gossip about.

I had threatened her with a much worse kind of disapproval, because she had broken her promise to Papa. 'I'm going to make my First Communion, Mamma,' I said. 'It's my choice.'

She had no more choices, except to fend off Giovanni. But in the end she would do what he wanted, or else leave the house and the land. We all knew it, without the words to say it. The house was charged with combat, lust, denial and refusal. Time was running out. The house was a coliseum like the one Papa had told me about in Rome. It was not a home any more, but a place for gladiators. That was why Papa had told her to leave.

But Mamma was strong, too, and she wouldn't give up without a fight. She fought Giovanni and she would fight me. Her voice softened as she tried another tactic. 'I know it's hard for you, Marietta.' She shook her head. 'Alessandro is not so nice any more.'

I bit my lip. She wouldn't make me cry. I hated the way my old friend spoke to me these days. He was like his father, but it was much worse from him.

'He'll do his military service soon,' she said. 'Don't fret, Marietta.'

I was a hair away from giving in to her. She was appealing to me. Giovanni would be worse, without Alessandro. I would escape in the end, but she wouldn't. I could afford to give in now, for a little while. Just a little time, then Alessandro would be gone. Was it so much to ask?

It was. Too much. If I waited, it would never come. Nothing would come. We'd be finished together. I didn't blame her. Her instinct wasn't to sacrifice me, not exactly. She had no choice but to use me to save herself, and the others

'Mamma,' I said as gently as I could. 'It's all arranged with

Elsa. The Countess Mazzoleni won't be pleased with us if I'm not there.'

I delivered the name like a blow: *the Countess Mazzoleni*, whose long hair was braided and twisted and held with a darkly shining tortoiseshell comb above her shining earrings. I couldn't look directly at her. It was like looking into the sun.

'I owe the Count a lot of money,' Mamma said.

Her voice made me forget the Countess. Mamma had never spoken to me about money before.

'There were many expenses when your father died, and from before. And after,' she said. 'If I left without paying him, the Count would send the police after me.'

I wanted to cover my ears and sing to drown her out. That was why she had broken her promise to Papa! Now she had told me.

'Couldn't we leave at night?' I asked her. 'Couldn't we pack up everything and leave while everyone is sleeping?' I knew from the well that it sometimes happened.

'Giovanni would stop us,' she said. 'If we left, Count Mazzoleni would make Giovanni and Alessandro pay. Someone always has to pay, Marietta.'

'We left Senator Scelsi's land,' I said. I couldn't believe her. It was too terrible.

'That was different, Marietta. Scelsi threw us off his land. Mazzoleni paid him for us, in the end,' she shrugged. 'We owe Count Mazzoleni everything.'

The name helped me. 'But it's all arranged with Elsa and the Countess, Mamma,' I said. I knew when to soften my tone, too. I had learned from her. 'We can't offend them now. It would be ungrateful, and they'd be angry with us.'

'We can try it for a time, with the lessons,' she said. 'It won't hurt you to learn some catechism, in any case.'

She was too tired to fight any more. She went back to her sewing and I turned to mine. Once I started down the road to Conca, I wouldn't turn back. In my mind, I was leaving

Mamma and the house forever. After my First Communion, things would be different. I hadn't worked out the details yet, but if I could do this, I could do anything. I would not go down into the fire's maw.

Maria's Memo

Mamma was desperate. She wanted to spare me, too, if she could. She saw the danger if I showed myself off in a dress and veil, a danger I was blind to.

She wanted me to blend in with her. We were like a married couple, even sharing the same bed. That way she was safe – or safer – from Giovanni. By insisting on making my First Communion, I was asking for a divorce.

My eagerness to make my First Communion would be used later as an example of my piety. No one noticed that it gave me my only education, my only way out of prison. I was said to be dutiful, without ambition. But I wasn't. I craved adventure.

No one gave me credit for anything except piety. But I had embarked on a battle of wills with Mamma. I would fight her to the death for my chance of a little life of my own. No one saw it that way.

She had broken her promise to Papa, a promise made on his deathbed. She was in debt. She was struggling. She was drowning. It was the only way I had of not going under with her.

First Holy Communion meant dressing up and being someone else. I would wear a white veil and like a bride, I would escape my mother's house. The shape of my new life was cloudy. But I had to take that first step.

Jesus would hear me on my First Communion Day. Miracles were easy for Him. Besides, First Communion was fun! No one talks about fun in the same breath as Saint Maria Goretti. But I wanted my share. I still watched the birds from the landing. There was sky and somewhere there was sea. I would have God on my tongue, like a bird with a worm.

9

Mamma stood with her back to me, stirring the pot hanging over the fire. I had laid the fire and made the gruel. I had cleaned the baby and fed her.

'I'm going to Conca now, Mamma.'

Teresa started to cry. Angelo and Sandrino were fighting and there was a smell of the bucket that needed to be emptied.

'Mamma?'

She waved at me without turning around. 'Go, then, Marietta.'

'Goodbye, Mamma.' I blew kisses at my brothers, not that they noticed, and my sisters. Ersilia blew one back at me.

I walked over to the door, opened it and slid outside, closing it behind me. Giovanni might be around somewhere, making his morning pipi. I walked quickly down the road that led away from the house, and then I ran.

When my side hurt I had to stop running but I walked fast, panting. There were buds on the trees, though it was still cold and the March wind blew. I needed to keep moving in order to be warm. But mostly I wanted not to see our house any more, not even the chimney with the smoke coming out of it. As long as I could see that, I saw Mamma at the fireplace and I heard the children's voices and smelled the morning smells.

But they were still there inside of me, Mamma especially. Her big back blocked the road, as she stood looking at the fire. The boys' voices rose as they fought. Giovanni would hear them and then there would be quarrels over breakfast. Mamma's face would turn white and the baby would cry. Little Ersilia would stand sucking her thumb and looking puzzled.

141

I stood not knowing which way to go. Mamma would hit the boys and rock Teresa against her if she cried. She would forget about Ersilia, who would be wet and cold. If Angelo or Mariano or Sandrino shouted, she would put her little hands over her ears.

I put my own hands over my ears and screamed as loud as I could until I couldn't hear them any more. Then I dropped my hands and stood in the ringing quiet, breathing hard. I was on the road to Conca. Everything else was gone.

There were no houses, only trees. I went behind a tree at the side of the road and let the pipi flow out of me. My brothers and sisters left me in a yellow stream, Mamma and Giovanni and Alessandro. Last of all, Ersilia left me in a little green trickle. When I stood up, I was empty. I wiped myself on some leaves and walked back to the road.

There was no smoke and no sound. I started to walk. I could keep on walking forever. I could walk to Rome, where the women wore gold in their ears.

I could go to the sea, if I could find it. Papa had promised me we'd go there one day. But promises were not always kept, and I'd known when he made that one that he might not keep it.

Besides, I was on the road that led to Conca and the Mazzoleni house, where I would learn my catechism. I had gone to Senegaglia and Rome because of Papa and Mamma. I had come to Ferriere because of Giovanni being drunk on Senator Scelsi's land. But I was going to Conca because of my First Communion. Papa and Mamma had left Corinaldo and the Colle Granturco because they had to. That was why people like us travelled, because we had to.

But I was breaking that rule with every step. I was leaving Ferriere behind, and not because I had to. Whose footsteps were these, on the road to Conca? They were the footsteps of someone I didn't know yet, a stranger who was also me.

Mamma had said the walk was too long. I'd be tired. It was dangerous. But it was these footsteps she was afraid of.

142

What danger outside the house could be worse than the danger inside? What could frighten me, when I lived with Giovanni? He was shrunken and stooped and drunk, his hand shook and he thought nothing of making hungry children watch him eat. He watched Mamma with hungry eyes and said she'd given Papa too many children to feed and driven him into his grave.

I flew down the road watching the birds fly over my head. I'd been too busy for them lately. But now my feet felt like birds and the road was a sky. I started to sing, at first in a low voice and then loud

The hymns I'd learned for my Confirmation in Corinaldo made me think about the Holy Ghost, who was also a bird. He was supposed to have descended upon me then, but maybe He had waited until now. I was filled with courage like a sail filled with wind, the kind Alessandro used to talk about when he told tales of his seafaring life.

He no longer did. But as I took the road to Conca, it was my turn to set sail. The trees around me shook. The world shivered and gleamed around me. What made it do that? *God's will?*

I had a will. It was a fierce thing. I had used my will to get this far along the road. This was what I wanted. To walk on a chilly day and see the buds that would burst soon. My shivering meant nothing. I would shiver anyway.

I would get there. I would knock on the door. Things that had been beyond me yesterday were not beyond me today. This was *will power*. It told me more about *God's will* than anything I had ever heard in church, or from Mamma's lips.

Down in the valley there was moss and grass. There were more trees and birds. I had left the swamp and smell of Ferriere behind. Everything around me was different, only a few miles away from our house.

Before I was ready, I had arrived. I stood at the back door, where I had been told to go. I could hardly believe the big white door would open. Faith was different from will. At the last minute, I almost turned around and went home. But I reached up and knocked. The door opened and Elsa Schiasi's smiling face looked out.

'Marietta, come in,' she said. 'Aren't you a big, brave girl, walking all this way on such a wild day! Come in and get warm.'

She bustled me into the kitchen and into a large, comfortable chair in front of the fire. The fire was brighter than ours. There was so much light, it made me blink. I felt very small in the big, shining room.

'You're the first to arrive, that's good,' Elsa told me. 'I've made some food for you. Now you sit there and eat, Marietta. I'll come back in a little while – I have some things to do for the Countess,' her kind glance said she knew I couldn't swallow, if she stayed. 'Eat up, we don't want it to go to waste.' She opened another door and passed through it.

I was alone with enough food for my whole family. I ate and ate. Porridge with honey, delicious and sweet and plenty of it. I licked it from my fingers with my eyes closed.

My stomach hurt. Where could I put the food to carry it home? It would feel like stealing and I could hardly sit with the other children, my pockets full of Elsa's good porridge covered with honey.

Elsa bustled back. 'Now, we'll put the rest of that in a basin so you can take it home with you,' she said. 'And there are a few more things, if you would do me the favour of taking them. Not too much for you to carry, on your long walk. But the Countess doesn't eat so much, you know, she worries for her figure.'

Someone tapped at the door and she went to answer it. The idea that anyone would not eat as much as they could was new to me. Couldn't Elsa let out the Countess' clothes, or make new ones? I was certain she could sew. But more children were coming through the back door and besides, I couldn't ask Elsa about the Countess' clothes.

The other children were all given breakfast, too, as well as sacks and basins to take things home with them. I had never seen so much food. Elsa was here in the middle of it, every day of her life. Her round, full body said she didn't worry about her clothes like the Countess. She ate as much as she liked. People liked her well-padded figure.

It might be better to be Elsa than the Countess. Teresa said she was the housekeeper. That's what I was, at home. I was the housekeeper. I could keep the Countess' house instead of ours, when Elsa got too old. She was quite old already. She might get sick. If only she would cough as Papa had done, or look pale and drawn instead of smiling and round and red-cheeked. If I took her place, I'd be as fat and full as she was.

I was learning more about the world than God. The catechism was the same as it had been in Corinaldo, with more words to learn by heart. But they meant the same thing. They told me nothing new. There was more to learn, commandments of the Church, different kinds of sins and virtues. No one mentioned will. I sat listening to Elsa, more interested in the lesson she was than the lesson she taught.

Because we were going to receive Our Lord in the Eucharist, she talked mostly about Him. But I thought about the Holy Ghost. I had been too young for Him in Corinaldo. But He was the one who gave what I needed most. The Holy Ghost came down in tongues of fire on Pentecost and filled the apostles with courage. Huddled in the upper room, they were not afraid any more. They threw the door open and went out, just as I had done that morning.

Giovanni had no will. The devil had taken it when he entered his hand. Alessandro had less will than he needed, because of Giovanni and his devil and maybe because his mother and his brother were mad. Mamma had will, but it was blind and tired since Papa died, because she had broken her promise.

Elsa's will was to feed us and teach us and still do her work in the house. I thought she might be a saint, even though

145

she didn't look like the ones in church. Women saints always looked young and thin like the Countess. Men saints and apostles were often old. They were plump and grizzled, with grey beards. Why couldn't women saints grow old or fat? I'd thought of another question already, on my way home. If Elsa was a saint, she might die and go to heaven soon and I could take her place.

I carried Elsa's food back after the lesson, planning as I walked. Giovanni slept in the afternoon, so I could hide it outside to share with my brothers and sisters and Mamma. I'd watch her eat what I had brought.

I'd pray for the Holy Ghost to inspire Elsa. She could take me on and train me before she died. It was no small thing, to be the Mazzoleni's housekeeper. I'd wash carefully every time I went to Conca. Somehow I'd find the time to bring back extra water from the well, so Giovanni couldn't complain.

The trees shook in sympathy. The air was warmer and the sun shone like the fire in Elsa's kitchen. Everything was different in Conca. Everything was green, not grey, and the air smelled of recent rain and rain to come.

Then I started up the slope towards Ferriere. There were fewer trees and the air was heavy, even before I could smell the swamp. I went over my plan as I walked back, trying not to drag my feet.

My plan worked. Giovanni had had his midday meal and most of everyone else's, I was sure. He always took his wine to finish under a tree and then slept heavily. I had to watch out for Alessandro, who could no longer be trusted.

I kept guard while my family ate. We were soldiers in a war. I was really confirmed in the Church Militant now. My brothers would obey me, because I fed them. Mamma ate her share hungrily. When you brought food, people looked up to you.

I went to Conca twice a week and it changed our lives. Elsa always gave me food to bring home. I told the children

146

to act hungry, so Giovanni wouldn't be suspicious. They loved the game.

Giovanni sensed our strength, though he didn't understand it. He kept a slacker grip on the food and there was even more to share. He backed away from Mamma, who was less tired and more at ease. I had changed things, instead of waiting for things to change. I had used my will.

I prepared myself carefully for my trips to Conca. I had to look like a real housekeeper. On my walk, I practiced what I'd say to Elsa. I always arrived first, so that I could talk to her alone.

'I lay the fire the night before, so it's ready in the morning,' I thought that was a sign that I knew how to prepare things well, though Mamma had taught me. 'I light it as soon as I get up and put the big pot of water I got from the well the day before to boil for gruel.'

I stopped on the road to think. Should I say *gruel*? It made us sound poor. But if I said *porridge*, it would be a lie. Elsa might think there was no need for me to come into the Mazzoleni household, if we had porridge. No, I'd say *gruel*, although I hated the word as much as the coarse and lumpy stuff itself.

I was distracted by the thought of the honey-coated porridge that awaited me. I walked faster. When Elsa let me in, always with a big smile, I started describing my duties at home to her as soon as I could. She listened and shook her head. None of the other children worked as hard as I did. Many of them had fathers. I learned quickly about the differences between us. I was the only one who could do what Elsa did.

Elsa hadn't told the other children about the Countess not eating so much because of her clothes. I wanted to ask her if the Count ate more. But maybe she would tell me, if I kept on getting to the back door before anyone else did.

I didn't tell anyone what I was thinking. Mamma couldn't imagine even daring to come to the Mazzoleni house. But things couldn't go back the way they had been. As the first week passed, then the second and third, I prayed for Elsa to take me under her wing. I stopped at the cemetery and pleaded for my Babbo to help me.

I also enjoyed myself. At first the lessons made me shyer than ever. My tongue was thick and slow in public, and I wasn't used to other, cleaner children. I preferred to watch and listen, rather than speak.

But Elsa was very patient. I started to get the knack of memorizing. It was work, and I was used to that. It meant doing the same thing over and over, like the oxen in the field, pulling the plough. I made myself recite my catechism on the way home from Conca.

'Marietta has a fire in her belly after all,' Giovanni said one night at supper, surprising me. 'Eat, Marietta, tomorrow you go to Conca, eh? Put in a good word for us with the Count!' He was smiling, his grizzled face falling in new folds. 'Alessandro, don't you still have your old catechism? Why not give it to Marietta, and help her learn? She can't read, but there are pictures, and she could begin, eh? As you yourself said, how to learn if one doesn't begin?'

Alessandro nodded and we sat waiting for what would come next. Giovanni had not repeated himself, for once. That alone made us listen.

'I remember my First Communion.' Giovanni's voice was thick. He took a gulp of wine and continued. 'My hand was good then,' he said. He looked at it, then put it under the table. There were tears in his eyes. '*I* was good then,' he said. 'You might not believe it, but I was. I had my Mamma and my Papa, and my hand.' He drank more wine. 'The priest taught us. I memorized my catechism, just like Marietta.' He sounded like a man in a dream. 'None of this had happened,' he looked around without seeing us. 'I lived in Loreto and I had my life in front of me.'

It was as if baby Teresa had begun to speak. Giovanni had not always been Giovanni. Or – there had been another Giovanni before this one, who still lived in him.

148

Alessandro went to get his old catechism for me. He moved like a sleepwalker. He had only known the drunken Giovanni of the withered, shaking hand. He didn't know this stranger, either.

'I'll help you all I can, Marietta,' he told me when he returned with the book.

'Good, good,' Giovanni sat sipping his wine and wiping his tears. 'I'll go to sleep now,' he left us at the table, which was not his habit. He seemed to forget that without him we were free to eat.

'Let Alessandro help you, Marietta.' Mamma said. She sounded like someone in a dream. She smiled at Alessandro.

I stayed at the table with him while Mamma cleared away the supper things, took the children upstairs and put them to bed. Alessandro began with the first easy questions in the catechism, reading them out to me and testing me on the answers. I got them all, and he admired my memory.

Then we came to the harder ones and I began to stumble. He was kind. He didn't mock me. He explained and went over things many times, agreeing that it was the only way to learn.

'I remember these questions even now,' he said in surprise. 'I lay on my bed at night and repeated the answers in my head. It was before I went to sea,' he seemed amazed that there had been such a time, as his father had been.

I understood them. There was *before* for me, too. Before Papa died. Before Giovanni and Alessandro came to us in Colle Granturco. Before we left Corinaldo. Before our own Alessandro, my brother Sandrino, was born, or Mariano, or Ersilia, or Teresa. Each of these things had changed my world. There was also *before* I found my will and decided to make my First Communion.

Alessandro became my friend again. He remembered the catechism very well, and told me stories about the time when he had learned it. Giovanni sat with us sometimes, in the evening. It became less startling to think that he had once

149

been young. Only Mamma held back from these conversations. She worked around us and said nothing of her own childhood.

I admired Alessandro's quickness. It was clear I was a worse pupil than he had been. But he was interested in my struggle to learn. He liked being a teacher. I saw that he was at his best without Giovanni and I understood that they struggled too, like Mamma and me. But their struggle was different, because they were men.

'I might teach you to read, Marietta,' Alessandro said one night when Giovanni was absent.

I nodded. I held my breath. Maybe my future would be in Ferriere after all. The Countess had not appeared in the kitchen and Elsa seemed to think I was complaining when I went on telling her about my work at home. I didn't want her to think badly of me, so I had stopped.

Could I have a future with Alessandro? It was not impossible. There was no one else. God's will might point me in his direction and him in mine. I would have to ask Him, when I made my First Communion.

Maria's Memo

Poor Mamma. She had nothing to gain from my new way of life except the food I brought home from the Mazzoleni kitchen. It took a whole year for me to learn the catechism well enough to make my First Communion, a year that meant a lot more work for her.

It was the best time I had, after Papa died. Maybe my best time ever. I was blossoming. I was growing. We were all happy. My First Communion gave us something to look forward to. It gave Giovanni and Alessandro something to look back on, and Alessandro had something to do besides sweat in the field. Only Mamma had nothing she wanted to look back on, and nothing ahead to look forward to.

I was still hoping for the Countess to come down into the kitchen in Conca or, more likely, for big, kind Elsa to give me her life. But then things changed again, and not in the way I'd planned.

10

'Maria, come to the barn with me,' Alessandro came up
behind me one morning early, when I was feeding the chickens.

He made me jump. Another me was waking up in Conca,
starting her duties in Elsa's warm, bright kitchen. I could
taste warm honey as I rubbed the silky grains of corn.

'Why aren't you snoring, Alessandro?'

'Come with me,' he insisted. 'Giovanni says you should.'

Why did Giovanni want me to go to the barn with Alessandro?
He had something to tell me. Maybe they were leaving Ferriere!

We would have to leave, too. We could go back to Corinaldo,
as Mamma had promised Papa. I would make my First
Communion where I had made my Confirmation, so long
ago. My future would not be with Alessandro, or in Conca.

Once I was inside the barn, Alessandro slammed the heavy
doors shut. It was very dark and I stumbled forwards towards
the animals. They were warm and I liked to nuzzle them. But
Alessandro pulled me to him, close and rough. I felt his
breath and then I knew why I was there.

I pulled myself away from him with all my might. I threw
the barn doors open and ran back to the kitchen. When
Alessandro came in, he barely looked at me. He scowled and
sulked for the next few days, while I tried to find a way to
tell Mamma what had happened.

But she avoided me as if she knew. Then one day when I
was bent double looking for a hen that had run under the
hedge, Alessandro came up behind me and pushed himself
against me. I almost fell into the scratchy thicket when I felt
him. Then I twisted away.

'You'll do as I say, Maria,' he shouted after me as I ran.

He called me *Maria*, like a stranger. But he was the stranger. I had to tell Mamma now.

'Mamma,' I whispered to her as we lay in bed that night, before she started snoring. 'Mamma, Alessandro has – twice he has tried to –'

'I'm too tired, Marietta,' she said. 'Tomorrow, we'll talk tomorrow.'

She fell asleep and I did, too. I waited all the next morning and when she came in from the field to help me with the noon meal, she spoke quickly and harshly.

'You're too young, Marietta,' she said. 'But you have to learn not to make Alessandro angry, eh?'

'But how, Mamma?'

'You have to smile and ask him to wait.'

'To wait for what, Mamma?'

'Listen to me and stop asking questions. To here,' she drew her right hand across her waist, 'it's not such a sin, and nothing can come from it. Make him wait as long as you can and then – to here,' she drew the line again. 'And no further.' She looked hard at my chest, where breasts had begun to grow. 'I should have bound you,' she muttered. 'I never thought of it. You've grown too soon, Marietta,' she said. 'It's all this nonsense about Conca.' She shook her head. 'I knew no good would come of it. There's nothing for it now, he's seen you. Giggle and be a little girl with him and make him wait. And then, later, to here,' she drew the line at her waist again. Her eyes were hard as she said, 'you wanted to grow up, Marietta. This is what it means.'

She made it all my fault, for wanting to make my First Communion. Was my triumph a mistake? I left the house for Conca the next morning full of questions. How could I giggle and act like a little girl, when I was a housekeeper?

It was warm. The buds had burst, the leaves had come back on the trees. Spring had even come to Ferriere. I stood by the roadside, put my finger in my ears and screamed.

Then I walked to Conca, listening to the birds and breathing

154

in the warm air. I tried to enjoy the deep greens of the valley. I tried not to think about what had happened. I had to prepare myself as best I could for Conca, though I felt very unprepared when I arrived at the Mazzoleni house.

'Come in, Marietta,' Elsa smiled at me. 'Today is a very special day for you.'

My heart beat fast. She'd been talking to the Countess about me. Now they'd tell me I could stay, after I made my First Holy Communion.

'The date for your First Holy Communion has been set,' she announced. 'The Countess is coming today, to congratulate you.'

'To congratulate me?'

'To congratulate all the children,' she said.

She had never looked at me before as if I disgusted her. I had tried hard to be clean when I came into her kitchen, but I was dirty and tired today. I had had no time to wash. My hair crawled with lice, and she had seen them. I wanted to turn around and run out the door.

'We'll brush your hair again, Marietta, after your long walk,' she said kindly. 'So that you can look your best for the Countess.'

Her disgusted look had gone. But I had seen it and I went on seeing it as she led me into the scullery and placed me on a stool by the sink. She doused my head with water from a jug and began to scrub my hair and my scalp, using a comb to remove the small black bugs.

'It's the eggs,' she murmured. 'I'll use this cream, Maria, and rinse them away.'

I said nothing. I was shivering under the chilly water, even though I burned with shame. We had no water at home for hair-washing, though we did it once in a great while, when Mamma remembered or Giovanni roared that we could live on our bugs, we had no need for food.

'Ooph,' Elsa made little noises as her fingers dug into my sore scalp. She rubbed over the places where I had scratched at night and torn the skin. I folded my lips tight as she worked. It seemed to take a very long time, as her hand went back and forth from my head to the little pail she had brought.

'My goodness,' she said once, and 'you poor child.'

I wanted to put my fingers in my ears and scream again. But I sat like a statue.

'Now,' she dabbed at my ears. 'It won't hurt to take some of this dirt away too, eh?'

She left me in the scullery with a thick towel on my head while she let the other children in. I heard her giving out apples and pears and my stomach growled. I wanted to bury my face in the towel.

When she came back she smiled but she looked busy and didn't really see me. She began to dry my hair, rubbing my sore scalp with the towel.

'Elsa,' I said, my voice loud in my clean ears. 'Elsa, I have to –'

'Come,' she pulled me up and led me through the kitchen to the little room off the scullery, in the back of the house. I knew there were other, better little rooms in the house for the same thing. Some of the boys in the catechism class had gone through the house while Elsa wasn't looking. But this cold, dark little room was the one she always took us to. The other children looked up as we passed through the kitchen, and some of them giggled.

I shivered as I crouched on the wooden box fixed over a bucket like the ones at home. Someone, not me, would empty it. The thought made me more ashamed than before.

'Marietta,' Elsa knocked on the door.

There were no leaves in the little room. Then I saw some strips of newspaper, and used those.

'All right, Child?' Elsa sounded breathless. When I opened the door she took my hands and washed them with an edge of the towel she had wet. Then she quickly dried my hair as best she could and combed it out.

'There. You look very nice, Marietta,' she smiled without

looking at me. 'Remember to curtsey and be very polite to the Countess. Don't tell her about this,' she gestured to my hair.

She thought I was simple. Why would I want the Countess to know I had arrived crawling with lice? *Was this a mistake? Was Mamma right?* The thought churned in my head under my damp hair. I wanted to run away.

Instead I stood as Elsa arranged us in a semi-circle, as she called it, like a half-moon. I heard a soft cough and then the Countess was in the kitchen with us.

She looked as beautiful as the Blessed Virgin, and as strange to me. I could hardly breathe and I was relieved to think there was nothing crawling in my hair, and my hands were clean.

'Congratulations, children,' she said in her soft, smooth voice. 'You've studied and learned your catechism well. Elsa is very proud of you and so am I.'

Elsa pronounced our names as the Countess moved around the half-circle. Everyone curtsied or bowed, then she shook our hands.

I waited my turn, hoping to drop my curtsey without falling over. I did. Then I shook her hand, but my hand was weak and hot. It belonged to the old, frightened Marietta. After she'd gone round the circle, she left the kitchen.

The catechism lesson was a hard one, and I was hungry. When the time came to leave, Elsa pressed a bag of apples and pears into my hands. I walked home in a daze. Who was I? Where was my will?

I bit into an apple as I walked. The sound of my own chewing roared in my ears. I had not told the Countess I was Mamma's housekeeper. I'd barely forced a smile. The old, shy Marietta had wasted my chance, and it might never come again.

If only I'd washed my hair. If only I hadn't used the bucket in the little hutch behind the scullery. If only I didn't do everything wrong and forget to do the things that might help me. If only I wasn't on the way home with nothing but apples and pears to show for my hard work.

The afternoon was filled with work. After the evening meal I sat in the firelight turning over the pages of Alessandro's catechism. What good was it to me? What had the Countess seen but a small, dirty child with damp hair? She had probably guessed the reason. And now Elsa would never want me as her replacement.

Alessandro wanted me only as one beast wanted another. Even then, I sensed he only wanted me because Giovanni goaded him. He wanted to use me to gain his father's respect, just as Mamma wanted to use me to fend off Giovanni.

Tomorrow I'd stay at home and work. Everyone was tired. The work in the field was harder in the heat. Giovanni slept more, drank more, made Alessandro work harder. He was too tired to help me with my catechism, and his father was spiteful to him in the old way, which made him spiteful to me. Besides, he was angry with me now for not doing what he wanted. I rubbed my eyes. My scalp hurt where Elsa had rubbed it. Her white towel would have my blood on it. I pictured her disgusted face when she saw it.

'I'm afraid you'll never know your catechism well enough to receive your First Holy Communion, Marietta,' Mamma said. She was watching me for signs of weakness.

'The date has been set,' I said. 'Elsa told us today. The Countess came to congratulate us for learning our catechism so well.' I couldn't tell her Elsa had washed my hair. She hadn't noticed and if she did, she'd never let me go to Conca again.

'I know how hard you've tried. But sometimes the things we want are simply not to be, my sweet child. You've had your walks and your instruction. It's not as though it's been a waste of time. Things were against you, that's all. If Papa had lived,' Mamma sighed, 'then it would have been possible.'

She had found a last shred of will. It would not break mine. 'Mamma,' I said quietly. 'I've learned the catechism

158

perfectly. I can answer any question. You've heard me reciting it and even teaching the little ones what I've learned. How can you doubt me?'

'Oh Marietta, my darling, it isn't you I doubt. It's just the way things are for us.'

'But God expects us to help ourselves,' I remembered Papa's voice long ago, telling her we had to leave Corinaldo.

'Yes,' she said. 'But sometimes it doesn't happen as we wish, Marietta. Not even when we try our best.'

I felt something crack in me. I wouldn't let it break. I had worked hard. I had learned my catechism. Alessandro had helped me and when he stopped helping, I went on alone. I had struggled and made my memory strong. I was at the point of making my First Communion. I had the date.

'Take me to the parish priest and have him test me on my catechism,' I said. 'Then let him decide.'

'I hardly think the priest wishes to be bothered with our little concerns –'

'It's not a little concern, Mamma,' I replied. 'At any rate, he can refuse to see us if he wants to.'

She was caught.

We both knew the priest would not refuse to see us. She thought I was the old Marietta. What she said next proved it.

'Think of your Confirmation, my poor darling,' she said.

That was back in Corinaldo, back when Papa was alive and I was a baby. I had had no backbone, no will. Didn't she know it had all changed? That very Confirmation, which because of her had come too soon, had finally forced its way up in me.

I pushed away the sight of Alessandro's eyes glinting in the dark barn, the weight of his heavy body as he came up behind me by the hedge. I pushed away Mamma's answer when I went to her, which was no answer. Most of all I pushed away what had happened today, in Conca.

'That was a long time ago, Mamma.' I hated her for

159

reminding me how weak I had been. But I knew what made her cruel. It was fear. I could be cruel, too. 'That was back in Corinaldo.'

There was silence in the kitchen, a silence of two wills. I dared her to try and stop me. She dropped her eyes and sighed.

'We'll go to the priest,' I said.

'I suppose it won't hurt,' she mumbled.

Her face was white. It was over, for now. But she had betrayed me, and not only by trying to stop me making my First Communion.

She refused to talk about Alessandro or the way he hunted me as Giovanni hunted her. Mamma, who complained about the pictures on Alessandro's wall! She had not done her duty, just as she had broken her promise to Papa to take us back to Corinaldo. She knew I'd be stronger if I made my First Communion. Besides, then I'd have to go to Confession, and I could tell the priest everything.

Mamma was afraid of Giovanni. Things had changed since the night he had surprised us with his memories. He had become his old drunken self again, small and cruel. His eyes glinted when he looked at Mamma. But I didn't care. I wouldn't let go of my plan. No one would help me now, not Alessandro, not Mamma, not even Elsa or the Countess. I'd go straight to Jesus and He wouldn't fail to rescue me.

My will had returned and I wouldn't lose it again. This time it was a darker thing. I'd seen how small Mamma made herself, how small she wanted to make me.

Even Elsa seemed smaller. Even the Countess was small, as she shook hands and smiled over a damp head that had crawled with lice half an hour before. What if I told her, or Elsa, about Alessandro? Would they shake their heads, and then forget?

In the days that followed, I prepared for my test. Mamma thought I'd change my mind and beg her not to take me to the priest. She was willing to humiliate me, if she had to.

160

I made myself imagine the test, instead of my First Communion day. Even as Elsa talked to us about that great day, I took myself in my mind into the church house, into the priest's office, which I had only glimpsed before. I'd face my ordeal.

If only Mamma had died, instead of my Babbo! I could keep house and watch the children for him, my dear kind Papa. It was not God's will and it was a sin to think it, but I still thought it and Mamma knew. We'd all be better off with Babbo instead of her. He could go on working in the fields and keep control of Giovanni and Alessandro.

'I can make my First Confession on the day of the test,' I told Mamma. Let her quake. I was merciless, because she was.

She shook her head, then nodded. I wanted her to know that I had failed in my duty to honour her, just as she had failed me. How could I honour someone who had broken a deathbed promise to my Papa? Who refused to protect me? I wanted her to be afraid of what I'd say in the secrecy of the confessional. Let her think I'd expose her to the priest. Let her think I'd tell him everything, about Giovanni as well as Alessandro. Then he'd know the kind of house I lived in.

It was Mamma's first rule not to speak about such things. She'd been afraid I'd tell Elsa how the Serenellis hunted us, father and son, mother and daughter. But she couldn't beg me to be silent without speaking, and she would never do that.

The priest took me not into his office but into the sacristy behind the altar, where we stood facing each other.

'Now, Maria,' he said kindly. 'I'm certain you know your catechism. I'll dispense with the easy questions, my child, and go straight to the harder ones.'

'Yes Father,' a great peace came over me. The sacristy was very quiet. It smelled of wax and incense. It would make a lovely little bedroom like the one I'd dreamt of, in the Mazzoleni house. The drawers behind me held the flowing

161

robes that Father wore at Mass. I longed to open them and put on the holy silk and satin vestments. They'd be even softer than the clothes the Countess wore, and they were big and loose. I could wear them and eat as much as I liked.

'Ready, Maria?'

I shook myself awake. 'Father?'

'Yes, Child.'

'Afterwards, I'd like to make my first confession.'

'Of course, Child,' he said quietly.

Though he said *Child*, he said it with respect. I knew no one was ever refused confession. The priest had to respect the conscience of the sinner, and he had respected mine. I was ready now.

'What are the seven deadly sins, Maria?'

'Pride, covetousness, lust, anger, gluttony, envy and sloth,' I rattled the list off.

'Well done, Child. These you must avoid with all your might.'

'Yes, Father.' I had no chance of committing gluttony or sloth. Pride was almost unknown to me, and lust. I couldn't remember what covetousness meant. Anger, envy, these I knew.

'What are the Ten Commandments, child?'

'I am the Lord thy God thou shalt not have false gods before thee. Thou shalt not take the name of the Lord thy God in vain. Thou shalt keep holy the Lord's day. Honour thy father and thy mother. Thou shalt not kill. Thou shalt not commit adultery. Thou shalt not steal. Thou shalt not bear false witness against thy neighbour. Thou shalt not covet thy neighbour's wife. Thou shalt not covet thy neighbour's goods.'

'Can you see how the commandments and the seven deadly sins go together, Maria?'

The question surprised me. It surprised me even more that I could. 'Yes, Father. The sins are all the things that lead us

162

to break the commandments.' I had failed to honour Mamma as the fourth commandment said, because I was angry. But how could I not be angry?

'Very good, Maria. It's important that you know the meaning of these things. What are the seven gifts of the Holy Ghost?'

'Wisdom, understanding, counsel, fortitude, knowledge, piety and fear of the Lord.'

'Yes, my child. Now, can you tell me the twelve fruits of the Holy Ghost?'

I took a deep breath.

'Take your time, Child.'

I couldn't take my time, or I'd be lost. I plunged in. 'Charity, joy, peace, patience, benignity, goodness,' I stumbled. 'Long-,' my mind went blank. Long what?

The priest nodded. 'It's the ability to accept the crosses God sends us over time, Maria.'

'Long-suffering,' I sputtered on, 'Mildness, faith, modesty, continence and chastity.'

'Excellent, my child,' he looked surprised. 'Really, Elsa has done a wonderful job! I congratulate you, Maria, and I only have one more question.'

I thought we were finished. I looked at him, trying not to show I was afraid my mind would close over so that I couldn't get in. Would he ask me what all the words meant?

'Can you tell me the six commandments of the Church, Marietta?'

He had asked me all the hardest questions. Did he want me to fail, as Mamma did? I was angry now, and I wouldn't stumble again.

'To hear Mass on Sundays and holydays of obligation,' I began. 'To fast and abstain on the days appointed. To confess at least once a year. To receive Holy Communion during the Eastertime. To contribute to the support of the Church.' I paused for breath.

He nodded at me. 'Only one more, Child.'

'Not to marry anyone who is not a Catholic, or who is

related to us within the third degree of kinship, or to – marry at forbidden times.' I took a deep breath.

The priest held out his hand. 'I heartily congratulate you, Maria. I asked you the most advanced questions and you answered them perfectly.'

'Thank you, Father.' *Perfectly.* The word made me shy. Had I ever done anything perfectly before? Would I ever do anything perfectly again? But I refused the shadow that came with that question.

'I can tell your mother all is well. Now come, I will hear your confession. We'll go through to the church and you can genuflect with me on the altar, as a reward for your hard work.'

I was almost frightened. I trailed after the priest and stood in the sanctuary where no grown-up woman was permitted except on her wedding day, unless she was cleaning it. The red light gleamed, proving that Jesus was present in the tabernacle. I longed to be with Him in that little house. If only I could become small and climb in through the tiny door. It must be warm and light in there, better even than the sacristy.

I genuflected and we left the altar and the sanctuary. Father clicked the altar rail closed behind us. There were so many sanctuaries I had glimpsed and then been locked out of. We walked towards the confessional in the back of the church. Father motioned me into a pew while he took up his place. Mamma was already there. I didn't look at her. Then Father cleared his throat and I went into the confessional.

'I've been guilty of anger towards my mother,' I told him as my first sin.

'And why is that, my child?'

'Because she doubted that I was ready to make my First Holy Communion, even though my teacher said I was.' I couldn't tell him I had wished her dead instead of my Babbo, or even that she had broken her promise to him.

'Your mother only wanted to be certain,' he said gently.

164

'She was worried, afraid to send you to the altar unprepared. It's not something to be angry about, Child.'

'Yes, Father.' I hesitated. 'Father –'

'Yes, my child?'

'Alessandro, who lives with us, with his father Giovanni –' I stopped.

'Yes, what is it, Child?'

'Alessandro sometimes – approaches me.'

'I see.' He sighed. 'The devil works very hard on young souls like yours. He wants to wrest you away from the path of purity and virtue.'

'Yes, Father.'

'Have you told your mother, child?'

I was silent. How could I say yes? Mamma would go to confession after me. He would reproach her for not doing her duty.

'You must confide in her. She is wise and she will help you,' the priest said.

'Yes, Father.'

'Pray to Our Lady with all your might and strive to be pure in thought, word and deed. Men respect pure women. If you don't tempt Alessandro, you won't be in any danger, Child.'

'Yes, Father.' I left the confessional wishing I hadn't spoken about Alessandro. The priest would tell Mamma, and then what would happen? Mamma was right. It was better not to speak. I went up the aisle to say my penance of three Hail Marys before Our Lady. I couldn't keep my mind on them and I had to say them over and over. What would happen now? But maybe it was still better that something should happen?

Mamma came from the confessional with a heavy tread and I wondered if Father had told her. But then I remembered the Seal of the Confessional. He couldn't tell her anything I'd said. But I faced her wondering what she knew.

All she said when we stood outside the church was, 'Father

165

says you're prepared, Marietta. He told me to entrust you to the Madonna and have no fear for you.'

'Yes, Mamma.'

'I'll make your dress from one of mine,' she said. 'It isn't solid white but it's the best I can do.'

'Thank you, Mamma.'

We walked home talking about the dress, the veil, the shoes. It seemed Mamma already knew where they were coming from. Had she planned to give in all along? How could she give with one hand and take with another?

I was tired of people changing and wearing different faces. Tired of the Countess whose face said she was kind, but who refused to let me into her world, tired of Giovanni who wept over his First Holy Communion and then was cruel, tired of Alessandro who became my friend only to turn his back on me, and worse. I was even tired of Elsa, who had something I wanted, and most of all I was tired of Mamma, who thought I shouldn't want anything.

I had won. I would make my First Holy Communion. We walked home in the heat and I tried to feel triumphant. But I only felt tired.

'Marietta, you can wear my earrings for your First Communion,' Mamma said. 'I think Papa would want you to have them now.'

I was frightened. Mamma's earrings were the only precious thing we owned. Why was she giving them to me? Was she going to die, like Papa?

But I wanted them, because they came from Papa. Besides, they were a peace offering. Mamma thought I deserved them. But it was more than that. She had broken her promise to Papa, and I had broken her.

'Come, Marietta,' Mamma took out her needle and thread when we were home. 'I'll pierce your ears for you. You can wear threads in them for a few days, while they heal. Then we'll put the earrings in.'

She had to do it right away, before she lost the will to give

166

me the earrings. I sat in the chair and let her push her biggest needle into my ear. I didn't make a sound.

'You're brave, Marietta,' she said. 'It's good for a woman to be brave.'

She pulled the loop of thread through and then pushed the needle into my other ear.

'You will have to keep the earrings in,' she told me. 'Otherwise the holes will close again.'

I thought of Teresa and my other brothers and sister pushing through her when they were born. Did she close over every time? I had pushed through her, too. I tried not to shiver under her hands. Then it was done.

Giovanni, canny old drunk that he was, understood the cost of my victory.

'Marietta will make her First Communion,' he observed. 'Look at her ears! Lift up your hair, Marietta.'

'What?' But I pushed up my hair, eyeing Mamma as I showed off the white threads.

'There, you see?' He announced to the table. 'The ear of the bull is given to the bullfighter, but the bullfight is over and in this case the bull has won, eh?'

'It was not a bullfight, Giovanni,' Mamma said.

'No,' he agreed, pleasantly enough. 'It was bloodier, I think.'

In the days before my First Holy Communion everyone was kind to me, even Giovanni, who blinked back tears again as he recalled the time before his hand was ruined, and his life. Alessandro smiled at me. But even as I smiled back, I knew I'd see his other face again.

Mamma was busy sewing my dress. It was red, with big white spots like snowflakes. I loved it. When she'd measured me, she seemed surprised how much I'd grown, as if she hadn't noticed. After I'd worn the white threads for five days, she took them out and pushed her pearls into my ears.

'They look lovely, Marietta,' she had tears in her eyes.

Were her tears for me, or her earrings? I looked like a woman, in my dress. A small one, but still a woman.

Mamma didn't want me paraded before Alessandro. She was watching him. She still wished I'd stayed down, for safety's sake. She'd done her beat to beat me down, to keep things as they were.

But it was too late. Things were already changing. I'd outgrown my life. It would close around me again, tight, without the trips to Conca. I wouldn't be able to breathe. I could only throw myself on Jesus' mercy and hope He would tell me what I had to do.

People said their First Communion Day was the best day of their lives. Giovanni swore it. Alessandro said he hoped the best day of his life was yet to come, and Giovanni grunted and looked at Mamma when he said it.

I practiced my clothes. Every time Teresa brought me something else, shoes, socks, snowy white shift, I put everything on. Mamma delayed finishing the dress, as if she still hoped I might not need it. In the end she had to hurry.

I used her delay to stretch the day out further. There was nothing she could do to me now that I couldn't use against her. My day had already started without her or her dress and it would go on without her, somehow, even after I had changed back into to my old clothes.

The day came. Mamma came to help me dress, watching me as I put on her dress as if it belonged to me and I belonged in it. I'd taken the time to scrub myself and I was free of lice. The Countess would be in the church, and Elsa. I prayed that they might see me and think I could fit into their world. But that was an old dream, and I didn't linger over it. When I looked at myself in the glass with Mamma beside me, it was my own reflection I smiled at.

My reflection smiled back. We were not so beautiful but not so ugly, either. Mamma had drawn the veil over my head, with its crown of flowers. The veil made me more beautiful than I had ever been, the secret of brides.

I whirled in my dress. 'The earrings are so beautiful,' I said to Mamma in the mirror.

168

'Be careful, Marietta,' Mamma said.

'Why? You pierced my ears, Mamma. They won't fall out.'

'I'm not talking about the earrings, Child.' Her face was white and frightened in the glass. 'You look so grown up, Marietta.'

She made it sound like a sickness. 'I'm going to ride to the church with in the cart with Teresa, Mamma,' I told her.

She nodded. 'I'll go and tell Giovanni and Alessandro,' she turned and left the room. She would have to ride with my brothers and sisters and the Serenellis, all crowded together. It felt good to punish her. She had done her best to see that this day never happened.

It also felt bad. In the end she'd done her best for my dress, if not for me. She'd given me her earrings. I wanted to forgive her. I told myself I had forgiven her, but it was a lie. There was nothing in the catechism about things that were both good and bad, or lies you told yourself.

When I came down the stairs, Alessandro was the first person I saw. His eyes lit up and he smiled. I went to him and asked his pardon for any wrongs I had done him, as was the custom. I gave him my hand and he held it tight, then lifted it to his lips in forgiveness.

'Come, Marietta,' Mamma said behind me. I went to all my brothers and sisters, to Giovanni and Teresa and Domenico to ask their pardon for my faults. I hugged Teresa hard and then I turned to Mamma last of all.

'Please forgive me any wrongs I've done you, Mamma,' I said to her. I was still thinking of Alessandro's lips on my hand. It had never happened before. Mamma took me into her arms and I stayed stiff, thinking of him and not her.

I had never thought of being a nun, after all. That was not something poor girls dreamt of. There was no reason for me not to dream of a husband. Alessandro was there, he was tall and strong. He'd been to sea. He could teach me to read! Then I'd be above Mamma forever.

'My Marietta,' she hugged me tight.

I smelled her sweat. She'd been up early to feed the hens and clean their cages on my special day, to cook and feed the children and the men their breakfast. I pulled away from her to climb up on the cart and ride to church with Teresa.

I was still distracted by thoughts of Alessandro. My life with him wouldn't be so different from my life now. I was wearing a white veil, how could I not dream of being a bride? Alessandro was the only groom around, even though he was older and could speak to me as harshly as his father.

We lived in the same house. We breathed the same air. We were not related by blood. If Papa had lived, Alessandro would have seen me through my Babbo's eyes, his wild flower of the field. I glanced at the flowers and smiled as we drove towards Conca.

'You're thinking of your papa, I know,' Teresa said tenderly. 'I'm sure he's looking down on you and smiling.'

'Yes,' I said half-guiltily. There was nothing in the catechism about half-lies. I *was* thinking of Papa, but only because he would have made Alessandro see me as a wild flower.

I was no wild flower to Mamma. In her eyes I was a cook, a cleaner, someone to watch the children, mend their clothes and do a thousand other chores in the course of a day. I was what she had been, a slave, dirty and sweaty with work. But I had wrested something from her grip. I touched the pearls in my ears as we rode along. They had come to me from my Babbo.

Teresa was happy for me. We laughed and chatted on the way to the church. She told me many times how beautiful I was. All the other children looked like strangers and I wondered if I did, too. I was the only one without a white dress, but no one said anything, though they looked.

'Your dress is the prettiest of all,' Teresa said. 'And your earrings are lovely.' She said it when Mamma was there, so we could both hear.

Mamma smiled. I kissed her on the cheek and then I felt better. Had I forgiven her, after all? I felt lighter as I stood in the line to go into the church. I was the shortest and also the youngest, so I went first. Elsa, who was lining us up, told me I looked lovely. She didn't mind about my dress not being white.

There were flowers in the church, wild flowers arranged with sheaves of wheat and grasses. I wondered who had picked them and fixed them like that, Elsa? Or the Countess? I liked to think of her hands fixing the stems the same way she fixed her hair.

The organ was playing. Elsa and the Countess were both in the choir loft, singing for us as we walked up the aisle. I saw Mamma see me. There were tears on her face and she lifted a handkerchief to her eyes. I saw other mothers doing the same. Giovanni smiled as proudly as if he were my papa, and I could feel Alessandro's eyes on me as I passed him.

I was sorry when I reached the front pew. I had never liked being looked at until today, and I might not ever like it again. I looked at the flowers and candles as Father began the Mass. When it was time for his sermon, he talked about how hard we'd all worked, and Elsa, how kind the Countess was to give us this opportunity. He said some of us had had great obstacles to overcome and we had shown great Christian persistence and courage. He looked at me and I looked down, my heart pounding. I hoped Mamma realized she had been my biggest obstacle.

I tried to follow every bit of the Mass. It was always my favourite moment when the priest held the host up and genuflected – where I had been, on the altar! – and people bowed their heads and tapped their chests over their hearts. I read their lips that said *My Lord and my God!*

Today I loved the moment more than ever, but I kept my eyes down. I made a fist and tapped my own chest softly, trying to be truly sorry for my sins. The moment belonged to me in a way it had never done before. Jesus was coming to me.

I prayed twice with all my heart *Oh Lord I am not worthy*

171

that thou shouldst come under my roof, and then the last time, *Oh Lord I am not worthy that thou shouldst come under my roof, but say only the word and my soul shall be healed.* I knew the story those words came from, of the young girl who was dead and whose father sent for Jesus. He brought her back to life without even touching her.

I had been first into the pew, so I was not the first one at the altar rail. I listened to the beautiful music and tried to pick out Elsa's voice, and the Countess'. I told Jesus I did forgive Mamma. I forgave everyone. I even forgave Him at that moment for not making Elsa and the Countess take me in. Besides, He could still do it.

When it came my turn I knelt down and hid my hands under the starched white cloth as we had been taught. No naked hands could be near Jesus. When the priest came to me I put out my tongue and the priest put the host on it, the little round slice they called bread that was like no other bread. I closed my mouth and bowed my head and rose to my feet to make my way back to the pew. I was impatient. I couldn't really talk to Jesus while I was struggling to find my place again.

Finally I was there. I buried my face in my hands. I didn't know how long Jesus stayed, but Mass went on again after a short time so I didn't think it could be long. I felt He might be slipping away, and I had to tell him everything quickly. *Dear Jesus thank you for coming to me even though I am unworthy and made a bad confession please help us not to starve because of Giovanni and maybe he could die.*

I was amazed on two counts. First I had asked Jesus to kill Giovanni and secondly, I had found the solution to all our problems. If Giovanni died, everything would change, just as it had changed when Papa died, but for the better, this time.

I'm truly sorry for my bad thoughts and You know best Jesus but remember he has a bad hand already. And please let Elsa think of me as her replacement and send for me to train me, if it should be Thy holy will. I love you more than anything Jesus and please

172

look after my Babbo in heaven and don't let him be sad without me and Sole too even though cats can't go to heaven you could let him in if you wanted one for company.

I was in a kind of trance as I spoke to Him. The host didn't taste of anything and it was stuck to the top of my mouth, but I thought it better to wait till after Jesus had gone to try and get it down again. I knew it would be wrong to chew it.

I took my hands away when Father went on with the Mass and we had to stand up. My Communion was over. Now it would be all right. I felt dizzy. I had fasted from midnight, but I was used to fasting. After all, Jesus Christ had come under my roof. He had stuck to the roof of my mouth, but that didn't matter. He seemed to be melting there.

I was last in line, as I had been first when we walked in. I had lots of time to look up at the choir loft, where the Countess was singing with her eyes closed. She looked like a saint in heaven or the women in the pictures on Alessandro's wall, but not indecent. Elsa was dressed in her best, but she still looked like Elsa. The music rose and I saw her smiling at me. I smiled back, hoping she saw how clean my hair was underneath my veil.

Mamma dabbed at her eyes again. Alessandro looked bored until he saw me. I pretended not to see them. I wanted to go on seeing Elsa and the Countess and hearing them sing. I was like a bride, changed forever. Now things had to change around me.

Mamma came up to me outside the church and hugged me. 'You were lovely, Marietta. I was proud,' she said. 'Now we have to hurry home, so there will be some breakfast left for you.'

'I hope those boys haven't eaten it all. If they have, they should be beaten,' Giovanni said, coming up to us.

Mamma frowned. But Giovanni couldn't beat anyone, with his hand. He reached out his good hand to me and we shook hands like strangers.

'Congratulations, Marietta,' he said.

I thanked him. We were turning to go home in our cart when Elsa appeared with the Countess. Elsa hugged me into her big, warm body and I felt how I would miss her. Then she stepped back and the Countess came forward.

'Congratulations, little one,' she said and offered me her hand.

I dropped a small curtsey when I had her hand in mine and she smiled brightly at me. Her delicate gold hoops shone under her hair. She was wearing a blue costume with a jacket and a skirt. It was made of pale, soft stuff shot with gold, and it looked so smooth and silky I longed to stroke her skirt. Her hand left mine and I stood trying to keep myself straight and not stoop and cringe with shyness. She was tall as the Archangel Gabriel and even in my finery, I felt small and grubby.

The priest came over to us. He towered over me when he wasn't bending down to put the host on my lips or sitting down in the confessional.

'Marietta, what a wonderful day for you,' he took my hand and pumped it. 'We're all so proud of you, aren't we, Mamma?'

Mamma nodded. She was speechless in such grand company. I was more used to it than she was. I had been in the Countess' kitchen.

The Countess, Elsa and the priest went to shake hands with the others and then I was on the cart with Teresa, on the way home through a world refusing to admit that anything had changed. If only there was a way to tell the trees and the fields, the houses and the sky, that transubstantiation had happened to them, too! When Papa died the world had stayed the same, just like this. Only when I'd walked the road to Conca, alone and strong, it had changed along with me.

Of course my brothers had eaten most of my breakfast. Mamma gathered up what she could for me and I realized that between the fasting and my brothers, my conversations with Jesus would cost me a lot. Today it didn't matter. Teresa had brought my favourite soft rolls and yellow cheese. On ordinary Sundays, any unclaimed food would go quickly and Giovanni, for all his tears and handshakes and congratulations, would not protect my share.

True, he had punished us less with hunger, lately. I started to stuff my mouth with bread and cheese when Mamma stopped me, grabbing my arm and pulling it away from my body, hurting me a little bit but offending my pride a lot more.

'Marietta, go and change your clothes,' she commanded.

Even though I hated taking my dress off, I changed quickly, because I was hungry. I left my veil on, and my earrings. They wouldn't get dirty, on my head.

Mamma and Teresa laughed when they saw me in my old dress with my veil and earrings on. I sat down at the table and started to eat. I had got the better of Mamma again, if only in a small way. I was still beautiful, at least as beautiful as I could be.

I had risen to a new height, small and stumpy as I was. My shoes helped. I wasn't used to shoes. We wore them only on Sundays and sometimes not even then. I sat tall and ate slowly, like a lady. Alessandro came in for his breakfast and Mamma served him. Teresa was still there.

I didn't look at him but I felt his eyes on me sideways, as he ate. Then I looked and he was smiling at me in my veil. He chuckled.

'Will you wear your veil when you sleep, Marietta?' He asked.

He was treating me like a child. I shook my head. I didn't mind being teased by Alessandro like an older brother, but when I had finished my breakfast I went to the room I shared with Mamma to take off the veil. Alessandro had taught me something, and Mamma and Teresa with their laughter. This was what grownups did. They let things go.

I was clumsy, taking off my veil. I thought of the pale blue costume the Countess had worn with flecks of gold in it and

175

the thick hoops in her ears, the delicate shoes and silk stockings. She wore fine clothes and gold earrings every day. The world would always show her its changed face, the one I only saw when I had walked the road to Conca. I could keep my earrings in, at least. I had to, otherwise the holes in my ears would close up again.

'Mamma,' I asked as I came back to the kitchen, 'how do you get to be a countess?'

Everyone laughed, Mamma, Teresa, Alessandro, and Giovanni, who had come out of his room.

'The child wants to be a countess!' he roared. 'Still,' he added more quietly, 'it's a good question, Marietta. Alessandro, tell the child what she wants to know, you're the reader. How does one get to be a countess, eh? Tell her, my boy!'

'You have to be born one or marry one, Marietta,' Alessandro said with authority. 'It's the same for a count. Mazzoleni isn't noble, not really. Only because of his wife.'

'And the rest of us can go to hell!' Giovanni said. His face was red. 'What do you think of that, eh? Doesn't it tell you we should do something besides scratch a living from their land? Eh?'

'It is as God wills,' Mamma said. 'Don't put ideas into her head, Giovanni.'

'And why not, Assunta?' Alessandro turned on her. 'What is a head for, if not for ideas?'

'It's to bow in prayer,' she said. 'As we will do tonight in the holy rosary – I hope you will join us, you two.'

'So if you marry a count?' I asked. I could see they were going to leave the kitchen, muttering about Mamma. 'That makes you a countess?'

'Now she's marrying a count,' Giovanni roared again. 'Where's your veil, Marietta, eh? Put it on quickly, here comes the count!'

'I took it off, and besides, he has a wife,' I said. 'But there are other counts, aren't there?'

I knew I'd make them all laugh and I did. Alessandro and

Giovanni, Mamma and Teresa laughed and laughed. Baby Teresa laughed too, and that made them laugh more.

'The little one wants to be a countess too,' Giovanni cackled. 'But you keep away from counts, Marietta. Don't be too nice to them, you'll end up on the streets.'

'Giovanni!' Mamma said in her sternest voice, and he raised his good hand, shaking his head.

He and Alessandro went to their rooms. It was Sunday, there was no work in the fields. Mamma cooked and I looked after the children. I took them outside to play, enjoying the freedom from the kitchen. I usually worked on Sundays as well as other days, but not today. I ran and hid, my heart beating fast as Angelo looked for me. I was glad to have my dress off, not to care if I fell. My shoes were gone and my feet sprang from the firm ground.

I was not a woman yet. I was still a child and glad to be. I stayed outside late into the light evening. I wanted to hold on to this day. That was what a child did.

Mamma called us in for the rosary at dusk. When Giovanni and Alessandro didn't come to pray with us, I was glad and sorry. Then they came, after Mamma had led the first decade, the Annunciation, when the angel Gabriel came to tell Mary she was with child. It made me think of my own announcement to Mamma that I would make my First Holy Communion, and how it had been one thing to say and another to do. I wondered if all annunciations were like that. It seemed like a long time ago, when I first set out on the road to Conca.

I led the next decade, the Visitation, when Mary went to visit her cousin Elizabeth. I thought of my visits to the Countess' kitchen, and Elsa. Already Elsa and the Countess seemed like the statues in the church or the stained glass saints on the windows. Giovanni and Alessandro's voices stood out, deeper than ours.

At the end of the decade when Mamma began the Nativity, the birth of Christ, I lost my way. My visitations were over. Elsa wouldn't open the door and smile at me. She wouldn't give me food and leave me to eat it in her warm kitchen looking at all the dishes and glasses and pans, imagining the food she cooked in them.

I led the next decade, the Presentation. Mary took Jesus to the temple and the prophets Anna and Simeon told her He would suffer *and thine own heart a sword shall pierce.* I was pierced with the sorrow of losing Conca. I felt tears in my throat. I tried to clear it, but my voice shook. I needed courage, but I'd used it all up and there was none left. I'd be here night after night, saying the rosary, and it wouldn't even be like this. I wasn't so tired tonight. I'd eaten more food than I'd have in the days to come. Night seemed to close over me. I could feel it, dusky in my throat. The fire was almost out. Once it had frightened me. Now I wished it would blaze up, fierce and bright.

Mamma led the last decade, the Finding of the Child Jesus in the temple. He stayed behind to teach in the temple and when his worried parents caught up with Him, He said *Did you not know that I must be about my Father's business?*

I had also left Mamma to be about *my* Father's business, preparing and receiving my First Communion. But now I was back. Had Jesus gone back to being a child again? The story didn't say, but He did go home with Mary and Joseph. It made me feel better to think He might have been sad, too, when he had to go back. I wished for another decade of the rosary, a better ending. Had He gone all that way only to return to his old life? I wanted to say the whole fifteen decades, to dip down into the sorrowful mysteries. I was sad enough for them. We could pray them slowly and sadly. Then we could do the Glorious mysteries and be glad again. I wanted more prayers, more mysteries, anything to keep this day from being over.

But our rosary was finished. Giovanni tried to stop Mamma hurrying upstairs to our room, as she told me to hear the children's prayers. I often did, though I wanted to be alone with my dreams tonight.

178

Giovanni told Alessandro to help me, but I waved him away as I waited outside their room for the boys to undress and settle. Giovanni was drunk and the smell of wine on him sickened me. Even Alessandro seemed too big and real, standing there. I wanted my veil back. I wanted to see the world through its lacy mist, not like this.

'Come on, Marietta,' Angelo called. I went into their room and Alessandro followed me. I shook my head at Angelo, who stood by his bed looking ready to fight. Mariano and Sandrino imitated Angelo. My brothers would get hurt. Besides, Alessandro wasn't hurting anyone. He was watching us with hungry eyes. He had no mother or older sister to hear his prayers.

'More prayers?' He asked when I gestured for the boys to kneel by their beds.

'The rosary isn't night prayers, Alessandro,' I told him. For once I knew better than he did. We all knelt and only he was standing. He left the room soon afterwards, maybe because Angelo stared at him with hard eyes. Angelo was right, it was not his place. But I was glad there was no fight. I was grateful to Alessandro for that and I hoped he had gone away to his own room when I left the boys' room, and closed the door so they could sleep.

But he was outside, waiting. He stopped me on my way to the girls' room.

'You were lovely today, Marietta,' he said. 'You were like a real woman, and I liked you a lot.'

'I'm the same now, Alessandro,' I told him. It wasn't exactly true, but I wanted him to laugh at me as he had when he saw me eating breakfast in my veil.

He shook his head. He seemed about to say something else but I walked into my sisters' room, my heart pounding. As I was closing the door, I saw Giovanni skulking away from Mamma's room, red-faced. He grunted as he saw me.

'It's the Countess, eh? You and your mother will learn you're not countesses, Milady!' He bowed to me from the

179

waist, then he went up to Alessandro and started talking to him in his loud, drunken voice.

I didn't want to hear what he was saying. As he started to do up his pants, I closed the door.

'Close the door all you want, the pair of you!' Giovanni bawled. 'It won't help you in the end. No door can keep us out, eh, Alessandro?'

I heard furious whispering, then footsteps and more of Giovanni's blustering from down the hall. I looked at my little sisters' frightened faces and we prayed together, kneeling on the floor.

Maria's Memo

I had gone to war with Mamma and won. I had felt the full force of my anger against her, even if it was a sin, a sin that made me more alone than I had ever been. I had used it as a weapon against her. I had turned her silence against her, and it felt good.

Alessandro also fought a war with Giovanni. But it was a different one, because they were men. The weapons were different.

We were their weapons. Giovanni knew how to use other people, especially women, as weapons. Alessandro didn't. This is his story, too, and it's important to know what was in his head, or what might have been. We lived closed, locked lives. No one ever asked us what we thought or felt. If we made a sign it was a slip, an accident. Even so we were people, and there were many slips and accidents.

Alessandro knew how to read. He was the only one for miles around who did. It set him apart. He was also big and shy. It was one thing to be a shy girl. To be a shy boy was less acceptable, and people didn't know how to approach him. They thought his reading made him put himself above them, and perhaps they were right. But even if he did, he put himself beneath them as well, in the way of the proud who are also desperately humble.

He should have been taught. He should have had more education. He should have been anywhere but in Ferriere, living with us in Count Mazzoleni's old cheese factory. Wherever he belonged or might have belonged, it wasn't there.

I'm not excusing him. I'm not even forgiving him. I'm far beyond all that. We're simply characters in the same story, Alessandro and me, and not the one that people tell.

11

'We'll go and join the women on their knees.'

Giovanni's breath stank. Alessandro made a face.

'Eh, you don't want to pray. I don't either. But we should be there with the pig-ignorant women who go down on their knees so easily for priests. Women's knees are made to open for men, not priests. But they think they can have counts to marry and be countesses,' he spat on the ground. 'Assunta knows better than that, and Marietta will soon learn, eh? They'll go down on their knees for us,' he subsided, muttering. 'Down on their knees for us, not the priests, eh?'

He talked to himself. But he'd laugh suddenly, watching to see if you laughed with him.

'The pearly gates, eh? The knees of women?' Giovanni roared. 'The gates of paradise, eh? You know what I mean, Boy, eh?'

Alessandro laughed. He had no idea what was funny, or why. He hadn't entered the gates of paradise yet, pearly or not. Marietta's's knees were far from pearly. They were dirty, dented gates. He wanted to make a joke of it with Giovanni, but he was afraid it would come out wrong and give him away as a virgin boy, a freak.

He had only come through those gates when he was born. His father had signed him up for the Merchant Marine after he had had enough schooling to learn to read, so that he could go away and become a man. He was twelve.

There were times on board ship when one of the men came to him. It was over quickly. The other, older man would go with a woman when he had the chance. Eventually he would marry and father children. Going with women and fathering children was what men did. When there were no women they used each other, on ships, in prisons, in the army. In school they did it in a circle, each one with his hands on his own cock but laughing together and competing for speed. Alessandro hadn't liked these circles, but he'd taken part. Everyone did. He liked the speed and darkness on board the boat, where things happened so fast and secretly that you forgot immediately and nothing was ever said.

Men had to be men. He was treated like a boy on the ship, though they worked him hard. He sidled into the kitchen behind his father, who must never find out his son was not a man. He did a man's work, which was more than Giovanni did. But there were other things one had to accomplish, to be called a man. It was easy for women. They bled between the legs and it was done.

They went to kneel behind the Gorettis. Assunta looked up and then down. Marietta was beginning the second decade. Alessandro took his rosary from his pocket, crossed himself and kissed the crucifix.

'The second Joyful Mystery,' she piped in her childish voice. 'The Visitation. Our Father who art in heaven hallowed be thy name thy kingdom come thy will be done on earth as it is in heaven –'

'Give us this day our daily bread,' the words came mechanically as he reflected on the need to embark on a *visitation* to the dark place underneath Marietta's rough, stained skirt. 'And forgive us our trespasses,' One *visitation* would be enough. 'As we forgive those who trespass against us.' One time, and then he'd be a man. 'Lead us not into temptation,' If only she'd be still and let him do what must be done. Then he could hold his head up and look his father in the eye. 'But deliver us from evil, Amen.' He could take a rock and dash her head with it. She'd fall on the ground and then it would be easy. But he might kill her. Did it count if you did it with a dead woman? Were you still a man afterwards?

'Hail Mary full of grace,' the childish voice went on. 'Blessed

184

art thou amongst women and blessed is the fruit of thy womb –'
Prayers and hymns to the Virgin Mary were always about her
womb. Giovanni said all women were whores except
Alessandro's mother, who was too pure and delicate for this
world. It had driven her raving into the next one.

'Holy Mary Mother of God pray for us sinners now and
at the hour of our death amen.' The womb was hidden deep
in the mysterious bodies of women. What did it look like?
A little field where babies grew in their own soil? Or a marsh
like the one outside, a swamp where the ground oozed and
stank?

*That one slept like the ground sleeps when Luigi planted his
seed in her*, his father had said more then once, before Luigi
died. It would be simple to lift up a shift and make a *visitation*
while your wife slept. But for that you needed a wife. And
Marietta shared Assunta's bed now. He saw Marietta behind
her veil, eating her breakfast at the table that morning. She'd
made him laugh and given him a quick throb of feeling for
her, not wanting to go back to the usual, dull way of things.

'Now and at the hour of our death amen.' In the morning,
she looked a little bit like the pictures of singers he'd stuck
up on the walls of his room. They made him think of his
mother, not crazed and ranting but beautiful and still, like a
candle. Assunta said his pictures were indecent, but she was
pig-ignorant. Giovanni said so and he was right. Who would
want a wife like that?

Marietta might sound like a child and run around with her
brothers, but her breasts had swelled under her white blouse
today. Giovanni said she hid behind her age. He said the age
in years didn't matter so much, peasant girls grew up fast
and any fool could see she was a woman.

'Hail Mary full of grace...' how did one persuade the knees
to open? It seemed like a mechanical problem. The high,
childish voice went on and he saw Marietta kneeling at the
altar rail and holding out her tongue.

A little bolt of heat shot through his groin. After all, he

185

went down on his knees for her, working in the field like a beast. His father did nothing. Assunta did her best, but she was a woman. Giovanni was fond of pointing that out, without drawing the logical conclusion that, of the three of them, Alessandro did the most work.

Giovanni rolled his eyes, grinning. Alessandro grinned back. He helped Giovanni dress and undress. His father waved him away when he tried to help the old man wash. More and more often, he stayed dirty. No wonder Assunta shrank from him, not that she was so clean.

Giovanni blustered about manliness, but he whimpered and sucked from his wine bottles like a baby at the breast. The thought of him with Assunta made Alessandro feel sick.

Assunta's eyes were closed, Marietta's open. When Mariano reached out and tickled Sandrino, she was ready. She whispered furiously to him and Alessandro saw the back of his neck blush red. Assunta's eyes stayed closed while Marietta's voice kept on, calm and soft. Baby Teresa cried and her hand shot out to rock the big wooden cradle Luigi had made, as she finished the decade. 'Glory be to the father and to the son and to the Holy Ghost,'

'As it is now, was in the beginning and ever shall be, world without end, Amen,' he answered. Marietta was a busy little thing, a hard worker.

'The third Joyful Mystery, the Nativity,' Assunta began in her deep voice. 'Our Father who art in heaven –'

Why hadn't he done it when he had the chance? But he knew why. He hadn't wanted to then, just as he didn't want to now. But it would have been easy then, and he'd know how.

When the ship docked, the men went to the women in the ports. Alessandro was young enough for the others to laugh it off when he hung back, and luckily his father wasn't there. He'd stayed in his hammock reading. At thirteen and fourteen, he was still young enough to make them laugh when he shied away from invitations to the whorehouse.

Then he turned fifteen and they decided it was time. *High time*, they said. Someone found out when his birthday was, probably by asking the captain. It must have been in his papers. In any case, they set up a special treat for him.

Stella specialises in virgins, eh? They told him. *Stella Maris, star of the sea*, they laughed as they half-pulled him through the dark streets of the port.

Stella Maris was another title of the Virgin with the famous womb and breasts who had never opened her knees for anyone. Alessandro had gone with a strange sense that they were taking him to the Virgin Mary, somehow combined with his mother. He was drunk of course, *but not too drunk*, as his comrades had insisted, carefully rationing his drinks.

'Holy Mary Mother of God pray for us sinners now and at the hour of our death amen.' He listened to the voices drawn together in the chorus of prayer. The Gorettis were a family. His own voice muttered darkly underneath theirs and his father's voice was thick and guttural. Their voices stood out from the rest. They didn't belong.

He had never belonged. He had wanted to run away from the loud, drunken sailors in the port that night. He had looked for a chance to escape, but none came. He tried to escape now, listening to Assunta's tired voice. Seven children had come from that *womb* and fed from those *breasts*. They had come from the act she must have performed, or at least allowed, with poor Luigi.

He had let the sailors steer him, because he had no choice. He was always being steered by someone else, in what was called his life. When the door had closed behind him in the drab little room with the bed in it, he could only stand there, not looking at the woman. *Stella*.

'Hail Mary,' Assunta's voice was heavy with drowsiness. Stella's voice had been more like hers than Marietta's and she was probably Assunta's age, though not so worn. Being ploughed was easier than ploughing. He'd remember to say that to Giovanni.

You look like a little calf, staring at me like that, the woman had laughed, a farm girl come to the city. *Stella Maris.*

Alessandro wanted to strike her for laughing at him. He wanted to close her eyes forever for seeing him looking *like a little calf.*

She shook her head and motioned him to sit down on the bed. She kept her distance as she asked in her husky voice, *What is it, eh? What's happened to you?*

My mother tried to drown me, he heard his own voice with shock, then and now, as though hearing the story for the first time. *I was only two, but my brothers told me.*

'Blessed art thou amongst women and blessed is the fruit of thy womb Jesus.' *She sounds like a man*, his father said of Assunta. *I'd better do her a favour and keep her a woman, before she crosses over!* Alessandro had laughed with him, wondering what he meant. The hairs that bristled on the chins of old women? The round belly on old men, like the bellies of pregnant women?

Stella was a woman. She had shaken her head and said *Tell me.*

She was mad. She ran with me to the sea and my brothers ran after her. One of them held her and the other one grabbed me.

They saved you.

Yes.

And your mother?

Died in the madhouse.

Come here, she motioned to him. *Come here, if you want to. Just for comfort. Sometimes it's just for comfort.*

He had stayed where he was, rigid in all but one part of his body. She came to him in the end and rocked him like a baby while he wept. She had unmanned him like his mother, shamed him. No one could ever, ever know what had happened in that room.

I don't care but they will, your friends, she had said. *I won't tell, but you have to pay me extra for that.*

He had paid her what he had on top of what they had

already given her for him. He felt no resentment over the money, in fact he was grateful to her for demanding it. It seemed to restore his manhood a little bit.

'Hail Mary full of grace,' Assunta's voice began again. *A tough old bird*, Giovanni said. At least she wasn't mad. Before Alessandro, between his three older brothers, his mother had lost four babies. Giovanni had kept her *womb* and *breasts* busy, all right. Scarlet Fever had snatched some of them from her, the rest had died of something else, un-named. Babies died. Sex and death came together often, for women. Assunta had also lost her first baby. Luigi had told them that, back when they were still on Scelsi's land. But she had only lost one, not four. Luigi said she had never forgotten Antonio, or got over his loss.

They never do, his father had answered. *My poor wife ran mad because of it. She was possessed.*

Possessed. Had she killed the four dead babies? Drowned them like kittens in a bucket? Wrung their necks like birds? If so, no one knew. Giovanni only talked about her when he was drunk. Then he blustered and blubbed about her beauty and purity. His brothers had told him the real story.

'...and blessed is the fruit of thy womb, Jesus...'

She had not run to the sea with the others in her arms, as she had done with him. Pietro and Vincenzo had seen her and followed her, otherwise he'd be dead and buried like them.

His mother had been locked away. His brother Gaspare had fits and he was also locked away, in the same hospital where she had died.

'Now and at the hour of our death Amen.' She was gone, her suffering ended like Luigi's.

'Glory be to the Father and the Son and the Holy Ghost,' Assunta's tired voice came to the end of her decade.

'The Fourth Joyful Mystery, the Presentation of the Child Jesus in the Temple,' then it was Marietta's voice again. She began the Our Father and Alessandro tried to remember who

189

was presented, and why. He had been *presented* to the woman in the brothel, and he had cried like a baby. The woman had kept her promise.

Tell them how good I was, she had smiled at him as they parted. *I'll say the same about you.*

She had won him respect. But it was based on a lie and there would be other visits in other ports. Not all the women behind closed doors would hold their tongues. He saw Marietta's tongue again, held out for the host at the altar rail, and felt another little stab in his groin. Then he remembered: the Child Jesus was taken to the temple, like a newborn for baptism.

Had his mother wanted to baptize him again, when she took him into the sea? Had he slipped from her by accident? If she was so holy, as Giovanni said –

But that was not the story his brothers told.

Better for you to drown, she had shrieked as she waded into the water. *Better not to know the sorrows of life. I will spare you!* Then she'd held him under, praying to the Virgin to give him peace instead of pain.

'Now and at the hour of our death amen.' Vincenzo had held her while Pietro took him from her grasp. They had brought her home, but not for long.

Possessed. No woman in her right mind killed her child, not when she had a husband and a home. His brothers had told and re-told the tale. They were the heroes, after all. He owed his life to Pietro. He came into the rest of his life with a debt he could never repay. To him it was only a story, but the debt was real.

'Hail Mary full of grace...' Marietta sounded tired now. One day without hard work would show her how tired she was. Giovanni said Assunta was lazy, but she wasn't.

Alessandro never contradicted him. As a child he'd been afraid of his father's loud voice and sharp wit. His father made people laugh at others' expense and he didn't spare his children. Alessandro hated being made to look the fool.

190

It was worse than Giovanni's beatings, far worse. It made him want to lash out.

But his own tongue had never grown quick, sharp, dark or harsh like his father's. Words danced away from him when he opened his mouth. He liked them on the page, where they stayed still.

'...and blessed is the fruit of thy womb Jesus.'

There were too many Gorettis. They fidgeted around him now, bored and restless. Assunta's womb had borne too much fruit.

The Gorettis are nothing now, without the Serenellis, Giovanni liked to say.

It was a half-truth. The Gorettis could survive very well without Giovanni, better in fact. But not without Alessandro.

Marietta owed him. What would it cost her? She could go to confession. She would do her penance and God would forgive her. If she had a child, they could *drown it like a kitten*. He could imagine holding the ugly little thing under until it was still. He had drowned kittens, to see how it felt. They squirmed for longer than you expected. Some squirmed longer than others. But they all stopped squirming in the end. He had strangled birds. That was quicker.

But could he make a baby? That would make a man feel like a god, the Father not the Son. Jesus had never opened a woman's knees. He had remained the Son, always.

Assunta would weep and rail at him. Giovanni would laugh his dark, bitter laugh. Perhaps a child would be born and all would continue as before, with another mouth to feed.

'Hail Mary full of grace,' the high, tired voice began again. Would the priest and Mazzoleni make Alessandro take Marietta to the church and marry her? She could wear the same veil she had worn today, and the dress.

But she was too young to marry, and he didn't want her in the same bed with him every night until he died. He'd rather go on reading as he'd done on board ship. Better to read the papers that said the Church and the State together

191

kept men down and turned them into beasts with hard work, hunger and dirt. The priests were in league with the landowners and together they were strong. But what was to be done? If an army of workers with rakes and picks and shovels and ploughs carved their way across the land, then things would change.

They'd march to Rome, where he had been before he went to the Colle Granturco to help his father work the land of Senator Scelsi. They'd string Scelsi up first. Bernardo had met him in Rome, shown him the fountain at Trevi. He'd given him a coin to throw into the water and shown him how to stand with his back to it.

What had he wished for? Marietta's voice went on, the womb and the fruit went on and on, the hour of death came and went. Alessandro swayed on his knees. The Serenelli family was unlucky. But he had lived with his grandparents and gone to school. It wasn't such a bad life. It was very quiet, with only his grandmother's complaints to disturb him. But he had grown used to them. *Women complain*, his grandfather had said. *It eases them. Pay no attention, it's their nature.*

Marietta didn't complain, or Assunta. Did they complain to their God, the one they went down on their knees for? It was Him they knelt to, not the priests. Giovanni said it was the priests to make a point. But really it was God they went down on their knees for, and it was God the Father every man wanted to be, except for Jesus who remained the Son.

If only he'd gone with Stella, who knew what she was doing. (Or not doing with him, because he was a calf.) It would serve him well now. She might even have told him how to avoid sowing fruit in the womb. Then again, the child might be born dead, or die like his four brothers and Marietta's one. Did it matter so much, one more or less? Unless you were the one?

If only he'd stayed at sea. He would have gone ashore with the others and done what they did. He had been too young, that was all.

192

But Pietro had written and asked him to come home. It was hard for Giovanni to work the land, with his hand. It was a chance to repay his debt. Pietro had a family and couldn't be spared. Alessandro could hardly say no to the brother who had saved his life.

Besides, the sea had begun to frighten him. He glanced around as if someone might overhear his thought. The Goretti boys were winking and smirking at each other. Did they laugh at him, behind his back? Did they think he was less than a man, for all his hard work?

He'd kill Angelo first. He'd squirm the longest. The rest would be easy. On board ship, the bodies could be rolled over the side. The women would do as they were told, or join them.

Another, younger sailor on Alessandro's watch had drowned, just after he'd been to Stella and just before he got his brother's letter. Stella Maris, the star of the sea, had led him to a cold death under the waves. Some sailors wore a gold earring, to save them from drowning. But he had no money for earrings. His pay went home to his family.

'Now and at the hour of our death, amen,' he prayed. The dark wash had taken the other boy. It could have taken him. Pietro's letter had come and taken him instead.

'The Fifth Joyful Mystery, the Finding of the Child Jesus in the temple,' Assunta began.

It was the last decade. His eyes flickered over Marietta. He thought he saw her cringe. It was good that she was shy and frightened. Was it good? The women the sailors went to were neither.

Pietro's letter had given him an excuse to run away. He hadn't asked himself what he was running to. You never did, when you ran.

He'd been spared from drowning twice, even without an earring. Not for this. He knelt back on his heels, daring Assunta to open her eyes and look at him disapprovingly. He hated his low, meek voice. *Holy Mary Mother of God pray*

193

for us now and at the hour of our death Amen. Gabbling prayers like a woman. Giovanni was right. Much good it did you.

You worked and you died and some other fool worked the swamp, sweating and swatting at mosquitoes or shivering with cold, listening to his belly growl and groan while the land said *no.* But it said *no* to everyone. Would Marietta go on saying *no*? Would she dare? She was only a filthy little bitch (though not today), not beautiful and not possessed.

Assunta guessed how Giovanni goaded him. It was in her eyes when she nagged at him to take down the pictures in his room. She was really talking about Marietta, warning him to leave her alone. He and Assunta watched each other and Marietta together. Occasionally their eyes met.

He had seen Marietta asleep on her knees, but now she twitched under his gaze. She was keeping herself still, like an animal that knew it was being hunted.

'As it was in the beginning, is now and ever shall be, world without end, amen.' They came to the end of the last Gloria and he made the sign of the cross with his rosary. He got up from his knees and helped his father. Giovanni's knees cracked and he groaned.

'I wonder if our prayers would be so much worse if we sat down when we said them, eh, Assunta?' He grumbled. 'Like this, it's another day's work.'

'The Lord makes us kneel for a reason.' She replied. 'To keep us humble. Goodnight, Giovanni. Good night, Alessandro.'

'Assunta,' Giovanni stopped her, his voice hearty but darkening with warning. 'On a day like this, you want to brush us off so fast? This is a great day! Look at these two excellent women, Alessandro! I ask you, could any man ask for more?'

'Marietta is a child,' Assunta said. 'And I'm tired, Giovanni. Marietta, will you hear the children's prayers? You're close to God today,' she added piously.

'Of course, Mamma. Go and rest and I'll come soon.' Marietta replied.

194

Giovanni chuckled, 'Soon but not soon enough,' he whispered. Then he winked at his son and turned to follow Assunta as she went out of the door and up the stairs, towards the room she shared with Marietta.

'Why not give the child a hand?' he said over his shoulder. 'They're a wild lot for her to handle alone.'

Alessandro nodded.

'I can manage,' Marietta said quickly. 'Thank you, Alessandro,' she added. She didn't look him, or at Giovanni.

'Go on, boy,' His father hissed.

He hated that *boy*. He followed Marietta. The Goretti *boys* didn't look at him. At least they were smaller and younger than he was.

But there were yet more prayers! He was surprised as they knelt by their beds, and he said so. Marietta looked at him.

'A rosary isn't the same thing as night prayers, Alessandro.'

She spoke as if to a child. She knelt with them and he thought again of her knees and how he must enter them. He went on watching her, the little mother. But Angelo's eyes burned him, and he had no heart to fight. He turned and left the room to stand outside the half-open door, listening as her voice murmured, soothing them. Angelo had watching him watching Marietta, his eyes smouldering. Everyone watched everyone else, in this house.

He thought he heard her kiss one of them, a little noise that made his heart beat fast. His grandmother had not been one for kisses. She was too old to raise a child, she told him. She blamed her mad daughter-in-law for making her work so hard in her old age. His life had incurred another debt. But she and his grandfather had died.

He turned away from the doorway. It was Angelo's room, shared with his brothers. He could never be a brother to Angelo, or the others. He could never be a brother to Marietta and have those kisses. He must have the other thing, instead.

'You were lovely today,' he said when she appeared and closed the door. 'I liked you very much,' he added awkwardly.

He reached out blindly, hoping she would take him into her arms, if not her legs. But she shrank away from him.

'Alessandro,' she laughed. 'I'm the same, look at me!'

You're not the same. Don't be the same. He stared at her, wanting her not to laugh at him. *Like a calf staring.* He heard his father's voice, and Assunta's. Then the door opened and Giovanni came out of Assunta's bedroom with a red, angry face.

'The Countess,' he roared, when he saw Marietta. 'You and your mother will learn you're not countesses, Milady!' He flopped over in a clumsy bow, his hands fumbling at his flies. 'Countesses, pah,' he muttered. 'A few too many countesses, eh? Eh?' He went on mumbling as he struggled with his buttons.

'I have to put Ersilia and Teresa to bed,' Marietta said quickly. She whisked away into the girls' room.

Giovanni was red-faced and unsteady, waving the bottle in his good hand as he spoke. 'Assunta has insulted me for the last time. She ordered me to leave Luigi's room, can you imagine? Luigi's room! I looked around and said to her, I said "Where is he then, eh? If it's his room?" I'll take care of you again,' he told his cock in a resigned voice as he succeeded in buttoning his pants over it with his shaking hand. 'But you deserve better.'

'Come, it's time for bed,' Alessandro took his father's arm to lead him away and let him sink into a stupor. Marietta heard her brothers and sisters' prayers and kissed them goodnight while he wrestled a drunken, stinking cripple into bed and waited to hear him snore.

'Marietta's a scrap of a thing and you're a big ox. Use your tool on her, for God's sake, use your weapon! Make these women see what they have to do!' Giovanni muttered as he allowed himself to be led.

His tool? His weapon? Alessandro looked up at the pictures in his room after he'd put his father to bed. His bed felt like a ship on still waters. *He leadeth me beside the still waters*, the psalm said. It sounded beautiful, but still waters were treacherous. Ships were becalmed.

196

Ships ran aground. They were left in dry dock. Something had to fill their sails. Where would his following wind come from? It would never come from Marietta. Or from Giovanni. Wine was Giovanni's sea. He drowned his sorrows there. But sorrows were strong swimmers.

Military service. The army. That path was open to him and not to Giovanni. He was young and strong. There was nothing wrong with him.

He would have to obtain Mazzoleni's consent. Giovanni would be angry, but he was already angry. It was time to leave him to his complaints and his memories.

Alessandro had held back from asking Mazzoleni before. Luigi was dead and he was needed. They wouldn't be able to work the land without him. The harvest would fail. Mazzoleni would throw them off his land. They'd starve quickly, instead of slowly.

Let them starve. Let his father drown himself in wine, instead of his sorrows. Let Assunta and her children beg their *daily bread.* Could it be worse than this?

Marietta might die. She might become a whore, another Stella Maris in a port where business was good. She might even marry. Let her find an illiterate sharecropper, as her mother had done.

He was finished here. He was not safe and no one was safe from him. Soldiers killed. He'd be sent far away and taught to fire his rifle at strangers. That would *be his tool, his weapon.* He might make a good shot, with a rifle. Or he might die. What of it?

They had come for him. They had said he was *fit for service.* He only had to ask the Count, to put his case like a man. He'd be delivered from this life of servitude to sour soil and his sour father.

Marietta would escape, the little water rat. Plump and filthy. Throw her back like a fish that was too small, a fish for another line, another day.

Ferriere was a swamp where he'd had been stuck in filth

197

and mud for long enough. He fell asleep rubbing himself and woke to find he had achieved relief. It seemed like a good sign. He'd speak to Mazzoleni right away, today if he showed up on his horse.

Maria's Memo

Stories turn in a split-second. A smile, a nod, a shake of the head and everything is different. Alessandro strides away in his uniform. We never see him again.

We pack up our belongings and go back to Corinaldo. Giovanni comes with us, or stays behind. He becomes unimportant.

We might be beggars now. Or: my brothers grow up quickly, free from the low roof of the old dairy and Giovanni's tyranny, Alessandro's sulks. They find work, in Corinaldo or elsewhere. They help Mamma. She remembers her almost-mother, and she finds work sewing. She teaches me. Above all, she keeps the promise she made Papa on his deathbed. Good things come from that.

We prayed for these things, all of us, even Alessandro. We all wanted the trap to open and let us out. Only Giovanni didn't pray. There was nowhere else for him to be, nothing for him to hope for.

The catechism taught that we were made in the image and likeness of God. It meant that we were good, of course. How could we be otherwise, when God was all-powerful and all-good?

But I wonder who was listening to our prayers, and Giovanni's mutterings and ravings? In whose – or in what – image and likeness were we made?

12

Mazzoleni rode high in his saddle. He wasn't a count, though. Only through his wife. A man who needed a wife to make him a *Count* didn't *count*! Alessandro carefully wiped the smile from his face. The upper classes, like the priests, became suspicious if you looked too happy.

Alessandro would ask and he would receive. It said so in the Bible. No one would ever teach Marietta to read. If she was truly unlucky, her husband would die and leave her a widow with children to feed, like her mother. *As it was in the beginning, is now and ever shall be, world without end, Amen.*

He'd got up early, surprising her in the kitchen. It was time to get on with the rest of his life. Marietta was sleepy in the early morning light, still cleaner than usual from her First Communion, a few days ago. Soon enough, she'd be filthy and stinking.

But soldiers were clean. His fortunes were rising. He didn't waste a smile on her as she served him his breakfast. There was nothing to gain from her now. He had eaten quickly, before the others woke. His father would sleep the longest. At least in the morning, Marietta fed her family well.

He watched the figure on the horse ride closer, as he worked. It was important to be seen to be working *hard*, like a man. Soon he'd be beyond reach of this backbreaking labour that produced so little. It was a good sign that he'd got up early, almost as if he'd known the Count would come today. He was dizzy with sun and optimism. The signs were all good. He had his following wind.

At least he didn't need to nudge his father awake under his favourite tree, as Mazzoleni rode in. Giovanni hadn't appeared yet. Alessandro would make some excuse, if Mazzoleni questioned his absence. The Count let his chestnut mare canter gracefully around the field, taking the long way round to where Alessandro worked, showing off his horsemanship. When he was almost there, Alessandro went to meet him.

'Good day, Count,' he said politely, taking off his old felt hat and putting it on again.

'Good day, Alessandro,' he looked down from his horse. His face was grizzled. He was not only less noble than his wife, but also much older. Giovanni said it was his land she'd married. 'You're doing a fine job.'

'Thank you, Count,' Alessandro paused, gathering his thoughts. He shaded his eyes as he looked up.

'I'm very grateful to you for staying on my land. I would have had a hard time after Luigi Goretti died, but for you.' He glanced around the field at the other workers, including Assunta.

My father is unwell. He'll come as soon as he can. A little stomach disorder, something he ate. Nothing to worry about, not like poor Luigi Goretti. He's a strong man, my father – Alessandro waited, preparing his defence of Giovanni.

'If it were not for you, Alessandro, I would have had to send Assunta and her family away and get new tenants, sorry as I would have been,' the Count was saying. 'Many a young man would have been selfish and gone off to the army and adventure without a thought.' He looked Alessandro in the eye and smiled. 'Good day to you now, Son, I won't hold you up any longer.' He dug his stirrups into his horse's sides and with a 'Ya'! he was gone.

Alessandro watched him ride off. *Son.* The count's praise stung. There would be no escape. *Good day to you now, Son.* Why didn't he speak up, interrupt Mazzoleni? But the grizzled old count was crafty. He knew very well what Alessandro wanted. He had outfoxed him. Left him standing with his cock in his hand, Giovanni would say. Mazzoleni had stuck him up the ass without breaking sweat.

Assunta sidled up to him, still holding her fork. Her brown eyes squinted from her brown face, the skin tough as hide. 'He said no, eh? The old swine,' she shook her head. 'He'd like to be gone himself and escape that young wife,' she said with a coarse laugh.

Alessandro smiled to show he understood. Men demanded, women submitted, old and young, wasn't that the way of it? Apparently not. The Countess demanded, and so did the old witch in front of him, probably the same age in years but ancient in looks. The sun had shrivelled her up and bad food had taken most of her teeth.

'Never mind,' she clamped his wrist with her free claw. 'You can ask him again. Wait, then ask him when he's not expecting it, that's the way.'

'I will,' he said. Did she want him to go or stay? If he went, Marietta would be safe. But the Gorettis would be ousted from Mazzoleni's land. He looked into her face. She wanted things to stay the way they were, the one thing that could never be.

'Next time he won't refuse me,' he answered her with certainty, the way men answered women.

'That's right,' she said. 'That's right, Alessandro,' as she walked back to the field with her fork, in her black rags.

She thought he'd never get away. Somehow he knew that. She was only flattering him. But she was wrong.

Giovanni had staggered up. 'She was quick off the mark, the old crow,' he said. 'Caw, caw. Quick to tell you not to give up hope, eh?' He grinned at his son. 'I saw you with Mazzoleni. I knew he'd say no. Caw, caw,' he said in the same high-pitched voice.

Had he always hated Giovanni, the millstone around his neck? 'It's only the first time,' he said.

Giovanni shrugged. 'First time, last time, what's the difference? Come on, let's get to work.'

He was sly as Assunta, working for once as if to show he could. Damn the pack of them. Let them all starve together and burn in hell afterwards.

'Turned you down flat without giving you a chance to ask, eh?' Giovanni straightened suddenly to ask.

'How did you know?' They always knew, the old ones, they had eyes in the back of their heads, Giovanni and Assunta. How alike they were, and how they disgusted him.

'I saw it coming, boy. I saw it coming, of course I did,' 'Saw it coming, didn't I? He'd never let you go. But I will,' he grinned.

'You will?' Never mind that he looked like what he was, an old drunk. Never mind that he raved and stank. Never mind if he had driven his wife mad, driven her to try to drown Alessandro, never mind anything, if he could get out of Ferriere. 'You will?' He repeated.

'I have a wager for you. Luigi would never wager with me. Too high and mighty. If you ask me, it was that old witch who stopped him. She wanted it all for her brats, eh?' He made a hoarse, juicy noise as he gathered spit and mucous in his throat and spat it out in a long whoosh. Then he wiped his mouth with his hand and left a new streak of dirt to join the rest. 'If you can plough the young one before I plough the old witch, you can go back to sea or to the devil or whatever you please. I'll fix it. How's that for a wager, eh? Eh?' He extended his hand, still grinning. Spit foamed from the corners of his mouth. 'Or are you afraid I'll overtake you, eh? A tough old cock like me?'

Alessandro's hand shot out and he shook hands firmly with his father. Now he'd make it happen with Marietta. The Count had seen to that. It was on his head. The old ones were pushing him right into the pit and into the pit he would go.

'Now we'll see,' Giovanni muttered as he dropped his hand. 'Now we'll see how much juice is in the old cock, eh? Eh?' He went on muttering to himself as he slouched back to his tree, where he threw himself on the ground.

His life was an interrupted nap. One day Alessandro would be just as ugly, ruined by hot sun and bad food. But first he'd win the old man's wager and his freedom. He'd go back to sea, or join the army. For once he'd choose and not be chosen for.

Maria's Memo

One story ends and another begins. It's a very old story. It started before, but it stopped. Now it starts again and this time, it doesn't stop. But even the ugliest story has moments of beauty, because the world is never one thing, just like the people in it.

13

'You're a woman now,' Alessandro told me.

He had said it before, when I made my First Communion. But now his voice was shy, like the boy I used to know. He turned bright red when he said *woman*. It was such a funny idea. What was a woman? How could I be one and not know?

'Don't be silly. I'm me, Marietta.'

He shook his head. 'I need to show you something,' he whispered.

Oh God, oh Mary and all the angels. I shook my head.

'I've seen my brothers', Alessandro.'

He looked surprised, then he laughed. 'I want to show you my pictures. The ones your mother wants me to take down – I want you to see them, how beautiful they are. They're pictures of singers, Marietta. You know how much you love to sing.'

'How do you know?' I didn't sing any more.

'Little songbird,' he said. 'I heard your father call you that, many times.'

I fought back tears. I heard my Babbo say *my little songbird*. How dare Alessandro use the name that belonged to my father and no one else?

'I used to hear you singing when you thought no one was listening, little one. Come, have a look. I'll leave the door open, Marietta. I won't lay a finger on you.'

Little songbird. Little One. He sounded like Papa, for an instant. But my Babbo knew better than to talk about my singing. He knew it was secret.

But he had known what it meant to me and now no one knew, unless Alessandro did. I followed him like a little lamb, because he'd used my Babbo's names for me. I would have followed the devil himself, if he had called me *Little One* or *Songbird.*

I had been in his room once or twice, when I was younger. It smelled different from our rooms. It had a man smell. We were like two armies pitched against each other, men and women. This was the smell of the enemy. My brothers were still on our side, not men yet. But standing there with Alessandro, I felt I was in the presence of my old friend. I was stiff, guarded. But I was guarding myself more from Mamma than him. She would hit me, if she found me there.

'Look,' he said in his old, soft voice. 'Look at the pictures, Marietta. Aren't they beautiful, these songbirds? Just like you on your First Communion day. You looked like one of them, that day.'

I laughed. 'I could never look like one of them,' I said. I felt he wanted me to wish it, but I hardly knew how. Looking at his pictures was like seeing the Countess. I had only imagined myself as her housekeeper, no more. But I had to say her name.

'Just like the Countess,' I murmured.

'Better than the Countess! She keeps us down, don't you understand that? She's one of *them.* She's a bitch,' he said in his new, harsh voice, 'a filthy bitch!'

'But no, she's kind. And clean. It's only that she forgets us.'

'Forgets us! She exploits us, she takes the food from our mouths!'

'But look how thin she is. How can you say she eats our food?'

He laughed. 'People like her are thin because they eat good food, Marietta, not horrible grain that makes their bellies swell. They come to me in my dreams, these beauties,' he said, his voice changing again. 'They come to me when I lie on my bed, Marietta.'

210

'Do they sing to you in your sleep?' It sounded stupid, but I didn't know what else to say.

'Oh, yes, they sing,' he said. 'They sing to me of such things – I'll tell you the things they sing about. Or I'll show you,' he moved closer.

'No, Alessandro,' I left his room quickly. I could hear Mamma returning from the field.

'Marietta? Where are you?' She called me.

Alessandro still had a smile on his face when I looked back, but it a different smile. He pursed his lips at me in a kiss, but it was a big, ugly kiss.

Ever since my First Communion day, he had watched me like a snake watching a bird. I'd never been afraid of snakes. There were lots of them in the fields. Mamma was afraid of them and when we walked to Mass I went ahead with a stick, whipping the grass. If I chased one and it slithered away, it made me laugh. They were shy, that was why they rustled away. I envied their speed, their way of slipping into holes in the ground and cracks in the rocks. Sometimes I found the skins they left behind, smooth and fine like the Countess' gloves. They changed their skins more than I changed my clothes. The long dry sleeves were clean as grass after rain, but dry.

Snakes couldn't really see us. They squirmed away from the noise we made. Alessandro didn't really see me, either, but he wasn't blind like a snake. But sometimes he showed his other side, like showing me the pictures in his room.

'Your pictures are indecent,' Mamma had already told him, many times. She told him again that night, as if she sensed something. 'You have to take them down, Alessandro.'

I tried to catch his eye and tell him I understood why he wanted his pictures. He wanted to pretend he could step into that other world, like a snake sliding into its hole.

He laughed, an ugly laugh. 'Is beauty indecent, Assunta?'

'Beauty!'

'If you don't like them, don't look at them,' he said.

211

He could read, and he had been to sea. He knew more of the world than we did. *Assunta is a pig-ignorant peasant woman*, I had heard Giovanni tell him, and Alessandro had grunted approval and laughed along with his father. They were always laughing at us now.

Mamma shook her head. I hated seeing her like that. She had no answer. I blushed for her. Giovanni grinned.

'That's right, Assunta. It's for women to be quiet and let men do as they like.'

'If I let you do as you like, my children will starve.'

A hush fell over the table. Even the boys stopped eating. Giovanni smiled, a wide smile. Then he yawned. 'I think you have it the wrong way round, Assunta,' he said.

We began to talk again, loudly, as he went on muttering to himself, saying that if Mamma would only do what he wanted, everyone would have plenty to eat and we would all be happy. Angelo's face was tight and white. He looked like Papa, but an angry Papa.

I crept into Alessandro's room alone the next day, when he was in the field. The women on his wall looked so soft, their skin like snakeskin. They dressed in long white gowns that showed their breasts.

I'd never look like that. I wanted to tear the pictures down, take them to the landing and tear them into tiny pieces, throw them in the air and watch them blow away. Did Mamma feel like that? Was that why she hated them?

I crept out. Let Alessandro look at his pictures and long for their world. Mamma was right, he should take them down. But not because they were indecent. Because they made us uglier and dirtier than we already were.

But I wouldn't think about Alessandro, or his pictures. I'd sweep him out of my mind as I'd learned to sweep away the devil, using my will as a broom. It was too dangerous to think about the singers on the wall and their soft, silky gowns.

Alessandro smiled less and less. He hardly spoke to me. Our moment in his room was over and there would be no more. He seemed to resent what he had shown me, or resent me for having seen it.

He was like Giovanni now, and it made me sad. If he would only speak to me the way he used to. But his voice never softened any more. Even when he told me I pleased him, it scratched me. He wanted something. He demanded it by right. He was hungry and I could feed him. That was what he felt. But he was wrong.

He needed to go away. We needed to go away. Something, someone needed to go away. Our house was ready to burst with hunger and anger. I told Papa when I managed to creep away to the cemetery that he was right, we needed to move back to Corinaldo. But how? Mamma still owed Count Mazzoleni money, even though the harvest had been good.

I had broken my silence about her broken promise to Papa, and now she used it to break my will and silence me again.

Everything we eat costs money, Marietta, everything we wear, the thread we use to mend and the soap we use to wash. Where do you think it comes from?

It made me dizzy and I had no answer. When I was little, she said everything came from God. But now our debts piled up like mountains around us, instead of the old, low mountains outside Corinaldo. These mountains would crush us. But I tried hard not to be crushed underneath them, as she was.

'Mamma,' I spoke out in the darkness and silence of the night. 'Mamma, Alessandro – I can't be left alone with him or he tries to do bad things to me.' It was clumsy and childish, but it was out.

Mamma said 'Alessandro – oh! Not again.'

'Not again, Mamma. Still.'

She sighed. Then, as if to herself, she murmured, 'he could have waited until you were a little older.'

He could have waited until you were a little older – and then what?

'I thought he was my friend.'

213

'He isn't your friend, he's a man. That's what they do, Marietta.'

'But he cried for Papa. He told Giovanni to let me learn how to cook and then he helped me with my catechism. He said he'd teach me how to read!'

'Forget all that. Men have something they can't control. And they have pride. You need to flatter him a little, I told you before.'

She put her hand on my waist in the dark. 'Nothing below here, and you'll be safe.'

'But I want him to leave me alone!'

'He won't. Tell him,' she thought for a moment. 'Tell him if you kissed anyone, it would be him, but you're not old enough to kiss. Giggle and be a little girl with him. Never toss your hair or smile.'

I threw my hair off my forehead because it was a heavy bundle that came down over my eyes. Often I hid behind it. But I had come out from the thicket of my hair, that day in Alessandro's room. Was that a sin? I tried to concentrate on Mamma's advice. I wasn't good at giggling or acting like a child. I had had grown-up responsibilities for a long time. *Tell him if you kissed anyone, it would be him.* But would it? It couldn't be the right thing to lie to him, could it?

'I don't know if it would be Alessandro I'd kiss, if I kissed anyone,' I whispered. 'I don't know anyone else, how can I tell?'

'Just say it. It will save his pride. Don't be rude, or you'll pay a price. But don't do anything bad either.'

'But why does he try to make me do these things?'

'Because. I told you, that's what men do.'

'But why?' It made no sense to me. 'Why should they?'

'God made them like that in order that the human race would go on,' she recited it like the catechism. 'Even when there's war or famine, they make babies.'

'But there's no war or famine –' I stopped. Our famine went on all the time.

'It's up to you to control Alessandro. That's all there is to it.'

It seemed a very bad way of arranging things. God put something in men and left it up to women to control it.

'But Mamma, how can I?'

'That's the way it is. No use complaining. And don't talk about these things any more, or even think about them.'

'But Mamma –'

'Maria, do you hear me? You'll get a reputation.'

A reputation from thinking? But when she called me *Maria* instead of *Marietta*, she was serious. I tried once more.

'Mamma, they talk about it at the well, when I go for water –'

'You don't talk at the well?'

'No. But I hear it.'

'Close your ears, Marietta.'

'Mamma, ears don't close like mouths.'

'But you don't join in with such talk?'

'Of course not.'

I still had no idea what to do about Alessandro, how to control the thing God had given him so that the human race might go on. I knew it must not go on through me.

But why was Mamma so stubborn and silent? She'd had babies. I'd seen animals have babies, and I'd seen them making babies. Why did she pretend it was a mystery? Alessandro looked at me a certain way and I trembled. Mamma knew. But she'd told me not to speak of it again, and I kept silent for a time.

I was living in a jungle. I had heard of them, places where the heat steamed and animals hunted one another. I was being hunted by Alessandro and I had to find places and ways to hide like a small animal. He was a bigger, stronger animal. But snakes escaped from us, and they were smaller. Rabbits got away sometimes, though they were often caught. Even Giovanni had once snared a rabbit for our pot. We were not supposed to poach Count Mazzoleni's rabbits. But

215

everyone did, and now there were few left. Even the squirrels were few.

But where did they come from, rabbits and squirrels and snakes, if not from the thing Mamma would never talk about? It was all around us. The oxen we ploughed with, the horses the Count and Countess rode, the Count and Countess themselves, all came into the world the same way.

Mamma, I tried again and again to get an answer from her. *About this thing men do –*

Hush, Marietta. Keep yourself from sin and pray to the Madonna for assistance.

I thought of the closed cold face of the statue in the church as I prayed to her. She had only known the Holy Ghost who *came upon her* in a mysterious way, and Joseph who took care of her and asked for nothing in return. How could she know what it was like to be hunted by a man?

I lay awake at night wondering if I could ask Mamma to speak to Giovanni about Alessandro. But she was afraid of Giovanni. And what if he said to her, *Give me what I want and I'll protect your daughter from my son?*

Giovanni smelled. He was crude and drunk. His withered hand trembled and shook. The devil had touched him. How could she want him near her?

She had nursed Papa on his deathbed after a marriage of seventeen years during which she had borne seven babies and buried one. She wanted her sleep. She had no wish for a man in her bed again, especially not a stinking drunk like Giovanni. I was young, but I could see these things.

How could she agree to spare me from a danger she had not yet admitted was real? – *If* it would spare me. These things went round and round in my head, and kept me from sleep. What could I do? Who would help me?

I tried to stay away from Alessandro and for a time I succeeded. But I couldn't stay in the kitchen all the time, and one day he cornered me in the field. I had wandered down while little Teresa was sleeping. I craved fresh air and

216

even wished for company. Being alone to think and dream was one thing, but you were not alone or free in the company of a fretful child. It was another kind of loneliness and when at last Teresa slept, I quickly ran outside where there were voices and laughter.

'Come, Marietta,' Alessandro took me by the hand. 'We can go now and no one will know.'

Did he want me to run away with him? I would! But where would we go? I looked at him. He meant not running, but rutting. I twisted away from him and ran. When I looked back he wasn't following me, but looking after me with his hard, jeering look that frightened me more than his hand on mine. He shook his head and walked away but he didn't look defeated, only determined. I began to avoid the field, the barn where he had approached me before, the quiet spot by the hedges. There was nowhere left where I felt safe. I had always liked my shady hiding places, but now I had to stay in the open, where there were others. I could never be alone, and it was suffocating me.

Mamma went to the field as early as she could and stayed as late as she could. I asked her with my eyes to stay with me in the house, but she ignored me. She was safer in the field. Giovanni kept up his attacks, and she went on rejecting him. I knew because he began to keep food from us again, watching her face.

'This is your Mamma's doing, not mine,' he'd say as he helped himself to the steaming food on the table, food I had cooked. He gave Alessandro even more than he took for himself, and doled out smaller and smaller portions for the rest of us. Bread and grain and even garlic were locked away, most of the time.

The little children cried, the older ones complained. The little ones sucked their thumbs raw and slept longer, whimpering from hunger in their sleep. Perhaps Giovanni wanted to make sure my brothers were too weak to challenge him. A life and death battle went on every day. My brothers

217

found ways of taking food. They became clever little thieves, stealing what was theirs. Giovanni was also cunning, and he sometimes outwitted them. Hunger became a kind of fog I could almost see closing in on us, inside the house.

Something had to cut through the fog and save us, or at least change things again. But all we could do was wait.

Maria's Memo

Starvation weakens you. I know sometimes girls choose it, and the thought terrifies me. I became weak and light-headed and a little crazy with hunger. Whoever or whatever was to blame for what was about to happen, hunger played its part. We had been less hungry for awhile and now we were hungrier again, with a whole new kind of hunger.

"Let Marietta go to Conca", the little ones said. They didn't understand why my going to Conca and coming back with food had come to an end.

We were moving towards something. We were on a cart in the snow with hungry wolves close behind us, howling and snarling. Something or someone had to be thrown to them, and there were too few rabbits and squirrels. We needed to sell the pigeons we caught, in the market.

I didn't offer myself, not for a moment. I fought. I tried everything I could think of, when I could think. I tried everyone. But no one could help.

Then and now, children under siege, kidnapped, starved, hunted. People, good people, seeing and not seeing, knowing and not knowing. People being timid and lazy, not wanting to interfere.

People being people. People don't like to think about the dark corners that might be all too close in clean, familiar rooms. I was crouched in a dark corner that was growing smaller all the time.

14

Mamma was already in bed when I finished hearing the children's prayers and giving them their goodnight kisses. I was tired after a long day of cooking and sewing and cleaning. It was summer and very hot, even at night.

I walked towards our room, hoping for nothing but sleep. As I approached our room, I heard a commotion from inside.

'Leave me in peace,' Mamma's voice was breathless and thick. 'Marietta will come and find you here. Go, Giovanni, and leave me alone.'

'You can't fight me forever, Assunta,' Giovanni's voice also sounded breathless and flustered, as if he'd been fighting.

I walked faster. I had to defend Mamma.

'Nothing is forever, Giovanni,' Mamma said. Her voice was lower this time and flatter, more hopeless. 'None of us live forever.'

'No, so why not live while we do?'

'What you call living to me is death.'

Giovanni came speeding out of Mamma's room towards me. He made a face when he saw me and pursed his lips, as though to kiss or spit. I knew it was no kiss he had in mind. But he only made a spitting noise and walked on, wiping his mouth.

I remembered the noise and his horrible wet lips as I sat beside Teresa on the ox cart the next morning, going to Nettuno. We would go to the market and then to confession. The horrible spitting sound Giovanni had made mingled with the sound of the wheels as we rolled along. Everything was spoilt for me, even my precious outings with Teresa. There was no escape now. Tears rolled down my face and I rubbed my eyes to hide them, but Teresa had seen.

'What is it, little one?'

I took a deep breath. The fresh air felt good after the stale, hot kitchen. Wild flowers were all colours, reminding me I'd been Papa's wild flower, once upon a time. But my tears spilled faster.

'Marietta, what is it?' Teresa pulled the cart over. She took me into her arms and held me while I sobbed out my story.

'Alessandro gives me no peace. He wants me to, you know – maybe I should, I don't know, there's no food for us and my brothers will cross him and then –' I sobbed harder. I was afraid Alessandro would hurt Angelo, or kill him.

'What does your Mamma say? You have told her, Marietta?'

'Mamma –' I couldn't look at Teresa. How could I tell her about the game of cat and mouse being played in our house?

'Giovanni,' she said. 'I thought so. Oh, Marietta, I'm so sorry.'

'It's all because my Babbo died,' I wept against her soft, warm breasts. 'Why did God let that happen? He knew what our life would be.'

She sighed and patted me and didn't answer. After a little while she flicked the whip over the ox's back. She looked sad and I was sorry I had told her.

'Maybe it will be over soon,' I said, not knowing what I meant.

'Over?' She repeated, louder. 'What do you mean, Marietta?'

I didn't know. The perfume of flowers in the air distracted me.

'Marietta?'

'If I did what he wanted, everything might be easier.'

'But you're too young!'

'I know. Teresa, I just don't know how,' I wanted to cry again but I didn't.

'Of course you don't, my darling. All that will come later, in a proper way.'

222

'Will it?' I looked out at the familiar countryside and remembered the green valley I had travelled so hopefully.

'Of course! Look at what a wonderful cook you are now, how well you tend Teresa and the others. There's nothing you can't do. You'll make a perfect wife, in time.'

'But what can I do now, when he –'

'He hasn't actually done anything?'

'No, no. I've always been able to run away. Sometimes I think he wants me to run away. He only brushes against me and talks of doing other things.'

'Thank God.' She crossed herself. 'Maybe he's just playing a game, trying it on as young men do.'

'Maybe.'

'Domenico could talk to Giovanni – or Alessandro –?'

'No!' I could imagine how furious Giovanni would be. We'd be hungrier than ever. Alessandro would sulk. Perhaps he'd stop hunting me for a time. But not for long.

'You pray for help, I know,' Teresa said. She looked out over the flat land as though searching for something. 'Have you spoken to the priest about this?'

'Yes.' I spoke to the priest before I made my First Communion. Things were different now. 'But I'll try again today.'

We were both silent, looking at the workers bent over in the fields. It felt all the more special, to be out riding.

I dreamed my old dream as we rode along. The priest would command the Countess Mazzoleni to take me in, to learn from Elsa how to be her housekeeper. I'd tell Elsa our trouble with Giovanni and the food. Before, I'd sat in her kitchen and let the warmth of it flood me.

Besides, I'd known I had to go back to Giovanni and the daily battles over food. What if Count Mazzoleni had come and spoken to him and then gone away again? Or the Countess, daintily sitting her horse at the edge of the field and then riding off after she'd had her say? What would happen to me then? What would happen to my brothers? There war in

223

our house was between the women and the men. So far, the children were mostly out of it. But if it became a war between the Serenelli men and the Goretti boys, there would be bloodshed.

I missed bringing food home to my family. It made me understand how Papa had felt when he couldn't feed us. I often felt I knew him better now than when he was with us.

The market was bustling and though I was shyer than ever, people were friendly. I tried to smile back at them and it became easier. I even sold a few eggs and pigeons.

'You're doing very well today, Child,' a woman I had seen before said to me. 'I see you're growing up.'

I smiled, but my heart sank. Did I want to be grown up? Wasn't that the source of all my troubles? I tried to shake off my sadness again, but this time it clung on. Teresa glanced at me, but said nothing.

In the early afternoon, the market finished. We shook out our clothes and placed our empty crates on the cart. Then we drove to the church. I was hopeful again for no reason, and I chatted about the morning. Teresa smiled to see me happier.

We went into the dark church and I waited my turn for confession. When Father slid the window back, I began immediately so I wouldn't have time to change my mind. My will was not so strong, these days. Will power weakened, when you had so little food.

'Bless me father for I have sinned it has been one month since my last confession – Father, I have a great problem.'

'A great problem!' There was a smile in his voice. 'For such a small soul. Well then, my child, what is it?'

'It's Alessandro, Father. He tries to lead me into sin and he won't leave me alone.'

'Yes, Child,' the smile was gone. 'You've confessed about him before, I believe.'

He remembered. I'd hoped he wouldn't.

'Yes, Father. But it's different now. I'm afraid of him.'

224

'You know it's up to you to control him. The devil tries very hard to tempt young men, and young women must be strong and help them.'

'Yes, Father, I know, but how?'

He cleared his throat. 'By your modesty. You must not be a temptress, Child. You must guard your every movement, your every glance. Men read women's faces. Alessandro reads something in your face that tempts him. Do not be vain or look for admiration. Think only of Our Lady and keep the devil away. Guard yourself from every impure thought.'

'Yes, Father.'

He cleared his throat again. 'Have you other sins to confess, Child?'

'Yes, Father.' He'd said *other sins*. I hadn't thought of what Alessandro did as sins of mine, but if the priest did, they must be. Otherwise I had the usual list of missed prayers I was too tired to say, rosaries dozed over until Angelo nudged me, giggling, impatience and anger with my brothers and sisters, unkind thoughts about Mamma, Giovanni, Alessandro.

I didn't mention the Countess and how I sometimes thought she might have come down more than once, when we were gathered in her kitchen. I didn't say that I could do what Elsa did, even better, and why didn't she ask me? I didn't say *The Countess is more vain than I am. Do you tell her so?*

I had forgotten to confess my blasphemous thoughts about how slow Jesus was to work miracles, these days. But it was too late. The priest was absolving me. There was always something I forgot. So many sins to remember! I made the Sign of the Cross, knowing it made no difference. My soul was not clean. I had made a bad confession and that was another sin. The devil was very busy in the dark confessional. Even as Father told me to keep him away, I had fallen into his clutches.

'Your penance is a complete rosary, fifteen decades,' Father said. 'And pray to Mary for a pure spirit.'

He banged the window shut. An entire rosary! We said

225

five decades nightly, all together. Did that count? I hesitated, but I couldn't knock at the window and ask him. I walked down the aisle to kneel in front of Our Lady's shrine with tears in my eyes. There would be no brand new, swept-clean feeling today. It was a feeling I only had after Confession. I felt confused, weak, lost and frightened. Wouldn't it be better to die and go to the cemetery?

Had I tempted Alessandro when I wore my First Communion dress? Did Father think that was why I wanted to receive Our Lord? Was it? It was hard to remember. I never looked in the mirror any more. Only today, because I was coming to Nettuno with Teresa. But I went nowhere near Alessandro. I had to look at myself on Sunday, before Mass. He saw me then. But I couldn't refuse to wash my face or wear the best clothes I had for Mass, could I? Mamma would have plenty to say about that.

I had no time to think of how I looked. I was barely out of bed before my day began, and I quickly became dirty and sweaty. When did I have time for vanity?

Father had said not to look for praise. I wept into my hands. Since my First Communion, Alessandro had said only harsh things to me. He made me go to the well after I'd already been, saying the water was too warm for him and not fresh enough. He took every chance to make a mess for me to clean up. He treated me as less than an animal and then he jumped out at me and frightened me. He never praised me. No one praised me except Teresa, and I hardly ever saw her.

I looked up at Our Lady's pale face. Did she think I was vain? Did she look down at me and see a temptress? But her cold face said nothing. Were questions sinful? No one liked them or listened to them.

'What did Father say?' Teresa asked when we were on our way home again.

'He told me to be careful of my modesty,' I said. 'And not be vain or look for praise.'

226

'You're always modest, little one,' she patted me. 'And no one could be less vain.'

Was that the sort of praise I shouldn't look for? I leaned my head against her arm and slept all the way home. I'd never done that before.

But the priest had been my last hope. Besides, for once my head didn't buzz with hunger and keep me awake. Teresa had bought me delicious crusty bread, soft inside, and cheese, yellow and rich and as much as I wanted.

There was another sin! It had come into my head as I bit into the bread that I could eat forever. I loved soft bread that wasn't like the bread we had at home, bread we hammered with our fists and slammed in the doorway to break. I loved the cheese that had such flavour it filled your mouth. I loved them more than I loved anything or anyone, including God and the Blessed Virgin. Food like that was heaven. It tasted much better than the flat, dry disc of the Eucharist.

'Teresa,' I raised my head to say.'The devil always comes when you're tired. Is it a sin to be tired?'

'Never mind the devil, Child,' she said. 'It's no sin. Rest, now.'

I slept fitfully, my sleep threaded with doubts and questions. The devil had led me into sin. But if I didn't receive Communion at Mass on Sunday, Mamma would ask why. I'd been to confession, after all. She'd want to know what had happened since then.

I couldn't receive Communion often. When I did, my brothers ate my breakfast and I risked fainting. Thoughts whirled in head. Would it be better if I stumbled and fell into the fire and my face was ruined? Would Alessandro leave me alone then?

But men didn't care about faces. He'd turn me around and do it like a dog. He might do that anyway. If I said no, we'd starve. If I said yes, I was damned. Mamma and the priest said so. Father would blame me, whatever I did. And even a burnt face wouldn't protect me.

227

There were no more walks, no more lessons. I'd forgotten everything I'd learned with Elsa Schiasi in her warm kitchen. I was uglier and stupider than ever. For a time I'd been bigger, and now I was smaller again.

Giovanni and Alessandro had been bigger too, and now they were smaller in one way and bigger in another. Alessandro lurked in the doorway when I kissed the boys goodnight. Angelo was becoming stronger and angrier. I wouldn't be able to control him forever.

Mamma and I lay together at night holding hands, but far apart. She slept sooner and deeper than I did. The silence in the house rose like a tide. When it was at its height, I slept. When there were stirrings, long before the dawn, I woke.

'Marietta, you're so silent and sad,' Teresa said when I woke up on the cart beside her.

We'd be home soon, and nothing had changed. Even she had no answer. The priest had blamed me. There was nothing more to say.

'Speak to your mother again, Marietta,' she said. 'It's the only thing you can do.'

I nodded. Mamma was hungry and hunted and she had to work every day. If she had to watch me live like a beast of the field, I had to watch her do the same. Somehow she went on, in spite of everything. She set her face. How could I take away her rest?

I'd gladly slip away like a snake, if there was any place to go to. I thought sometimes of going to the church and claiming sanctuary, like a saint. But the priest would turn me out and tell me not to be foolish. Saints had armies at their backs. They were fed to lions, beheaded or thrown into vats of boiling oil. No one would think I had the right to claim the church's protection because Alessandro was pursuing me. What was happening to me happened to many girls, I knew that from the well. They did their best. They held out until

228

they had to give in, and then things took their course. Men always won.

'Marietta,' Teresa said. Then she, too, was silent. 'We'll go to Nettuno soon again,' was all she said.

I nodded. The miles were slipping away. We were almost home. On Sunday I'd go to Communion and commit a sacrilege. At least I'd try not to think any more sinful thoughts until then, like giving in to Alessandro so that we could have food again. I wouldn't watch Giovanni eat and hate him, mouthful by mouthful. I wouldn't blame my poor exhausted Mamma for her silence or her snores at night. I wouldn't hate Alessandro, who had been my friend.

It was a lot not to do. But I was too tired to hate. The journey had given me too much time to think. I was sorry I couldn't make my mind blank as I rode beside Teresa. Even here, safe with her, I was chased by shadows and doubts. I was impure, or Alessandro wouldn't have bad thoughts about me. But if I was already impure, what was I saving from him?

Was everyone else stained by impurity, like the blood that still came only sometimes? Did women's blood come to the Virgin Mary? It was hard to imagine her blue and white garments stained with ugly clots that smelled like the rakes and forks used in the field. Mamma had slapped me when it first came. It was the custom.

The Devil is with us now, she said. She sighed and looked angry and somehow afraid.

We were home. Teresa patted me. I closed my eyes and tried to relax against her as she drew me into a hug. I couldn't let myself cry any more, or I'd never stop. She let me go and I got down from the cart with my provisions. I'd hide a few things away before Giovanni came to watch me. I had to be quick, before he heard.

I ran up the stairs and managed to hide some grain to make an extra loaf of bread. He came in quickly after me. He knew, but he said nothing. It was like a game, and I had won this time. But for how long?

Maria's Memo

People hurry over the details of my life except as they show my piety, my sanctity, my purity – never my liveliness, my livingness. But I'm still living. I'm a bit crushed by heat and hunger and hard work and silence. But I'm alive.

I stay alive through it all. And that's the one thing I wouldn't change, though I'd change almost everything else.

15

Watch the birds, Marietta, I heard my Babbo say.

I watched the high, swooping circles the birds made, so different from our tight, sweaty ones. We stumbled and pitched, Mamma and I, but we were also in flight. It was almost time for her to come in from the field with the others. Despite my heavy thoughts, I'd made good progress and the midday meal was done. The early afternoon was hot and bright and the baby slept. I could climb the steps to the landing, sit there and sew in peace.

The landing was my new hiding place. I didn't go to the cemetery any more. It was hard to find gaps in the day when I could run down the road and be with Babbo. It took a kind of hope to plot my small escapes, and hope was draining away from me.

If I sat down, no one could see me. It was a relief to be invisible but still out in the air, under the sky. I could still hear Teresa. I could look at the sky and breathe a little. If I stood up, I could look down and see Mamma and the others in the field. I couldn't see the cemetery, but I could see Sole's grave under the tree. Often Giovanni slept on top of it, but at least Sole was warm, in the cold ground. And he had always liked sleeping with a human being.

Mornings, especially, when no one else was up yet, I could climb the steps and look up at the birds that circled the flamingo sky. I could trace their circles with my fingers like writing and make it mean whatever I liked.

I loved the ceiling of the church painted with angels and clouds, but the sky was better. The birds reminded me of Papa. Sleep came easily to me, it was waking that was hard.

Sometimes in the evening when I was tired of my tiredness, I climbed the steps and watched the birds fly. They lifted me.

'A man can't work in this heat,' Giovanni came up from the field grumbling to himself. 'In this heat,' agreeing with himself.

I couldn't see him. I stopped myself from giggling as I listened, glad he couldn't see me.

'I'm sick, like that poor bastard Goretti,' he grumbled. 'Malaria will kill us all in this infernal place.'

My giggles died. Poor Papa. Giovanni was drunk and loud. He'd wake Teresa. I wanted to tell Giovanni he could do my work in the kitchen and I'd gladly do his in the field. But he did nothing. And he dared to speak of Papa, who had worked until he dropped!

Alessandro had told me last night at supper that his shirt needed mending in time for Sunday. I had said nothing.

Marietta, answer Alessandro.

It was Mamma. *Where's your shirt, Alessandro?* I had asked him, without looking up.

On my bed, Marietta, he said. *With the patch you need to mend it.*

Did he really think I was so stupid as to go into his room? Did the bird go down into the snake's hole?

Very well. What else could I say? But I'd decided to wait until he'd gone off to the field, in the morning.

He'd gone, and Mamma, along with my brothers. I had pleaded with her to leave Ersilia with me, but my sister wanted to leave the kitchen and play outside, and who could blame her?

I'd gone into Alessandro's room and found the shirt and the patch. I didn't linger, not even long enough to look up at his pictures. They would only make me sad. It was much more important that his little trick had failed and I was safe, for now.

Back out on the landing with my needle and thread, I

234

looked up at the blue sky. I began to stitch the patch carefully onto the shirt. It had to be perfect, or Alessandro would make me tear it out and do it again. He might find a way to force me into his room again, and then I would be lost.

The day after tomorrow was the feast of the Most Precious Blood. I'd go to Communion. I hoped my brothers would leave me some breakfast, but they probably wouldn't. I could hear yelling and laughing from the field. It was hard work to take the cart with the oxen and trample the husks. Then the beans could be harvested.

I looked up at the blue sky and made my mind blank, before I committed a sin by thinking of bad things. The sky helped me, but it didn't always work. Sometimes my blank mind took on a cast of colour like the sky in the early morning or evening, a streak of pink like sunset or dawn. It was so beautiful I had to look and then a sin committed itself. I wanted something God had not given me, more porridge and honey, soft clothes like the Countess', a white veil like the one I'd had for my First Communion. I put it on sometimes, but it made me sad. The wanting wasn't white, but deep pink. My pink sins streaked across my body like flamingos rising towards the sky. I had seen flamingos once, when they came to the swamp. They didn't stay long.

The priest would think my bright pink flamingo sins were ugly and would lead me down to hell, not up into the heavens. But I'd remind Jesus on Sunday that He still had miracles to perform for me. My old dream of being taken in as a housekeeper like Elsa by the Mazzolenis was still worth mentioning to Him.

In three months and ten days, I'd be twelve. I wasn't so young. I had nowhere to hide but here. It hurt Teresa when I spoke. What could save me? In spite of my flamingo thoughts that flew into forbidden places, I still didn't know how to please Alessandro. Did he know?

Was that a sinful thought, flying across my soul? The priest

235

would call it my impurity, the thing that made Alessandro come after me. He might be right, though I'd tried every way I knew to keep my modesty. But I was always tired. The devil had plenty of chances.

I heard the drumming of heavy boots on the stairs. Alessandro came bounding up. I hadn't heard him until he was there. I'd been dreaming again. Maybe that was a sin. But he brushed past me and went to his room as if he didn't see me. He never saw me, not even when he grabbed me by the arm and pulled me to him.

He might have forgotten something. I sat looking up at the blue sky. It made me feel dizzy, or maybe that was hunger. *Blessed Virgin Mary, help me,* I prayed.

'Marietta!' Alessandro's voice came from the kitchen.

'What is it?' I tried to steady my voice.

'Come in here.'

'What do you want, Alessandro?' Let him say it and shame us both. But he wouldn't speak of it, any more than Mamma would.

He came outside and took me by the arm. I clung to the top of the landing behind me, but he prised me loose. My arm scraped the concrete and I cried out.

'For goodness' sake, why did you have to do that?'

'I had to bring you to your senses,' he was breathing hard. 'Now, Marietta, now.'

He pulled me into the kitchen and then he shoved me down onto the floor. Before I could get up he was there, pushing me down, his breath in my face as he lifted up my skirt. I pulled it down again quickly. It couldn't be done without lifting my skirt, but I had to be modest. I wanted two things: *to live and not sin.* I prayed to Mary again quickly: *Help me to live and not sin. Could I have both, or only one? Which one would I choose, or would he choose for me? Help me.*

'Now,' Alessandro showed me the corn-cutter in his hand. Papa had sharpened it to mend the brooms with. It had a sharp point, which he put to my neck.

'Don't move,' he told me. His breath smelled strong and came in gusts, like wind.

I saw something slam shut in his eyes, like a gate. Alessandro still looked out through the bars of the gate and I reached up to him. He thought I was hitting his face and he slapped my hand down hard.

'Alessandro! Please!' The bars of the gate filled up and there was no Alessandro in his eyes any more. His face was locked like the faces of statues, with a terrible coldness iced over his eyes.

'Alessandro!' I tried to break the ice with my voice.

'Be quiet.' He didn't say my name again. He'd forgotten it, along with his own. I couldn't make him see me. I could only speak and hope he might hear my voice. His eyes were lost, but I might enter his ears and remind him.

'God doesn't want this,' I said. It seemed better than telling him I didn't want it. Mamma had said to spare his pride. 'You'll go to hell,' I said. *Help me*, I prayed to the closed face of the Madonna. It might open, even if his wouldn't.

'Be quiet!'

'But God doesn't want it,' I said again. I couldn't think of anything else. 'You'll go to hell.'

He pulled my dress up again and he took his trousers down. I saw something small and pink and curled like a tail. His eyes flashed at me.

'Don't move and don't look!'

He had the corn-cutter in his hand. I saw my brothers' and sisters' hungry eyes and Mamma's face. I saw the Countess with her hair and her gold earrings, Count Mazzoleni on his horse and Giovanni asleep under his tree with Sole underneath him. I saw the cemetery where Papa lay and I saw him as he was after his breathing had stopped, not tired any more. I saw the blue sky and the birds that flew in it. I wanted to go on seeing. I tried to move away, but he held me tight.

'Be still or I'll –' He showed me the cutter again, shining in his hand.

237

How could something bad shine like that? But I had no time for the question as if flew across my mind like a bird and disappeared.

My little songbird, I heard Papa say. I made a sound.

'Be still!'

'Yes, yes, yes, Alessandro, all right!' I didn't move. I closed my eyes and prayed. Time seemed very slow. Nothing happened and I opened my eyes. He wasn't looking at me. He was looking down at himself, and he looked angry.

'God doesn't want it, you'll go to hell, Alessandro –' I said it without moving, with my eyes closed.

'Be quiet!' he stuffed his handkerchief in my mouth.' Who cares what God w- Goddamn God!' He swore.

'Alessandro, shhhh, please.'

'Shut your mouth or I'll kill you, I swear.' Then he tried to stuff his curled-up pink thing into me. I felt it down there, but it didn't hurt. It wouldn't go in.

I tried to get away and as I moved, I wet myself like Teresa. I thought I might do worse, but it didn't come. I made a little sound instead. Time moved slowly, then faster. Alessandro pushed me down again. He didn't seem to notice I was wet, or smell it. I looked up at his face and saw the devil. He wore a gold earring, only one.

The devil was a mask. Anyone could wear it. I lifted my hand again to tear it away, but he grabbed my arm and pushed it behind me. I was in his grip and I fought, thinking of Sole as I scratched and bit.

I was in the devil's mouth. I felt his teeth. They tore my flesh. They tore it again. I fought more weakly. Blood poured from me and my claws lost their strength.

'Filthy stinking bitch,' he said, breathing hard. 'Filthy, stinking –'

'I'm sorry Alessandro, I couldn't help it.'

'Don't talk.'

'For God's sake, please –'

'I said don't talk,' he tore me again.

I prayed without words. God was a mask, too. Only Jesus had a face instead of a mask. But how could He hear me screaming from the devil's mouth? There was no host in my mouth, only blood and screams. The devil was hacking me with the corn-cutter as if I were a tough husk of corn in the field.

I screamed and screamed through the blood, but the mask stayed in place. He couldn't see anything now, and I saw less and less. The terrible sharp corn-cutter tore and tore at me. It left pain like fire.

He stopped. He stood up and looked down. He was breathing hard under the mask, but I couldn't reach it. Blood came from me, much more than the blood that made me impure. He walked away. He stood behind me. I tried to raise myself and the handkerchief fell from my mouth.

'Mamma! Mamma, help me! Teresa! Help!' I cried as loud as I could. A kind of strength came to me and I tried to stand.

He grunted like a wild pig. Then he came behind me and plunged the cutter into my back, again and again.

'Mother of God –' I screamed and Teresa started to cry.

'Don't talk, don't talk, don't talk,' he said as the corn-cutter plunged.

I heard footsteps on the stairs and that was all I knew. A mask came down over my face and I slipped away behind it.

16

Mamma came to the doorway and I saw her face turn white when she saw me in my blood. I tried to reach up my arms to her, but she fell down on the floor.

Then Teresa came running up behind her. I lifted my arms to her and she knew what I wanted. She pulled my clothes off gently, my shift that stung me like a thousand wasps. But the wasps went on stinging.

Then she dabbed my wounds with vinegar and they stung again. I knew it was to help me, as she sobbed with me. I was so tired I let her cry for us both and closed my eyes again. I didn't know where Mamma was. I heard voices and then they wrapped me in a sheet, to take me away in the ambulance.

I knew they couldn't take me naked but I wondered why, when the sheet hurt so much. I was alone in the ambulance with men who didn't look at me when I asked them for water, only shook their heads.

'Wait for the doctor,' they said.

Every bump on the road was like the corn cutter again. There were many bumps. I had walked them, a long time ago.

At the hospital, they kept a cloth over my mouth like Alessandro's handkerchief while they held me down and examined my wounds. I saw the doctor's face turn white when he looked at my back. I fainted once or twice. I hated waking up. That was my last sin. Little cries came from me. I had no strength to cry louder.

They heard my confession before the operation. It was hard to think about my sins when my back and my belly were

241

still tearing apart. I saw the devil and the corn cutter again, when I closed my eyes.

The priest asked me if I forgave Alessandro. Why was it important to forgive him so quickly? I thought of saying I'd forgive him for a drink of water. But no one had ever listened to me the way they were listening, now that words were leaving me and I was leaving them.

'Am I going to die?' I asked him. It seemed to surprise them, but I thought I had the right to know.

'We hope you will be with God soon, Maria,' he said.

I understood. They wanted me to go straight to heaven and not to burn in purgatory as I was burning now.

'I forgive him and I want him with me in paradise,' I found some words of my own and everyone seemed pleased. I thought they might give me some water, but they didn't. The word *paradise* made me think of streams and waterfalls. There must be water in heaven. There was milk and honey.

'Do you want to be a member of the Blessed Virgin's Sodality?' The priest asked me. 'I have a medal for you, Maria.'

No one had asked me to join the Sodality before, and I had never expected to. 'Of course,' I whispered. It was a great honour. But as the priest bent down to put the silver medal around my neck, I saw Alessandro's devil mask with one earring glinting. He'd come after me, he'd drag me down to hell with him again.

'Don't let him in! Don't let him in here!' I pointed to his shadow on the wall.

They put the handkerchief in my mouth again. The operation was like another devil cutting me, this one in white without an earring. Afterwards I burned with fever and when I asked for water, they said it would make me worse. I would have drunk my own blood, I was so thirsty, but they had bandaged all my wounds.

'How is it possible that you can't give me a drink of water?' I asked them politely.

They told me to think of Jesus on the cross and I was too

weak to reply that even He was given a sponge soaked in vinegar. I'd be grateful for that. That might be another sin, comparing my suffering to His.

Then Mamma came, and I was quiet. She was trembling and she looked at me for a long time. I asked her how the little ones were. I missed them. It was time to hear their prayers.

'They miss you too,' she said. 'Oh, Marietta, my Marietta.'

It was the same wail I had heard when she came into the kitchen and fainted when she saw me. She couldn't look at me. She couldn't stay with me.

'Sleep, Marietta,' she said, and I did.

In the morning Mamma came back. We talked about the children and I told her I was better. The pain was not so strong. It came through a mist.

A doctor came in, listened to my heart and said to me, 'Will you pray for me in paradise, little one?'

He looked quite old to me and I tried to be polite as I answered him. 'Who knows which one of us will get there first?'

'You will,' he seemed very certain.

'All right then,' I said, but I couldn't help hoping he was wrong.

Then Mamma came again. The pain was stronger, even though the mist was deepening. I was given the Last Sacraments, while Mamma cried. I received Communion. I had gone to Confession, after all. At least it wasn't a sacrilege. I had had no time for bad thoughts.

It wasn't very long before I felt weak and cold and my breath came in short gusts. I knew it was the end. It was a kind of wondering feeling, beyond pain.

It didn't feel like going *up*. Why do they say you go up? You feel yourself pulling apart, a ripping along the seams. I thought of Mamma ripping the seams of her dress for my First Communion.

It isn't exactly pain. More like a deep tickling that almost

243

hurts. You keep thinking it will hurt, the tickling inside where no one can reach. All the little bags and pouches your skin holds tear apart and split. Then they spill you out. You want to laugh but you can't, the bag of laughter has been spilt out along with the rest. People were crying around me, but my sack of tears was empty, too. I may have smiled, like they said.

Maria's Memo

They said I smiled as I lay dying. They said I must have had a heavenly vision, that the Blessed Mother had smiled at me and I had smiled back at her. They said I never moaned or complained when they cut me open and stitched me up again with nothing to blur the pain. They said I bore it all with perfect patience, even the great thirst I had at the end when they refused to give me water. They thought it would make me worse.

But they must have known that nothing could really make it worse, or better. They must have known that nothing they did made any difference. Perhaps it was precisely because they did know, that they had to try. I don't know why they couldn't at least soothe my thirst, or let me die in peace.

They said I accepted everything that happened to me, because it came from God's hands. These stories came from the priests and Mamma. First they told her about me, then they asked her.

'I never thought she was a saint,' Mamma said at first. Then: 'I knew she was good.'

Then: 'I never thought she would give her life.'

I didn't give my life. It was gouged from me.

I wanted my life. Poor as it was, I wanted it. It was mine.

At first Mamma said that Alessandro had approached me indecently the year before, then after my First Communion and several times in the months leading up to my death. Then she said he'd only tried in the last two months. Then she'd never known of anything at all, until I lay on my deathbed. When I told her that Alessandro had tried before, she asked why I hadn't told her and I answered that Alessandro had said he'd kill me, if I did.

For the first eight years of his prison sentence, Alessandro went on insisting that I had said Si, si, si during his attack. He said

245

he had killed me because he wished to go to prison, he was so ashamed of what he had done.

My Si, si, si was a problem for them. By then they wanted a Saint Maria Goretti. They were trying to make her out of my dead parts. But they needed Alessandro to give them the part they needed most.

17

1909–10, Noto Prison, Sicily

He had never wanted priests near him. Giovanni had hated priests and he agreed. It was all the fault of the priests. They had taught Marietta to say no. If she had made it easy for him, she would have lived.

Two years in solitary had only made Alessandro more himself, not less. He was stubborn, mute, like a mule. He even brayed like a mule sometimes, sending out his strange cries through the prison.

He refused to plead with them or listen to their bribes. Almost from the first, they had wanted something from him. It gave him an opportunity to refuse, to prove he was still alive. Besides, he liked darkness. He had liked the dark nights watching from the ship, until the other sailor drowned. He was not afraid of drowning here, in this other darkness where there were no winds or waves.

After the first year in Regina Coeli, outside Rome, they moved him to Sicily, to this godforsaken castle – castle! – to Noto prison, known as the worst in Italy. He had forsaken God already, why should he care? Besides, he got a trip to Sicily out of it, not that he was allowed to see anything.

But the solitary confinement at Noto was different. Buried deep in the bowels of the castle, there was nothing to see or hear. He made himself recall the books he'd read, the newspapers, finally, out of desperation, the catechism he had learned by heart as a child and taught to Marietta.

The words brought her back in spite of himself, her struggles to learn, his promise to teach her to read. He dreamt that she came to him, a grown woman now, and asked him to teach her. He refused, as he had refused before. *It's too late*, he said in the dream. He had the dream again, but this time he begged her to allow him to teach her to read and it was the grown-up Maria who replied, with dignity, *It's too late*.

An earthquake rocked the island, but left prison intact. Only God-fearing souls were killed. By then he had been taken out of solitary and placed in the open prison population, where was no silence and he was never alone. He was worse off than an animal. An animal had a stall to call his own. He had nothing, not even his body, and soon he wouldn't even have his mind. He felt it straining and knew it would give. The sea was coming in. He was drowning.

When he complained, they laughed. When he said he was raped, they shrugged. *The punishment fits the crime, eh, Serenelli?*

He couldn't very well tell them it didn't fit the crime, could he? He couldn't tell them he had put it in her but it was soft, it failed to do what it had to do. No one in here suffered from softness of that kind, or any kind.

But his mind was drowning and he wanted to keep that one last thing, his sanity. He went on refusing the priests. It was partly for Giovanni that he refused. He hated himself for still obeying the old man, dead now like his poor brother Gaspare. Giovanni had died in abject poverty and disgrace. He had killed Giovanni, no less than Maria.

'The bishop wants to see you, Serenelli,' they said one day when he had been there almost seven years. 'Imagine.'

He could tell they were impressed, and also uncomfortable. Why would a bishop come to see him? But they seemed to know why.

'What bishop?'

'The Bishop of Noto, of course. What other bishop? He's an old man, Bishop Giovanni Blandini.'

'He has the same name as my father,' why did he say that? He never spoke about himself.

'You can't say no to His Grace, then, can you?'

'No,' he said, surprising himself. 'I'll see the bishop.' Giovanni had never said anything about bishops.

They made him clean himself up and they gave him fresh prison clothes. He had stopped caring about himself long ago, other than hoping it might put off his persecutors if he stank. But he had stopped hoping long ago, too.

Then they took him to the visitors' room, where he had never been before. No one had visited him, though Pietro's wife Maria had taken it as her Christian duty to write to him once a year, sermons he read because she included news of the family. It was Maria who told him when Gaspare and Giovanni died. But now there was another Giovanni waiting for him.

'Alessandro,' the Bishop extended his hand.

The man was broad and white-haired. He looked more like old Mazzoleni than Giovanni, but he was much older. Alessandro knew what he had to do. He was no longer a mule. He was a dog now. He sank to his knees and kissed the bishop's ring. It gave him pleasure to think where his lips had been.

Blandini's face was a bag of wrinkles when he smiled. He had blue-grey eyes and white teeth. Signs of good food.

'You have refused to see a priest for a long time, Alessandro,' he said when they had both sat down.

'Refusing shows we're alive,' Alessandro said. 'It's what Marietta did, refusing me,' he was explaining it to himself as he spoke to the man with the cool blue-grey eyes, if a bishop was a man.

'Ah, you agree she refused you?'

'Until the very last, when I brought out the corn cutter,' he shrugged. 'No one could refuse then.' Blandini looked disappointed, but Alessandro went on. 'Mules refuse, everyone knows that. It's to show what they are. Not horses, not donkeys. Mules,' he explained. 'You see? That's what we do, people like us.'

'But you agreed to see me.'

'I feel my mind is going. I'll refuse that as long as I can.'

249

'I see. So this is another kind of refusal.'

Alessandro shrugged. 'If you like, Your Grace.'

Blandini seemed surprised when Alessandro used his title. Even a parrot could repeat a name. But he would hardly think Alessandro was a parrot. He was something much lower and dirtier. The Bishop would wash and wash his hands, when he got home to his palace.

'Perhaps you could tell me what happened, Alessandro?'

'I've told it and told it.'

Blandini waited. He was used to being obeyed. It was tempting to refuse, but Alessandro sighed and began.

'The ambulance taking Marietta to the hospital went past the police wagon. I was in handcuffs.'

' "You'd better hope she lives, Serenelli",' the policeman guarding me said. ' "Otherwise it's murder, eh?" He drew a line across his throat with his finger.'

'You have a good memory,' the bishop said.

'Yes,' Alessandro nodded. 'I could still recite my catechism if you wished, Your Grace.'

The pale eyes flickered as he shook his head.

'You know she died. It was murder. But the guard in the prison wagon was wrong. I was too young for the death sentence. Thirty years was the maximum allowed and that was what I got.'

'And the trial?'

He shrugged. By then he had been beaten and turned into a more obstinate mule than he had been before. He had wanted only to be left alone.

The bishop smiled, showing his clean teeth. It was rare for Alessandro to receive a smile. He was not in a place where people smiled and no mirror had smiled at him for a very long time. 'Are you sorry for what you did, Alessandro?'

They had asked him that question at the trial. He answered honestly, both times. 'I'm sorry for what I didn't do. I'm sorry I didn't put her out of her misery quickly. Even an animal deserves that much.'

'Have you no remorse?' Again, the same question.

'What's done is done. What's the use of being sorry?'

'But you must repent,' the bishop said. They had said that, too, in court. Then he added, 'To save your soul.'

'Do you care so much about my soul, Your Grace?'

'You know she is a saint,' the bishop said. 'You do know Maria's a saint, don't you? You're the killer of a saint, Alessandro. The murderer of a blessed saint. She isn't an official saint yet, of course. But it will come. The process has begun and nothing will stop it.'

'A saint?' The word confused him. It had little meaning in their lives. Rather it had meaning, but not one that applied to their lives.

'She will be. If you help us, Alessandro, we will help you.'

He almost laughed in Blandini's face. 'If she's a saint, didn't I make her one? Haven't I already helped more than anyone else ever could, by killing her?'

'Why did you do it, Alessandro?'

He was silent. What could a bishop know about the terrible necessity to become a man? He was well out of it. All priests were well out of it. It was not a choice, if you were poor. He had accepted his father's wager, and he had had to win. All it would take was one push into Marietta, one little drop of her blood.

You go on about Christ's Precious Blood. But it's our blood that's precious. The blood of virgins makes a man a man. The blood a woman sheds saves her from disgrace. The blood of battle –

But he didn't know about that. He never got there. Whatever way of life he chose, there was blood.

'You eat meat, your Grace?'

'Not on Fridays,' the bishop was startled. 'Do you miss meat, Alessandro?'

'How can I miss what I never had?'

'But you could have meat. You could have better food, and peace.'

'You know where meat comes from?' He didn't bother with

251

the title, this time. He wanted to make the bishop understand.

'Everyone knows that, Alessandro. God has given us the beasts for work and food.'

Blandini didn't understand what he meant, about eating animals and blood. He couldn't explain it to this bloodless bishop. It came to him suddenly that he was not so stupid, after all. Giovanni had always said so, because he could read. But he had never believed it.

'But about Maria,' the bishop said.

'She fought like an animal having its throat cut.'

The bishop winced. 'But she fought.'

'Of course she fought. I had to take the corn-cutter and plunge it into her again and again. Do you know how easily a human body tears? You have to do it again, it's so easy. And the blood flows and flows. Only a pig has so much blood. Maria bled like a stuck pig,' he had seen them, and he knew. He wanted Blandini to see it too. 'I thought she'd be better off dead, finished with suffering. My lawyer wanted me to plead insanity. There was a good chance, given the history of my mother and brother, that such a plea would reduce my sentence. The lawyer said in court that my refusal to make this plea was itself proof that I was insane.'

Why had he not made the plea? He couldn't be bothered. He was tired of trying to be a man, of trying to be anything. He would not try to be a madman. Let him be a murderer. That was enough.

'I was found guilty, of course. I had confessed to the murder. I was eighteen, I got thirty years.' He shrugged. What more could he want? Were they waiting for him to confess that the murder was not the only thing left undone? But they knew that. They had looked at her, of course they had! That was all they cared about, with any woman: was she a virgin, a mother or a whore?

They wanted him to speak about Maria, their saint. But what could he say about someone he had never known? They wanted him to talk about her purity. They knew nothing of moments like the last ones he had shared with her. There was no time for purity. Rather, they were pure in another way. They thought purity was good, always good. Purity was terrible. Death was purer than life. It was more absolute, more complete. Life had death braided through it but death was only death, forever and ever.

'You might have married her and made it right in the eyes of God and His holy Church, Alessandro,' the bishop said.

'I had no wish to marry her.'

'But why not?'

She did not have the sort of beauty that attracted me,' he replied.

The bishop smiled. The idea that Alessandro might know anything about beauty amused him. Very well. 'She was ugly and squat and dirty and reeked of sweat and sometimes of her women's blood,' Alessandro said, or spat.

The bishop blushed red, almost purple, at the mention of women's blood. What fools they were, these priests. If only he could rip into that face and let the blood spill. But he had made the bishop bleed, if only under the skin.

'Ah, my son,' Blandini said.

When you had the upper hand, they turned you into a child again. It was one of their tricks.

'She will be a model and symbol of purity for Catholic youth everywhere,' Blandini said. 'Just as the Holy Father wishes.'

The Holy Father? Alesssandro was startled. How had the Holy Father heard of Marietta?

'By the way,' Blandini went on, 'you had indulged in obscene reading, had you not? Before it happened?'

It was Alessandro's turn to be amused. He shrugged. 'This comes from the mamma.'

'Indeed, and who better to know about your bad habits and bad companions than Mamma Assunta, as she is now known throughout Italy?'

'Mamma Assunta,' he repeated. *As she is now known throughout Italy. Just as the Holy Father wishes.* He was beginning to understand what was happening. 'Ah, yes, of course. I wouldn't disagree with her,' he said politely. If Alessandro was the murderer of a saint, then Assunta was the mother of one.

Mamma Assunta. She had said nothing and he had said nothing. She had wanted to protect Marietta, but she had also wanted to protect herself and her other children from Giovanni, weakest of them all. The weak were merciless, when they had power.

But Giovanni was dead and *Mamma Assunta* had survived. She had turned a blind eye, even as she turned her stony glance towards him. She had played for time. Marietta was too young. He had understood her silent code, but he was in a hurry. He had a wager to win.

Mamma Assunta. The mother of a saint. Alessandro Serenelli. The murderer of a saint.

'It was all so long ago,' he said to the bishop.

'Not in the light of eternity,' Blandini answered.

Alessandro shrugged. If only Maria had let him become a man, how simple their lives might have been. No great saints or great sinners.

But time had run out for both of them. When had it become too late? When Luigi Goretti died? When Giovanni had his accident and his hand shrivelled and became useless? When his mother tried to drown him?

'Remember, we can help you, my son. If you help us.'

'But why should you need my help, Your Grace?' He still didn't understand.

Instead of answering, Blandini said sadly, 'I still don't understand why, my son.'

She'd seen his failure. He had had to silence her. No one could ever know, not Giovanni or Assunta. He could still see Assunta's dirty little smile when she talked about the Count and how he wanted to escape his wife. She'd grin and show

254

her rotten teeth when the truth came out about Alessandro. She'd throw her head back and laugh with malicious glee.

'Marietta was a good girl,' he said.

'Yes,' the bishop nodded encouragement. 'And you couldn't bear her goodness, could you, Alessandro?'

Marietta would have wanted to forget all about it. But she'd tell someone, some day, if only the priest in the confessional. She'd look at him and he would see it in her eyes.

'I couldn't bear it,' he said. Let the bishop misunderstand. 'But no man can. I'm not even unusual. I've been in prison long enough to know that. Men kill because another man looks at them in a certain way. Sometimes a woman,' he shrugged, 'even a child, but usually another man. A man kills because he *might* be looked at in a certain way. Or laughed at.'

'Finish the story, my son.'

'I heard my father's footsteps and realized baby Teresa was crying.' He had come up from the stream of blood to Giovanni's face, for once not flushed from wine but white as the bishop's face. If Giovanni saw him with the corn-cutter in his hand, he'd guess the splitting of skin and the spurting of blood was instead of the other, necessary blood. He would look at Alessandro *that way*, because he had spilt the wrong kind of blood.

'I went into my room. On the way there I hid the corn-cutter behind a barrel in the kitchen. I didn't want it with me in my room. It was filthy with blood. I lay on my bed looking around at the walls, at my pictures. Soon I would leave them, and I'd never be back.'

'I heard my father's voice. I heard her – Marietta – say 'Alessandro. Alessandro did this to me, because –' and then she was silent. I'd failed so miserably that she could still speak.'

He heard the bishop's breath. 'But my father was soon quieted and removed. They were taking her away and they were coming for me. A crowd had gathered outside.'

255

' "Come out, Alessandro, or we're coming in! We're going to give you what you gave the little one"!'

He shuddered as he'd shuddered then. The crowd was baying for his blood. Always for blood, his and hers.

'You were ashamed,' Blandini said. 'Do not be ashamed of your shame, my son. It could be the beginning of salvation.'

Could it? What was salvation? But he needed to save his sanity. 'The crowd went on shouting about Marietta, what an innocent she was.'

'And she was, my son, a pure and innocent virgin.'

He was struck dumb. Again the purity, the innocence. It was so important, the one bit of blood he had failed to shed. It was important even now, when it and she were no longer there.

'There is remorse, and penitence, and forgiveness from an all-merciful heaven.'

'Yes?'

'People change.'

Had he ever changed? He had changed on the ship. And he had changed when Mazzoleni tricked him out of joining the army and he took his father's dirty wager.

'Pray to Maria, Alessandro. Pray to her and she will help you change again.'

'Yes, Your Grace,' he said automatically, thinking the man was mad. One did not pray to the person one had killed. One tried not to think of her. Prison was a superstitious place. Every murderer feared the ghost of his victim. It was never joked about. It was not spoken about.

'Are you afraid of her, Alessandro?'

'Of course I am. I killed her.'

'Yes, yes.' The bishop sounded impatient. 'But if she forgave you.'

'Why would she forgive me?'

'Because she is a saint.'

They were going around in circles. But why should Marietta forgive him for taking away her life? Such as it was, it was all she had.

256

Suddenly he thought of her as she had been on her First Communion day. She was almost beautiful, that day. She was almost like the women in his precious pictures.

'What is it, my son?' The bishop leaned forward eagerly.

'She asked my forgiveness, on the day of her First Communion. It's the custom,' he said. The scene came back to him as he spoke. 'Before she went to the church, all dressed up,' it made his mouth twist. 'I forgave her – for what? For burning the soup and begging me to leave her in peace?'

The bishop's breath came. 'Your heart is not so hard, my son.'

'She was a child. She knew what children knew. She liked to laugh and play. She liked to eat. Only later, she became tired and sad. And then I killed her.'

A tear rolled down his face and he struck it away. He had no right to tears. But they came anyway, and he himself was not so pure as not to be glad the first ones had come in the bishop's presence.

'Weep, my son.' the Bishop urged him.

It dried his tears immediately.

Blandini cleared his throat. 'You saw her, I believe, my son?'

'Saw her?'

'In a dream?'

'What?' Then he realized what had brought the old bishop out to Noto prison. Alessandro had told someone about his dreams, when a grown up Maria had asked him to teach her to read, or he had offered. The story of the dreams had somehow passed to Blandini, and here he was. Alessandro shook his head. 'In any case,' he said to the bishop, quoting from the dreams, 'It is too late.'

'No. It's never too late, my son,' Blandini's face was pink with conviction.

'Maria said so. In my dream. About that, we agreed.'

'But what if you had another dream, in which she forgave you? You know that she forgave you at the end, when she was dying?'

257

'I know. They told me at the trial.' They had thought it would soften him up.

'You can give her this last thing,' Blandini said.

'What can I give her, when I took away the only thing she had?'

'No, my son. She has an immortal soul.'

My son. Giovanni had wanted him to be a man, and now they wanted him to be a child.

'You can withdraw your cruel slander against her.'

What *cruel slander*? He had nothing bad to say about her.

'You keep on insisting she said '*Si, si, si*' at the end, as you assaulted her. That can't be true, can it, Alessandro? Perhaps,' Blandini went on with difficulty, 'in her moment of terror, perhaps it was 'Hi, hi, hi,' that she said, Alessandro?'

Alessandro fought against the laugh that wanted to burst out of him. *Hi, hi, hi. Hi, hi, hi!* The bishop's face was pinker now. It was not disgust but effort that brought his blood to the surface. He was working hard, because he wanted something. But what did he want?

'Because she was a pure and holy saint and she resisted you even unto death.'

He nodded. It was another wager, like the one he had made with his father. But this time he could do what they asked. The freedom it would bring was not the sea, or the army, but quiet, dignity, peace. And meat, if he had the stomach for it. Maybe he was finished with blood. Or maybe it never stopped, whatever you did.

'It's hard to remember now, exactly what Marietta said,' he said slowly. 'It's easier to remember what she did. She struggled terribly. She was slippery as an eel, in all that blood. She was too young, she didn't understand. It wasn't her time yet. She couldn't want it.' He didn't want it, either. But their lives had never been what they wanted. Not his and not hers. They had both wanted to live, he knew that much.

'Of course it's hard to remember, my son. You must pray to the Holy Ghost to help you remember clearly.'

258

He nodded.

'And to Maria.'

The other *holy ghost.* That would be harder, because he was guilty and frightened.

'You will pray to her for forgiveness,' Blandini said.

'I will try.'

'If she grants you her forgiveness – and she will – you will write me a letter, describing it. I know you can write.'

'Yes, Your Grace.' But what would he write?

'She might come to you again, in your lonely cell.'

Once again, he thought the bishop was mad. Or did he really believe in ghosts?

'I mean in a dream, of course,' Blandini said.

'I prefer to sleep.'

'But you might dream of Maria again.'

He hoped not. The grown-up version he had seen was very distant, and seemed not to know that she was dead. But if she was grown up, then she wasn't dead, was she? 'In dreams all things are possible,' he said, following his own thoughts rather than the bishop's.

'Yes, my son. They are. Maria could come to you in a dream and give you a token of forgiveness. She might smile at you.'

She had smiled the day of her First Communion. But he had not killed her then. But the grown-up Maria was not smiling, whether or not she knew she was dead. Alessandro felt dizzy. But Blandini was smiling. Even the dull blue-grey eyes glinted a little.

'She might smile and give you fourteen lilies, one for each stab wound. Lilies like white flames, to burn away your terrible sin. You will write me a letter telling me about your dream, Alessandro.'

'If I have a dream, Your Grace.'

'Of course. If you pray to her to come and bring the fourteen lilies as tokens of forgiveness, I do not think she will disappoint you, Alessandro. Will you promise me that you will kneel down and do that?'

259

'Yes, Your Grace.'

'And now you can kneel for my blessing.'

He knelt down. It was a long time since he had made the Sign of the Cross, but it felt very familiar. The bishop blessed him and extended his hand for Alessandro to kiss his ring.

Then he stood up and Blandini swept out of the room. He was led back to his cell in a daze. But he kept his promise. He knelt where he had been forced to kneel many times, not for prayer – and spoke to her, in the night.

'Marietta, forgive me.' Why should she?

'Marietta, I never meant to hurt you.' What had he meant? To use her like a beast in the field, wasn't that to hurt? But she was only a means to an end. He had come to the bottom of his sin and there it was. A means to an end. Just as he had been to his father and his mother and his brothers, to the sailors and Senator Scelsi and Count Mazzoleni, just as he had become to the bishop and the Holy Father and Mamma Assunta: a means to an end. And Maria?

'I'm sorry, Marietta,' he whispered again and thought he meant it, for all of them.

Nothing happened. No one appeared. Did he expect her? Did he know what he expected? Yes, he knew. He expected nothing, and that was what he got.

He squeezed his eyes shut and tried to picture her. Instead, he saw the women in the pictures, in his old room. He tried harder, picturing Marietta on her First Communion day. Then he saw the grown-up woman of his dreams. The images swam together until it seemed that she, or someone, was there, someone beautiful and smiling. He went to sleep seeing her, whoever she was. He tried again and again and found he could bring her back, not always but sometimes. The lilies were harder, but he kept trying till they came. And then he wrote the letter.

Your Grace,

I humbly thank you for your visit. I have prayed to Maria Goretti asking forgiveness for the terrible wrong I have done her. I was very young at the time and I knew nothing of life. Maria answered my prayer and she has given me the grace of forgiveness.

Maria came to me in a dream and smiled at me. She gave me fourteen lilies, because I had stabbed her fourteen times.

When I took the lilies from her, they burned my hands. Of course Maria resisted me to the very end in my evil desires.

She was a pure and holy virgin and I will pray to her every day of my life. I humbly ask forgiveness from God, from Maria's family whom I have grievously injured, and I beg you for your blessing as a sign of hope that I may be forgiven finally for this rash and desperate sin of my youth.

Sincerely yours,

Alessandro Serenelli

He was proud of the detail that the lilies had burnt his hand. That was his own. It was more that the pen burnt him, as he wrote. *You can give this last thing to her,* the old bishop had said. But there was nothing he could give her now. This was something he gave himself, and them. He had help from the convict in the next cell, a quiet, intelligent man who also helped him request books. Now that the bishop had been to see him, he was allowed them.

His letter was sent and he went to confession, to the bishop. That also raised his status in the prison where he now occupied a strange position, half personage and half pariah. Most people backed away from him now, and he was grateful.

They would not allow him to confess to the ordinary prison chaplain. Perhaps they were afraid of what he would say. He confessed his assaults on Maria, her murder and his lack of repentance for so many years, and that was all.

Soon afterwards, he was allowed to work outside. He attended Mass and received the sacraments. He never swore or made trouble of any kind, and later he was moved to another prison where he worked in the gardens and enjoyed the fresh air. The work was much easier than it had been in Ferriere, and the food was much better. He went on eating meat, when he got it.

His dream was beautiful, they said. He could agree about that. It was true Marietta had wanted her life and fought for it. For her life, not their precious purity. But he had found it easy enough to change his words. Had he changed hers? He would never be certain. Did it matter? He began to think perhaps she had come to him and brought him fourteen lilies. Someone sent him lilies and their cool white flesh reminded him again of the women in his pictures, so long ago. He buried his nose in them and when they began to smell rank, he put them on the compost for the vegetable garden.

Maria's Memo

I can't help wishing Alessandro had left out the lilies. If only he'd changed them to tiger lilies, they might have been about me. But those white things weren't. They were about the other women, the ones in his room.

Then again, at least he was true to himself in that one thing. It was never about me, for him. None of it was about me. Only that one day, when I made my First Communion. Maybe. But now I'm about to be canonized. Or she is. And it's still not about me, it's about Mamma. She's about to meet the pope, for the second time in her life. She met him once before, when I was beatified. And I'm about to see his life again, deep in those walls that surround and shelter him.

18

The Pope's Apartments and Private Gardens,
The Vatican, Vatican City, Rome, Italy,
June 23, 1950.

'Holy Father,' Pasqualina rapped at his door. 'The day before a great day has dawned.'

'Deo Gratias. Every day God gives us is a great day, Sister,' he reminded her. One had to get up early, to get the better of Pasquilina. Luckily, she saw to it that he did.

'Of course, Holy Father.' She said it as though his reply gratified her.

'Thank you, Sister.'

Her footsteps retreated. Pasqualina was a good sparring partner. She kept him on his toes, when she was not busy fighting tooth and nail for him. She was invaluable, both as formidable ally and benevolent opponent.

Eugenio got up slowly from his large bed. The headboard was made of black iron and looked rather sepulchral. His predecessor had died in it. It was Cardinal Pacelli, as he had then been, who had had to carry out the ancient custom of tapping the dead Pius XI on the face with a little silver hammer and calling his Christian name three times.

Achille, Achille, Achille. There had been no answer. Eugenio had not met the ghost of Pio Nono he had imagined as a child, clad in the black cassock Pius IX had donned in order to disguise himself for flight. But a pope lived with his predecessors. They had rustled as he rustled in the exclusive

265

garments that only a pope wore. They and only they understood the infinite dimensions of the pope's role.

Eugenio pulled on his robe and went quickly into his bathroom to relieve himself, wash his hands and then walk out onto his balcony overlooking St Peter's Square, aware that there were some members of the faithful who made it their business to observe him, even time him. They might guess that a man of seventy-four, even a pope, even one persuaded by Pasqualina and his personal physician to be injected with the glands of simians to sustain youthfulness and vigour, would have to visit the bathroom before he could appear in public and pray in relative comfort.

He made the sign of the cross, noting that his hands had mostly retained their whiteness, with relatively few liver spots. Perhaps the glands were efficacious. He hated the brown stains on his white skin. It was more likely that his hands had preserved their purity due to the gloves he wore most of the time. Two gloves, unlike his father and grandfather.

Aware that his hands were naked now in the morning sun, he made his morning offering quickly and allowed himself a glance into the square where tall, white-ribboned posts were being set in place to hold the huge banners of Maria Goretti, tomorrow.

Pasqualina was not wrong. Tomorrow would be a very great day. It was his Holy Year of 1950. He looked over the Square and the venerable buildings that framed it. At least Vatican City, such as it was, had officially belonged to the papacy ever since the Lateran Treaty with Mussolini in 1929. His own brother Francesco was responsible for that. But he allowed himself a small sigh for the papal lands that had haunted his father and grandfather. He had dreamt of restoring at least some of them, and with them the temporal power of the Holy See.

Still, he had avoided Pio Nono's nightmare of exile. His grandfather's story of that ignominious flight, engraved on his memory, had served him well as a cautionary tale. Besides, he had vastly increased the influence of the papacy and the esteem in which it – and he, as its humble representative – were held. He had made the world respect the concentrated spiritual and moral power of the one, holy, Catholic and apostolic church, centred here in the Vatican where it belonged. He remembered his hands, made the sign of the cross with pious elegance and came inside, closing the balcony doors firmly behind him.

Back in his room, he went to the birdcage on its stand in the corner and lifted the cloth that covered it.

'Good morning, Gretel,' he said to his favourite canary, as he opened the little door and let her and her two companions fly free.

It was time for his fifteen minutes of physical exercises. Before he was seventy-one, he had used a rowing machine. Now he followed a Swedish Drill which involved stretching, bending and squatting. It was good for a man to keep his body trim and fit. The Nordic cultures understood such things, like the Teutonic ones. *Mens sano in corpore sana.* The Latin poet Juvenal was right about that, even if he had intended it satirically. Personally, Eugenio preferred Cicero.

He turned to the wall across from his bed and began to flex his arms rhythmically, using the wall-springs he had had installed. It would surprise many people to see the reed-slender pope pulling his springs until he was red in the face from exertion, especially those who accused him of decadence, of having an overly fastidious and even effeminate nature.

He cleared his throat, then made his way into his bathroom and turned the cold tap on full. A cold plunge every morning was a good practice. How many of the Jewish Bolsheviks who dared to call him decadent could claim to follow a similar regime?

Brother Ass, Francis of Assisi called the body. Fellow-lover of animals as he was, Eugenio preferred to claim kinship with his birds. He let himself down into the cold water, tightening his lips as he immersed. Human beings were not their bodies,

267

though many of them seemed to think so. The war was over and no one would wish it otherwise, least of all the pontiff who had suffered with the suffering while it lasted – but the euphoria of peace had its own temptations. People gloried in mere physical survival. War was terrible and ungodly. His personal coat of arms was a dove of peace. But at least during the war, the all-pervasive presence of death served as a reminder that this world was but a way-station.

He lathered his washcloth and ran it dutifully over his body. It was a good thing Pasqualina couldn't see how thin he had become, though she had sharp eyes and she urged and bullied him to eat. He ate very little and wished he could manage on less. But his delicate stomach did not permit long fasts.

He lay in the cold water enjoying the numbness it brought. He was temporarily bodiless. He closed his eyes to heighten the sensation, or lack thereof.

Oh to be a Teresa Neumann, the Bavarian stigmatist who lived on the Eucharist and nothing else! Or Padre Pio here in Rome, who had also received the favour of the stigmata, the appearance of Christ's wounds on his feet, hands and in his side. The wounds bled daily and Padre Pio had to wear bandages to say Mass. Eugenio had seen pictures, and the bandages and mitts Padre Pio wore to accommodate the wounds were most affecting.

He raised his own unmarked right hand – except for five liver spots, quickly counted on the balcony, no new additions today – regretfully, and let it fall. One could not pray for such privileges as the stigmata. He lifted himself out of the tub and hurried to take down one of the thick white towels Pasqualina made sure were fresh every day.

He dried himself carefully and quickly, then covered his body with his fresh white towelling robe and went to the dresser for his linen. Pasqualina saw to it that the pope's white linen was perfectly ironed, with just a touch of starch.

The birds fluttered round him in the bedroom, enjoying their freedom. He smiled at their lightness, the notes they

268

flung into the air. His body tingled, reminding him it was there. Soon it would weigh on him again. It didn't take long for the flesh to re-assert itself, even his. One day, he might be granted the grace of incorruptibility after death. His complexion, which had been described as ivory in the press, would become ivory.

If only God in His wisdom had allowed the body of the little Goretti to be found *in the odour of sanctity*, uncorrupted by death as it had been uncorrupted by sin. But when she was disinterred, there was nothing left but bones and the medal they had placed around her neck when she was dying.

He was ready to shave, a ritual he enjoyed. Gretel followed him and perched on his arm while he shaved, following the movements of his arm with her little yellow head. Like him, she had been slow to come to terms with an electric razor. But in the end she had also adapted.

His old wet razor had reminded him of a rapier. Fencing was another of the masculine traditions he found cleansing and compelling. Once while he still employed the other razor, he had lifted it to challenge a fellow-shaver across the courtyard.

On guard! They had both smiled and Eugenio knew he had given the man a story he could tell for the rest of his life, of the morning the pope had held up his razor and challenged him to a duel.

He mowed the first clear strip through grey whiskers and shook them into the sink, admiring the smooth white skin beneath the shadow and watching Gretel bob her head in concert with him. No, the little Goretti was not among the holy incorruptibles, and neither had she died in defence of her faith. Her killer had not offered her an idol to worship on pain of death, a strange faith to affirm. He had only wanted her body, not her soul.

It had taken a kind of verbal fencing, not so much to trace Goretti's path to sainthood as describe it. It was what he had done all his life, what he did with Pasqualina, what he had

269

done with world leaders, including Hitler – he frowned in the mirror.

Half of his face was clean and white – not snow white; ivory was, in fact, the best description. The other side was still sullied with overnight growth. Such was human nature, in its fallen state: half-angel, half-demon. It remained to the baptized soul to regain its purity, through the sacraments.

He buzzed a pathway down his right cheek. The answer in Maria Goretti's case had been an extended definition of Heroic Virtue. It had come to him after prayer and meditation that Goretti had died in defence of her virginity, making her the first martyr to holy purity. All the other virgin martyrs of the church had been threatened with conversion to a false religion as well.

He finished his shave and smiled into the mirror. A martyr to holy purity was exactly what the times demanded. In a world of permanent waves and lipstick – what were the words of the new, Godless babble? – *bebop. Bebop*! Catholic youth the world over – and especially here in Italy – needed a Maria Goretti, and God had sent her to them, through him. The godless secular press, the terrible filth that poured out of Hollywood, the American soldiers stationed in Italy, were all threats to the purity of Catholic youth.

He would say all this in his address tomorrow, commending her to the youth of the world. There would be many young Italian women and girls in St Peter's Square, some of them undergoing temptation at the hands of the American GI's billeted in Rome, and throughout Italy.

He had requested that the soldiers who came to occupy Italy should not be black, but he had been refused. He rinsed his face and brushed his teeth quickly and efficiently. It was well known that the darker races were more animalistic, more subject to ungovernable lusts. The United States House of Representatives had concluded the investigation into the Black Shame of 1920, when black French troops had raped German women and children in the Rhineland, by rejecting the allegations. That was democracy. It lacked the finer hand, the more discerning sensibility. It was the rule of the rabble. Besides, the Americans were tainted with mixed blood.

The fresh but discreet after-shave was a present from his sister Elizabetta. He had hoped his beloved sister might take over their mother's position, caring for his earthly needs and particularly his stomach. His mother had always known exactly what he needed. If Elizabetta had become a nun, she could have been his housekeeper rather than Pasqualina.

But it was not to be. She had married. Besides, Pasqualina organized his household with such efficiency, he couldn't do without her. He saw Elizabetta once a year now, at Christmas.

He walked into his room and Gretel followed him. She knew it was time for her return to the cage. After he had closed her and the others in again, he exchanged his robe for the immaculate cream cassock and cape laid out by Pasqualina. Now he was ready to pray at Our Lady's shrine. He knelt and made the sign of the cross.

His pectoral cross lay on the little altar, studded with jewels his father had bought his mother. They were small. His father's salary had never been large. They had never lived on the material plane.

He lifted the heavy cross to his lips and kissed it, as he knelt in front of the statue.

Holy Mary, Blessed Virgin Mother, I offer any bodily affliction I might suffer, now and in the future, for the souls in purgatory, particularly for the soul of my mother, your faithful servant Virginia.

Could his mother still be in purgatory? Surely not. But when St Augustine stopped praying for his mother, Monica, thirty years after her death, she had appeared and informed him she was still suffering in purgatory and required his prayers and sacrifices.

After Mass he would meet the little Goretti's mother. He had met her once before, at the Beatification. How had he addressed her? As *Mamma Assunta*? It would be an act of humility for him, the Holy Father and Vicar of Christ on

271

earth, to address an old peasant woman as his mother, even if the whole country called her that.

But she was the mother of a saint, a little virgin mother who had kept house, sewn and cooked and looked after her brothers and sisters. There was nothing more beautiful on earth than a young woman who was also a child. Maria Goretti would be raised to God's highest altar in celebration of her perfect obedience unto death, a pure, chaste virgin who had wanted nothing for herself beyond a touching desire to receive Our Blessed Lord in the Eucharist.

But she was not incorrupt, and absolute proof had been needed of her resistance unto death. Only Serenelli could provide that evidence, and he had refused for almost eight long years. But God had prevailed. The duel with Serenelli had been fought and won. Eugenio stared into space and saw the pure white lilies, frosted with fire, that had burnt her killer's hand when she handed them to him in a dream. The detail always made him wince.

But God had infinite mercy. Look how He had shown it to that brute, once he had recanted. Mamma Assunta had forgiven him and received the Eucharist beside him, in her village church in Corinaldo. Serenelli would be in his monastery garden tomorrow, no doubt watering the ground with his tears.

He made the sign of the cross and stood up. He had to finish his toilette, comb his hair and prepare himself to say Mass. His mind, his whole self, concentrated on the great mystery he was about to celebrate.

When he was ready, his valet, Giovanni Stefanoli, knocked on the door as he did at exactly the same time every day. The pope let silence be his consent and Giovanni opened the door and stood by it as the pope swept past him into the corridor. He knew better than to speak. The pope had entered the silence that would take him into the Mass.

Giovanni helped him vest, a simple matter today. Tomorrow, it would take four hours. Eugenio was on the altar quickly, immersed in the Mass. Giovanni served, discreetly and efficiently.

Eugenio genuflected beneath the white disc his hands had transubstantiated into the body of their Lord. How could any man not wish to give up every earthly vice and pleasure for this one, consummate power?

He plunged into the white blaze of his communion. The sensation of total union with his Lord was what he lived for. It suffused him and removed his bodily self more effectively than his cold bath. Joseph of Cupertino, Teresa of Avila, had actually levitated during their colloquies with Christ in the Eucharist.

Then the sensation was gone and he was earthbound again. Here, in most sacred part of the Mass, were inscribed the names of the little Goretti's sisters in martyrdom: *Felicity and Perpetua, Agatha and Lucy, Agnes and Cecelia, Anastasia.*

Some theologians doubted that these early martyrs were, strictly speaking, virgins. It was unlikely that they had not been violated. But the intention was there and for the early church, that was enough to grant them the ultimate dignity of sainthood.

It was not enough now. The process was more rigorous. One could not condemn the child if she were overcome, but one could not make her a saint for it, either.

It happened every day. And if, God forbid, she had tried to save herself by submitting at the end, or if Serenelli had fulfilled his evil purpose and then murdered her, hers would be one of the holy souls he prayed for. For surely God would not consign her to hell, even if she had weakened at the last extremity and lost the crown.

Agnus Dei, qui tolis peccata mundi, Miserere nobis. Lamb of God who taketh away the sins of the world, have mercy on us. God might gather her in, his little tainted lily. God was merciful. But God was just, and purgatory would have to cleanse her in its fires before she could go to Him and be a saint – a saint with a small 's'.

Agnus Dei, qui tolis peccata mundi, Miserere nobis. God and his Blessed Mother would have given her the strength to resist, if her faith had held. If her faith had flickered at the fatal instant, she could be called unfortunate, even tragic; but not holy. Not one of the elect.

Agnus Dei, qui tolis peccata mundi, dona eis pacem. Lamb of God who taketh away the sins of the world, grant us peace. Thomas á Kempis, author of *The Imitation of Christ*, had been buried alive as a martyr for the faith. A natural candidate for sainthood, he was found when disinterred to have scratched and clawed at the coffin lid until his hands were grazed and bloody, even raked his face in his frenzy. Despair was a sin against hope. Not that he was damned, of course not. But he could not be proclaimed a saint.

Still, the *Imitation* was a perfect book. Maria Goretti had been illiterate, of course, but tomorrow, when he raised her to God's holiest altar, the pope would commemorate it and remind the faithful to return to it, when he described her crucible: *In that moment of crisis she could have spoken to her Redeemer in the words of that classic, The Imitation of Christ: 'Though plagued by a host of misfortunes, I have no fear so long as your grace is with me. It is my strength, stronger than any adversary; it helps me and gives me guidance.'* He loved those words. How often he had said them, during the turbulent years of his papacy.

After Mass the pope sat down at the table where his coffee was already poured, his warm white roll waiting for him with butter and jam nearby. After breakfast, Mamma Assunta. Tomorrow she would receive the Eucharist from his hands, on the day her daughter was raised to God's highest altar. Had Pasqualina remembered that Mamma Assunta would also require some form of breakfast afterwards, having fasted from midnight? They hardly wanted the mother of the saint to faint during the ceremony.

The again, at eighty-two Mamma Assunta must be used to fasting. She had survived her daughter by forty-eight years, her husband by more than fifty. She had known a life of toil and tragedy, and survived. She could be held up as the model of a good Catholic mother, just as her daughter was an obedient and dutiful daughter of the Church. The country had need of a peasant saint, to hold back the deadly Communist threat. God would assist the Pope and Church Militant to fight against it. But God expected him to fight the duel. It was the pope against the devil, in whatever form he took.

Pasqualina came in to refill his coffee, and gave his half-eaten roll a pointed glance.

'Come, Holy Father. You have to keep your strength up, in these demanding times.'

'Thank you, Sister. Have you thought Mamma Assunta will be in need of some breakfast tomorrow morning, after the Mass in St Peter's?'

'Yes, Holy Father,' though her tone was respectful, she raised an eyebrow at him as if to suggest that only a madman would believe that she, Sister Pasqualina, could forget such a thing. Then she left him to his roll.

He finished every crumb and went to his private audience chamber. When Mamma Assunta came in, he stood to embrace her before he sat and allowed her to kneel and kiss his ring. As he looked down, he put his gloved hand on her ancient head under the black veil.

'Dear Mamma Assunta. We are much blessed in this meeting. Blessed, blessed mother of a saint.'

'Holy Father, Holy Father,' she stuttered, making the sign of the cross.

Her accent was difficult. She looked like an old tortoise, her neck just visible in the folds of black. He gestured for an armchair to be moved closer to his papal throne, in case she was deaf, and then she was helped into it.

'Welcome, blessed daughter,' he said. He was the Pope and she was his daughter, as she had recognized with her *Holy Father.*

'The mother of a saint,' he went on. 'You will be the first

275

mother to be present at the canonization of her child, do you realize that, my daughter? The mother of Aloysius Gonzaga was present for his beatification, but not his canonization.'

Tears had come into her eyes, dark, deep-set eyes that looked at him as if she could hardly believe what she saw. Did she understand what he had said to her?

'The first mother,' he repeated. 'To be at the canonization of her child. You,' he pointed at her.

'But my poor daughter,' she said finally, forcing the words out. 'My poor daughter, Holy Father!'

He put a gloved hand over hers on the arm of the chair, then withdrew it. 'Your daughter is in glory, and the whole world will know it soon, if they don't know already.'

It was hard for an illiterate peasant woman to comprehend the hugeness of the favour God and the Church had done her. He would be patient with her.

'But she is dead,' Mamma Assunta said. 'And she was only a child.'

'A holy child, a blessed child,' he said. 'One who gave her life for her chastity. A heroic child!'

'Yes, Holy Father.'

'Mamma Assunta, you must thank God for this greatest of graces.'

'Yes, Holy Father.' She hesitated.

'Yes, my daughter? Your blessed daughter wanted very much to receive Our Lord in Holy Communion,' he prompted her. He liked to hear the story of Maria's First Communion. It would form a major part of her hagiography.

'It's all she ever wanted,' Mamma Assunta nodded. 'How she fought for it, my poor darling!' She sighed deeply and tears came into her eyes. 'I wish –'

'What is it, my daughter?' He preferred not to enquire as to why exactly she had had to fight, or whom she had fought for the privilege of receiving Our Lord. It was enough that she had done so.

'I did not have a dress for her. And I was afraid –'

276

Tears filled his eyes. She did not have a dress. Really, it was a beautiful story.

Mamma Assunta shook her head. 'I wish,' she said again, and stopped.

'My dear child, you can tell me anything.'

She wept at being called a child as the elderly often did, in his experience.

'I wish that we had given her a drink of water. When she lay there, in the hospital. She was so thirsty,' Mamma Assunta wept. 'So thirsty.'

'Yes but not now,' he soothed her. 'Now her thirst is quenched forever.'

She bowed her head and nodded. There was something else, he could tell. Would he have to hear her confession? It happened sometimes, at private audiences.

'If only I could have done more, Holy Father. To save her,' she whispered, a tear snaking its way down her wrinkled cheek.

'You did what you could. And you made her what she was, a blessed saint.'

'Yes but if I could have said more, Holy Father,' she whispered. 'To –' she stopped again, overcome.

'Ah my child,' his hand, which had left hers, went back and pressed it again. 'Thank you for opening your heart to me,' he meant every word. He, too, had critics who railed at him precisely for *not doing enough* and especially, *not saying enough* to save the Jews during the war.

He had saved some. It was hard to say how many. Pasqualina had had charge of that side of things. He continued to press Assunta's hand as he gathered his thoughts. It seemed to him he saw his case clearly, through hers, with a rare simplicity.

'Did you ever think that Alessandro would strike Maria down?' He asked her.

'Never, Holy Father! Such a thing never came into my mind, only that he might –' she stopped herself and bowed her head in shame.

277

'Of course, my daughter,' he was flooded with compassion. 'Of course, you could never think of such an evil thing, because you yourself are pure.'

She looked at him uncertainly.

'Too pure to understand what was in his evil heart,' He said. 'Pray, my daughter. God sees all.'

'Yes Holy Father,' she took her rosary and made the Sign of the Cross.

'No one who is pure can understand evil,' he pronounced. Had Pasqualina said that to him? In any case, it was the answer to his critics. *It is my strength, stronger than any adversary.* 'Maria is part of you, and now she will be given back to you,' he concluded, thinking also of the baptized Jewish orphans, 'better than ever.'

'Given back to me,' Mamma Assunta repeated. Then she smiled at him, a bright if toothless smile. 'Yes, Holy Father.'

He stood to signal that the audience was over and his secretary came forward to assist Mamma Assunta. When she was upright, the pope embraced her again.

'Tomorrow,' he said to her. 'She will be given back to you.'

'Tomorrow. She will be given back to me,' she repeated, and then she was led away.

'You will wish to have your walk now, Holy Father,' it was Pasqualina, looking at him with concern. 'A taxing interview, I think. The car is here, to take you to the garden.'

He was glad. The ride in the car always eased him. 'I think I'll go to the zoo today,' he told Pasqualina.

She smiled broadly. 'Oh yes, Holy Father,' she nodded.

He walked out and into the car and gave the instruction to the driver, to take him to the little zoo. The driver closed the glass panel between them and the pope relaxed. It was good to be alone again. It was always good to be alone.

The fruit trees were finished blossoming now. At their height, he could smell them even when he was sealed in the car. The *odour of sanctity* must be like that.

The car drew up at the zoo and the driver came round to

open his door. The pope smiled and thanked him, then walked briskly. He was light on his feet, unlike Mamma Assunta. Even so, his body was a body. His spirit was restless in its fleshy cage. It battered at the walls.

The bodies of animals were innocent. They could not be anything else, even if they were not necessarily clean. But the two little lambs their keeper brought out to him, his current favourites, were snow white. He took his white gloves off to pet them and feel their fur under his fingers. It was a good God who had created such creatures. They were often more appealing than men.

But some humans were as unschooled, as innocent and meek as these lambs. Maria Goretti was just such a creature. *The Saint Agnes of our time.* The symbol of St Agnes was a white lamb. He sat on a bench and let the lambs nuzzle him. *Lamb of God who takest away the sins of the world.* Maria Goretti, a pure white lamb sacrificed to the honour and glory of God, would become a saint tomorrow, a bridge between heaven and earth.

He laughed as the lamb's pink tongue ticked his palm. The little saint's mother had been too pure to imagine the evil in the heart of her murderer, just as he had been too pure to imagine or credit the evils of Nazism. He had had such hopes of the Reich Concordat, signed in 1933 when he was Papal Nuncio to Germany. He had drafted it with meticulous care. Catholics would withdraw from all political activity. In return, the papacy would have absolute spiritual and ecclesiastical control throughout Germany.

He had seen the beginnings of a new world, then and at the start of the war when it had seemed the Axis powers would be victorious. Fascism did not proclaim that there was no god, or seek to prevent people from practicing their faith. Only Communism did that. On the contrary, fascist leaders were eager to sign concordats with the papacy. They recognized the pope's supremacy in all things pertaining to God. The Holy See might finally have reclaimed some of its stolen territory, had things been different.

But Hitler had turned. He had broken the terms of the Concordat. The pope had assisted in a plot to get rid of him, hoping another leader could save his plan for a new era. But he had had to withdraw from the plot.

What a terrible time it had been. The torment had cost him his health. How could a pope endanger the Church in Nazi-controlled countries, even endanger the papacy itself? How could he risk a forced retreat from the last bastion of the Holy See in order to protect those who had not only killed Our Lord, but continued to turn their backs on him, obstinately refusing salvation?

Could one entirely believe the most lurid reports of Nazi excesses? Communists were everywhere, spreading propaganda. Scores of Jews had died at their hands, certainly. One felt for the children. And those who were saved might become baptized Christians, to the honour and glory of God. Those, one would of course protect at any cost.

Pasqualina had been assiduous in protecting and sheltering as many as she could. She had found ways and means. She had opened the floodgates on his behalf. Others had helped, convents and monasteries, prelates and lay people alike. It was startling what she had achieved, even for Pasqualina.

He relaxed as the lambs nibbled the grass. That was all over now. It was his Holy Year. Tomorrow he would canonize Maria Goretti in St Peter's Square. Too many people would flock to the ceremony to fit in the basilica. They would stand in the great Square to celebrate a pure, chaste, holy peasant saint who would save them from impurity and the Communist menace.

Yes, and her mother's name was Assunta! *To them that love the Lord, all things work together unto good. To those who are called...* the Apostle Paul, to the Romans. Assunta was named for the deep-rooted peasant belief that the Virgin Mary had not gone down into the earth after death, not even to lie incorrupt in the odour of sanctity, but had instead been taken up to heaven.

In the South, in strange little backward but beautiful places like Monte di Procida, near Naples, there had been statues of the Virgin of the Assumption in the churches for hundreds of years. The statues were carried in annual festivals.

It was time for the Church to regularize the situation. In six months he would infallibly proclaim the dogma of the Assumption. It would be the crown and summit of his Holy Year. Of course Our Lady had been taken bodily into heaven, *assumed*. He could feel the great Pio Nono nodding with him, at the wisdom of that word. The Virgin Mary could not *ascend*, as Christ had done. She was flesh and blood, a mere earthly woman, though untainted by original sin, as Pius IX had proclaimed.

Assumed. That was the answer, that one word. Just as *Heroic Chastity* had been the answer for Maria Goretti, that and fourteen fiery lilies seen in a vision of forgiveness by Alessandro Serenelli in Noto prison.

There was always an answer for the pope, an answer directly from the Holy Spirit. Pio Nono had known that, just as Eugenio knew it now. He stood up, gloves in hand, nodding to the keeper who took the lambs away, respecting his silence all the while. The car pulled up immediately and the driver came around to open his door. The pope nodded to him and got in. Tomorrow would be a day of days, and there was much to do in preparation, both spiritually and materially. First he would visit the small white room immediately inside the door of the Vatican, and wash his hands.

Maria's Memo

All these preparations! And meanwhile I lie in the ground, a few bones left over from the reliquaries, and a medal. Or did they take that, too?

But even I feel the enormity of the day. How could Alessandro and Mamma not feel it? How could they not be overwhelmed? It felt good to have Alessandro on his knees to me. I think he should be there again.

19

Monastery Garden, Capuchin
Monastery of Ascoli, Piceno, Italy,
June 23, 1950.

Tomorrow was the day. It seemed like a dream, the dream of Maria with her arms full of lilies. He had asked her forgiveness. But what did it mean to be forgiven?

He knelt on the ground, digging the soil in the large, lush monastery vegetable garden. The soil here was good, much better than it had been in Ferriere. But it was better everywhere, than Ferriere.

Tomorrow he wouldn't work. They'd told him he could listen to the Canonization on the radio, if he liked. He probably would, if only to make it real. He might say the rosary as they'd said it in the kitchen where he killed Marietta. He might hear her voice leading the decades, as it led them on her First Communion Day. He might squeeze out a tear for her. It was the least she deserved.

He wouldn't be there at the ceremony in Rome, though it would be reported that he was. The newspapers had said that he was present at her Beatification, three years ago, but he wasn't. He was here in the monastery, grateful to be hidden away. He might have been recognized as the murderer of a Blessed.

He worked the soil and weeded, hoping he would wear himself out and sleep when night came. Tomorrow would be a day to live through, the day he actually became the murderer of a saint. He bent to his work again. He liked the feeling of the soil on his hands. If only they'd left Marietta in the ground, under the dirt. Dirt cleansed the dead, turned them into bones and then to dust. But they had dug her up and separated her bones. Some were in one church, some in another, as they did with saints.

It had not occurred to him she was a saint, or anyone else. But Marietta came to him again. He didn't tell them. They had wanted one dream and one dream only. He would keep this one for himself. She was not sad, like the grown-up woman who had come before. She came wearing her veil and her earrings but dressed in her old dress, as she had come to breakfast on her First Communion Day. He saw her clearly, just as she had been then. The dream had made him smile, and his smile was part of the dream. But he told no one.

They had given him a holy card of Saint Maria Goretti, smiling. Her mouth was closed but behind her lips he knew her teeth were lily-white. They were not Marietta's teeth.

But he could only thank her, this wraith with her perfect smile and her fourteen lilies, one for each stab wound. It was the kind of detail they liked. They loved wounds, starting with Jesus'. Always blood. Why would anyone want to be washed in it, unless they were frenzied as he had been, once, briefly?

And all this had come from that frenzy. Marietta was washed in blood. As he had been, in prison, though it hadn't cleansed him. All his life he had played a part in the dreams of others, starting with his mother. She had tried to drown him as part of her mad dream. It had meant something to her that he could never fathom. At sea he was part of other men's desires and dreams, and there were the incessant dreams of the sea itself, its storms and calms.

Then he was recalled to his father's dream, which had gone sour and become a nightmare. He had stayed in that nightmare, which in turn demanded that he play the part of Marietta's killer. He would never know why, but that had been the one role he had chosen for himself. A terrible role, a terrible deed; but he had done it.

Now the dream had changed again, and it was less than ever his. There had been lines for him to speak and write. He had spoken them and written them. Otherwise he would never be free again, even in his own flesh, and then he would lose his mind.

He had dreamt the alabaster dream of Saint Maria Goretti and her lilies. Because of him, the alabaster dream girl would replace Marietta, and Assunta would be saved from her silence. He would be cast into deeper silence, but he was not afraid of that.

The Capuchins were kind to him. The nightmare of violation had faded. That side of life had never been very real to him, and he was happy for it to become unreal once more. In his own way, perhaps, he was pure.

It still surprised him that he hadn't killed himself. But it would be difficult to stab oneself to death with a corn-cutter and besides, suicide took passion and his passion had ebbed away. The men he had talked with in prison, the ones who had also killed, agreed with him. The red mist cleared as abruptly as it arrived, terrifying and alien. None of them wanted to know it again. But they had known it once, and that set them apart.

After he left prison, he had seen Assunta, in Corinaldo. She had clutched his hand and he had let her grip him with her claw. He knew what she wanted from him. She wanted Marietta, as if she could reach her daughter through her killer.

He had let her grip him and then forgive him. He had gone to Mass and received Communion kneeling next to her, at the altar. He knew he had brought her some measure of peace. He had made her less lonely, because they had both known Marietta better than anyone else.

That was in the time before he found the monastery and withdrew into his life of vegetables and dirt. He had spent a year wandering and lost. He had been accused of stealing, put in prison again, then exonerated. He had been hired and then let go when people discovered who he was.

He had been approached by a married woman who knew who he was, and wanted him. His murder was part of her desire. He had shaken his head and she had scoffed at him, *Once bitten, twice shy?*

A *man bitten by a snake will run from even a lizard,* he had said, and left her husband's land. Only to be offered a poor young woman in marriage, at the next farm! It was almost unbelievable, but it had happened. He had said no and decided, then, to find a monastery that would harbour him. It would be safer that way.

Tomorrow Marietta would become Saint Maria Goretti. Assunta would become the mother of a saint and he would become the murderer of one. It was a dream in which he had a leading part. He would read of himself as he had played himself, with detachment.

Maria's Memo

Now, Mamma. Enough of popes and murderers. Enough of men.
It's you and me now. In some way, it was always you and me.
Now the day has come, and I want to hear what you say to yourself.

20

St Peter's Square, Vatican City,
Rome, Italy,
June 24, 1950.

Assunta looked down from a window of the Vatican at the people below in the great Square of St Peter's. So many people! It made her dizzy. Ersilia and her husband were on one side of her, Sister Teresa on the other. Her youngest daughter was a nun now. Angelo had come all the way from New Jersey, in America. Sandrino was not here. He had died of pneumonia when he was only twenty-two, also in New Jersey.

'Angelo.'

'Yes, Mamma,' he leaned forward for her kiss.

Marietta had come to him in a dream and told him to go to America. Then Sandrino was given the money to follow him by a friend, another miracle from Marietta. It was good for them to start a new life in America, and Assunta had given them her blessing. But then Sandrino died.

'Marietta, you're a saint. You must have known what would happen,' Assunta muttered as she clasped her rosary. 'If he was going to work so hard, in a dry-cleaner's with horrible things that ruined his lungs, why not leave him in Italy? He could just as well die here at twenty-two, and have his Mamma beside him!'

'What's that, Mamma?' Angelo leaned over to ask her.

'Nothing,' she waved him silent, him and his American accent. Sandrino's death had made her think of her dead baby, Antonio. Assunta crossed herself.

'And now Angelo will return to New Jersey after a few days, to the same town where Sandrino died,' she went on whispering to Marietta. 'How could you give them such bad advice?' She wished she had asked the Holy Father, who knew everything, how that could happen. But she had been overcome with other thoughts, thoughts of what had happened when Marietta died, and before. Her eyes swam and she rubbed at them. Ersilia leaned forward and put her hand on her mother's shoulder and Assunta leaned back for a moment in her chair.

She was in Rome. She had been here for Marietta's Beatification and before, on the way to work the land for that dog Scelsi. Marietta had held her orange cat and Assunta had held Sandrino, who was dead now, like Luigi and Antonio. She gulped back a sob.

'Mamma,' Mariano patted her shoulder. 'Marietta is safe now.'

At least Mariano lived in Italy, with his wife. 'Yes, you saved him from death in the First War,' she whispered to Marietta as her fingers moved along her beads. Mariano was the only one of his company who had survived. 'At least you did that well, if not the rest.'

Assunta had gone back to Corinaldo, after Marietta was killed. Mazzoleni had let her go. She had not paid off her debts. After all her worries, he had let her go. He seemed anxious to be rid of her.

Giovanni had also let her go. He was a broken man. Once she left Ferriere, she had never seen him again. He was dead now.

But she had gone back. She had gone back as a beggar, but she had kept her promise. People had been kind to her, because of Maria. They had found her a house and she had taken in sewing, like Mary. Only in the last five years, her eyes had grown too weak to sew.

Ersilia and Teresa had been sent to school by the priests. Her girls went away and left Assunta and their brothers, and

292

then the two boys left for America. Ersilia came back to Corinaldo and married. Now Assunta lived with her and her husband, as she had once lived with Mary and Victor. Like Mary, Ersilia took in sewing. But she had a Singer sewing machine, paid for by the children she was blessed with, unlike Mary. But she only had three. They were grown up now, of course. One worked here, at the Vatican.

'That must be your doing, too,' she whispered to Marietta. Another son was in the army, and Ersilia's daughter was married. They all sent money to their mother. 'Well, of course they would. You didn't tell them to go and live – or die – in America,' Marietta would understand what she meant. She had always understood.

Something was held up against the surging crowds below, and Assunta leaned forward. An enormous silk banner was hoisted into the air in front of her, right up into the sky.

'Look, Mamma,' Ersilia said.

Even Sister Teresa murmured as she looked at the beautiful young girl on the banner. Teresa, who had been there when Maria was killed. Seated next to Assunta, she crossed herself.

'Saint Maria Goretti,' she whispered.

Assunta leaned forward as far as she could without falling. They lifted the banner for her to see. It was a beautiful young girl with white skin and brown hair, wavy and shining. Everything about her shone.

'It's Maria, Mamma,' Ersilia whispered.

Assunta heard the Pope say *She is part of you, and she will be given back to you.*

'Of course it is, Mamma. They had to make her look different,' Mariano said, crossing himself.

'Santa Maria Goretti,' the crowd chanted. 'Mamma Assunta.'

'Wave at them, Mamma,' Angelo said.

Assunta waved, vaguely and helplessly. Tears fell down her face. Ersilia gripped one hand, Teresa another.

'She is in heaven, with Jesus and Mary and all the saints, Mamma,' Teresa said.

Assunta nodded through her tears. It was no use explaining. The Pope had told her the truth, and now she understood. The young girl on the poster was *part of her*, finally *given back to her*. Assunta stared at her and whispered her name.

'What did you say, Mamma?' Ersilia asked, and her two daughters bent to hear.

She said it again, but only in her head. It was a prayer, one that had been answered strangely and late. *Sunta Angiolina Ida*, she prayed to the banner. *Sunta Angiolina Ida*, as she wept and wept.

Maria's Memo

Oh, Mamma. Of course Angelo and Sandrino wanted to go, but they had to find a way that wouldn't seem cruel to you. I was the perfect alibi. If I told them to go to America, how could they stay with you?

Maybe it was easier for you to blame me, too. But let's go back to my canonization. You died four years later, in 1954. But I had to give you something, that day, or you might have died of guilt and sorrow and confusion right there in St Peter's Square.

That would have been a sensation: the mother of a saint, dead at her canonization. They would have made it into a triumph. You would have been a saint, too. A double canonization, like a double wedding.

Of course, it wouldn't have been. You would have had to go through the whole process of being made Venerable and then Blessed and then finally canonized, just like me. But you would have sailed through. There might even have been a miracle or two right there at my canonization, to help you along.

But you lived through it, and I'm glad. One of us should have. You needed something or someone to sustain you, and I bet on your old double, Sunta Angiolina Ida. She might as well claim the banners. They weren't mine.

I had always been a part of you, Mamma, in your mind. The Holy Father said I would be given back to you, as a saint. Sunta Angiolina Idu. Santa Angiolina Ida. Santa Maria Goretti. Does it matter, if it brought you comfort?

As for Alessandro, if I did enter his dreams, if I did stare down at him from the ceiling of his cell or up at him from its concrete floor, reminding him of that day – what of it? There were no lilies and there was no forgiveness.

Even my body wasn't my own, in the end. Alessandro was right about that. They carried what was left of me, those bones they love so much, along with the banners and pictures of Blessed Maria Goretti in all her finery, to Rome, to the high altar where she was exalted and lifted up to the heavens and proclaimed a saint. Or, let's be kind and say some hybrid mixture of her and me, a hothouse lily mixed with a wild flower to produce a strange wild lily – a tiger lily, the kind that grows wild like a weed in the swamp, orange with raised brown freckles, colourful and free.

It could have been torture for you, Mamma. You knew the measure of your faults and failures. You had a good memory, just like Alessandro. You knew what had happened and what had not happened.

Did you pray? Really, truly pray? Do we know what that means, any of us? I gave you back your Sunta Angiolina Ida, to pray to. Otherwise it might have been too cruel. No one who knew me, or you, was there, not even Alessandro. You would have wanted him there. Perhaps you had even asked.

They would have said no, it wouldn't do. Certainly not, no, they would have looked at you as if you had said something very odd. In their eyes, you had.

But not in your eyes, as you scanned the crowd and shivered because, apart from your other children, as bewildered and lost as you were, including Angelo but not poor Sandrino – apart from your lost little brood, you were among strangers.

You could have shared a small smile with Alessandro if he had been there and behind that, deeper still, a sly but baffled peasant shrug that testified to the strangeness of life. Shrewdness and resignation would have come together in that small gesture. It would have made you feel much less alone. But there was no one but Alessandro to exchange it with.

And he wasn't there. He was tending the garden of the Capuchin monastery, having served twenty-seven years and been let off the last three for good behaviour. Yes – I think a shrug would have said it all. There had been bloodshed and murder and neither of you could or would forget that. Still, a tiny lift of the shoulders

296

and the hands, for what was understood and never would be understood.

She was a chilly girl, Saint Maria Goretti, up there with her lilies and her lily-white complexion. She stared out into nowhere and perhaps she would have made you realize fully for the first time, Mamma, that I was really and completely gone, if it hadn't been for Sunta Angiolina Ida.

I couldn't leave you alone in that cold square, under the shadow of the big stone basilica. You don't belong there any more than I do. But I'm not there. I couldn't leave you there, with knowledge cutting through you like a knife. Does that make me a saint? Everyone would be, if they could look back and understand one human being.

Go home, Mamma. Go home, it's over at last for you and me. Go home with your holy cards and think of Sunta Angiolina Ida, who has been given back to you. Go home and be quiet in your bones, then rest in peace

And so you think – the rest of you – you think it's over for you, too. You think I'll go away now and leave you alone. But I won't. I'll come back and back again and tease and taunt you. I'll make you want to go out and play. Leave me on the road to Conca. Don't leave me, join me there. Your road to Conca will be different from mine. You will have to fight your parents and teachers, your families and lovers and friends, to set out. You will have to go without sleep and food.

But you will go. You will find that road. It's the road to learning and adventure and life, your life. It will make you thirsty and hot – or cold – or both – as well as hungry. But you will follow it to wherever it leads. It will take you where you want and fear to go. Fight your friends and enemies to find it. Once you've started down that road, there is no turning back.